A CATH KEITH MISADVENTURE

CATH KEITH: HISTORIAN DERAILED

RHONDA BELLOWS SUMMERFORD

Cath Keith: Historian Derailed

Copyright © 2025 by Rhonda Bellows Summerford

All rights reserved. No part of this book may be reproduced or transmitted in any form or by any means without written permission of the author.

www.rbsummerfordwriter.com

Library of Congress Cataloging-in-Publication Data
Summerford, Rhonda Bellows.
Cath Keith: Historian Derailed / Rhonda Bellows Summerford
Library of Congress Control Number: 2025927882

ISBN 979-8-9937475-0-7 (Paperback)
ISBN 979-8-9937475-1-4 (eBook)

Published by: Maple Dale Press
Printed in the United States of America

Cover & Interior Design: Kingdom Covers

This is a work of fiction. Names, characters, places, and incidents are either a product of the author's imagination; or are used fictitiously. Any mention of actual persons, living or dead, is in the context of an entirely fictional scene.

To my wonderful husband Keith, who has truly been my wingman in every way possible. His interest, input, and most of all patience have been invaluable. His ability to be funny when he is not trying to be, and his general willingness to be a good sport, have provided much inspiration! There's no one I'd rather travel with than the love of my life.

And in memory of my parents, Steve and Rosemary Bellows, who gave me many travel opportunities while growing up, as well as instilling a love of history and books. I am forever grateful.

Acknowledgments

THANK YOU TO my earliest readers – my first sets of extra eyes: my steadfast husband, Keith A Summerford; Beth Carney; Jeanne Dyson; Janet Goddard; Lee Guinn; Ann and Mike Silveus; Sheila Shunk; Linda Terry; and Tina Tine. Your input and comments were invaluable, and very much appreciated.

Thank you to numerous friends and family who showed ongoing interest in and support of my work. It's good to have a cheering section!

Thank you to my sister and Scottish brother-in-law, Stacey and Ian Anderson, for their character inspiration and regional input; and to my beloved granddaughters, Annabelle Summerford and Charlotte Summerford, for their unbridled enthusiasm and support!

I'd also like to thank professors Dr Brian Crispell, and Dr John Chappo, for continuing to fuel my love of history, way back when. And Mr Gary Chase – former analyst, senior official, Counsel, and Chief Counsel with the US Intelligence community – whose college course on Intelligence and US Foreign Policy proved fascinating, as well as an inspiration to delve further into research and writing.

Finally, I'd like to thank Alice Briggs of Kingdom Covers for her awesome cover and interior design, and her work in preparing my manuscript for publication.

To my readers: if you enjoyed Cath Keith: Historian Derailed, please consider posting a review on Goodreads. com, and on the site for the bookseller where you purchased it. Readers' reviews are crucial to authors.

Please feel free to contact me via my website. Stay tuned for my next release in the Cath Keith Misadventure Series, coming in late 2026. Thank you for reading my book!

Rhonda Bellows Summerford
www.rbsummerfordwriter.com

Contents

CHAPTER 1

"RUN! RUN!" I shouted, as we raced to catch the pack of Shih Tzus who were rounding the corner and heading for the main hub of Terminal C at Miami International Airport. "We're gaining on them!"

My husband limped up behind me. "Cath," he gasped. "We're not 'gaining' on them. They're a mile ahead already. And what, *what* in God's name made you think that was a sane move back there?"

Hands resting on knees, I caught my breath. "I thought it would make an interesting chapter for my book. The one I'm determined to write; the one which will make me a bonafide author; the one that will fulfill my biggest dream—"

Our little interlude was soon interrupted by a herd of angry dog owners on the chase. Specifically, they were pursuing ten international show dogs, fresh off of Crufts in England – the largest dog show of its kind in the world. Someone had opened their pen....

My husband was exasperated. "But why the need to enter their space?"

"To get an interview!" Sheesh. Why else?

Keith was incredulous. "From a dog?"

Before I could make my case any further, I was muted by the appearance of two TSA officers, who asked to see our passports.

Officer A looked over my document, satisfied that all was in order. He then questioned my 'harebrained motive for releasing several priceless show dogs'.

Officer B scrutinized my husband's passport, and his boarding pass for our next flight – the final leg that would take us home to the west coast of Florida. "Sir," he asked, "what's this? Your passport says Keith Keith – but your ticket says Keith Keith. I'm sorry, but those names don't match up. You'll have to come with us."

Oh, boy. Here we go….

Two hours and one missed flight later, all was right with the world again. Ten furry fugitives were back with their owners; my husband had successfully convinced TSA agents for the umpteenth time that his first and last names were, in fact, legally the same (he likes to claim that his parents were drinking when they named him); and I had escaped my little doggy mishap with a slap on the wrist, so to speak. We were good to go.

Pushing midnight – finally home from one of our first trips as empty-nesters – I began to unpack.

"AAACKKKK! Why is there a lizard in my suitcase?"

Keith wandered by, carrying a bag bursting with laundry. "Cath. You live in the subtropics. Reptiles happen."

The creature in question rolled a single cold-blooded eye at me, before leaping out of my bag and onto the floor. From there, it scurried up our bedroom wall and quickly disappeared.

"Well, great!" I looked longingly at our bed, which minutes earlier I couldn't wait to get into. "I'm certainly not sleeping in here tonight. Not until you catch that slimy thing." I shuddered, for emphasis.

My husband sighed. "I'll put it on my list."

I pressed on. "And, where could that creature have come from? Definitely not here; my bag hasn't been opened since leaving Provence."

"True," conceded Keith. "But there were lizards all over the South of France. Surely you haven't forgotten your nemeses this quickly."

I winced at the memory.

"Yeah, he was probably a stowaway." I thought for a moment. "Well, perhaps this French lizard will show some style to its drab American counterparts. It sported a coat of many colors, you know."

Meanwhile, a lizard in my luggage? The story of my life.

Technically, I'd say that I live a fairly smooth existence – if I overlook the little stumbling blocks along the way. Okay, most of them are boulders…but I'm an optimist.

I like animals – I just don't want them touching me. (Especially cats. Too schizophrenic; the stuff of nightmares.) My one exception is small, fluffy dogs. What's not to love? And, I do have an affinity for spiders – but I'm freaked out if one of the ubiquitous chameleons teeming outside my home gets indoors. Ditto for frogs. And snakes! It goes without saying: alligators are in this group, too.

I travel a lot, with my generally-willing husband – and every trip is a history trip! I'm a risk-taker when I'm not a chicken – and a stone-taker when I can be inconspicuous about it. When I set my mind to something, there's no changing it – especially when pursuing a historical nugget. Rome wasn't built in a day, and it didn't fall in a day – but it's not crumble-proof, either (so I've learned).

Keith is my biggest champion, but he can also be my biggest hurdle when I set my mind to something that he sees as a potential disaster. Of course, when it's his call – such as overloading a questionable elevator that last carried lions to the arena – he's all in.

Speaking of Hubby, flight attendants waiting at gates don't mind flirting with this man with the salt-and pepper-allure, oblivious to the fact that he has a wife mere steps away at the newsstand. (My smile may say *Hello* – but my narrowed eyes say *Off you go!*)

Job-wise, Keith is in the water treatment business – not the small stuff, but the big stuff. The kind of systems that keep third-world populations from becoming extinct. Much of our travel includes work for him; I get to tag along when his duties are on the lighter side. A good amount of my recent master's thesis (MA, History) was written in hotel rooms and on planes – a feat which required both determination and flexibility. And resilience, as obstacles and folly lurked around every corner.

Sometimes obstacles can reside next door.

I was mildly annoyed when my doorbell rang, as I rushed through packing for another big trip – occurring in just two days. (Normally I would have yelled, "Keith, you get it!" – but my husband was out, so I was stuck.) It was already dusk, and that brings a special trepidation to opening an exterior door in Florida, because it's guaranteed that slimy little geckos will be out for their evening meal. For some reason, they aspire to dart inside the house, under the misguided notion that succumbing to a slow death and subsequent mummification while skulking behind a piece of furniture, is preferable to the abundance of juicy bugs from the outdoor buffet that is our state.

I cautiously opened the front door, while scanning its perimeter for wily reptiles – only to find Osman Kose – our marginally-tolerable neighborhood doofus – at my doorstep. Great!

Osman is an interesting character. He hails from somewhere near Transylvania, and his first and last name mean, literally: son of a snake, and beardless. While I don't know his father, Osman is beardless. And he generally wears the expression of an eggplant.

"Hey, Osman," I offered, politely masking my aggravation while blocking the doorway from further invitation.

The eggplant forged ahead. "Greetings! What time do you leave for Scotland on Saturday?"

"Uh…well…why do you ask?"

He dove in. "I'm baking something from an old Romanian recipe, and I'd like you to deliver it to Nessie."

"Excuse me?"

Shocked by my obvious ignorance, Osman elaborated. "You know: Nessie. The Loch Ness Monster! Gee, I thought everyone knew her."

"Osman, I wouldn't say that anyone really *knows* her. Sure – there have been alleged sightings over the years, but that doesn't mean that she – or 'it' – actually exists." I went on to clarify the legend, explaining that the earliest report of some sort of water monster appears in an ancient text from the sixth century AD. An Irish monk, Saint Columba, who was staying near the mouth of the River Ness, sent one of his companions out to test the river. Upon the companion seeing the monster, the monk made the sign of the cross and banished the creature to Loch Ness. Later, in 1933, a water bailiff reported a monster sighting on the loch, and since that time numerous sightings have been reported. In 1934, an English physician captured a photo of the alleged monster's head and neck. It was speculated then that the creature was likely a plesiosaur – a marine reptile that otherwise went extinct 65 million years ago. "So you see," I concluded, "there's probably nothing there for me to feed. At least, not monster-wise."

Osman didn't hesitate. "Well, I'll drop off her treat on Friday – that way, you'll have it in time." And he was off. Egads.

I resumed packing. I threw in my smallest laptop – which I optimistically named 'Cath's Writer' – because I had high hopes of finding time on this trip to begin my long overdue literary masterpiece: the historical bestseller that I'd always wanted to write! Maybe I'd even start it in-flight.

By this time Saturday, we'd be on our way to the Highlands. Then eventually London: Henry VIII territory! Followed by a final stop in bonny Edinburgh.

What could go wrong?

❖

"Hold on; I forgot my bunnet." My husband hit the brakes as we were backing out of the driveway – our flight from Tampa just hours away.

"Your what?" Then I remembered, adding, "You do know that you're not actually British…."

'Bunnet' was the Scottish term for Keith's beloved tweed driving cap – at least, according to his dubious source. The correct authority – our soon-to-be brother-in-law, a Scotsman named Ewan – says it's called a Flat Cap. And he should know.

Speaking of Ewan, the happy reason for this trip across the Pond was to participate in his and my younger sister Sophie's wedding. Sophie was a long-time lover of all things Scottish, and she was about to realize her dream of becoming a British resident while having her Highland Prince Charming, too.

I waited anxiously while the car idled, resisting the urge to keep checking my watch. We had over an hour's drive north ahead of us, just to get to the airport. Or longer, with traffic.

The driver's door finally opened, the man wearing the wool cap in ninety-degree weather hopped inside, and we were off.

Planted at our gate in Tampa, I relaxed a little. We'd soon leave for JFK, then after a brief layover, we'd be on an overnight flight to London. From there, we'd catch an early morning flight to Inverness. Sophie and Ewan would be waiting at the airport, to drive us to their stone cottage – far up in the Highlands, on the North Sea. I couldn't wait! The pipes were clearly calling.

With just 20 minutes left before boarding, an announcement was made: there was a gate change. And it wasn't nearby.

"Criminently! We're at Gate 3 – and we now have to sprint to Gate 89?" I looked at our baggage – aptly named. Two roll-ons, two carry-ons, and my clown-car of a tote. All stuffed to the brim.

My gallant husband always bears the brunt of the burden, rolling both bags with carry-ons perched atop, plus the omnipresent Hudson News plastic bag dangling precariously from the cargo heap by its ripping handle. The News bag ferries critical supplies: water; Coca Cola (his, not mine); a bag of white chocolate truffles (mine, not his); and enough paper napkins to do a cursory cleanup of anything gross – because what would travel be without encountering something revolting?

Attempting to fast-walk – Keith ahead of me, turning around every few seconds to ensure I wasn't lagging – it was only a matter of time before I had a good reason for lagging. Somewhere around Gate 45, a crucial strap on one of my new sandals broke. (Yes, sandals. I know, I know… but they were cute. And comfortable. Until they weren't, because one was now flopping sideways off my foot like a confused salmon who was directionally challenged.) At any rate, I had a crisis to contend with, because I certainly couldn't continue my day with only one shoe.

"What the heck?" My long-suffering husband was dismayed, yet not really surprised, by my dilemma. "Cath! We're going to miss this flight! Why did you wear sandals instead of shoes?"

Men. They just don't get it.

"I know, I know! I'll pop into the next shop, and hopefully I can buy a pair of flip-flops." *Please, God, let them have my size.*

"There's no time for that."

One of Keith's less-endearing qualities is his fanaticism about not being late for a flight. It includes fear of being last to board; in fact, he must be as close to first on the plane as possible. Even if he's not in the current boarding Group, and even if he must cut off little old ladies with walkers. He must at least *feel* like he won't be left behind – and that perhaps he will somehow reach his destination before everyone else on the same plane. Oh, we've had many a small skirmish over this little quirk.

A few gates up, I spotted another newsstand.

My husband hovered impatiently at the perimeter of the shop, while I went in.

And back out I came – sporting the only size 9 footwear available: Minnie Mouse plush yellow slippers, featuring big red bows with white polka dots. Yep – at age 49, I was wearing a replica of the rodent's trademark shoes.

Keith was dumbfounded. I was near tears.

"Well," offered my husband, "they match the yellow in your outfit."

This was true. I was wearing black capris and a yellow cardigan, so it could have been worse. In a way, though, it already was worse, because it now appeared as though I had intentionally matched my footwear to my ensemble.

I blinked a couple of times to regain my composure, and we continued our trek to Gate 89 – arriving just as our plane for New York was boarding.

The flight to JFK was delayed…due to weather. Not good. We barely made our connecting flight to London. And worst of all, I had no time to purchase another pair of footwear.

"Now I'm destined to enter majestic England – land of history's most glorious monarchs – wearing mouse shoes!" I wailed, as we settled into our seats for the overseas flight. "Brits don't wear slippers in airports – they have more class than that!"

Keith wasn't listening; he was preoccupied. "What's the matter with this seat?" He fiddled furiously with his disembodied seat cushion. No matter what he did, it simply wouldn't stay put; it slid around with every move.

"Don't complain to me. Look at my knees!" We hadn't even left the tarmac yet, and the airline's logo was already embossed upon my kneecaps, courtesy of the seat-back in front of me. Ohhh, it was going to be a long flight to London.

Moving toward getting situated for the evening ahead, I began tapping around on the entertainment screen in front of me. I only require one thing: an in-flight map showing our route, our visual progress, and how many hours and minutes we are into the flight. I especially love a transatlantic flight map! Between bizarre plot points (Charlie-Gibbs Fracture Zone), shipwreck points (*Titanic!*), and the general awesomeness of literally seeing the world map pass below you ("We just flew over Nimes!"), it's somewhat like transcending time, for the historian in me. One of the reasons that I love history

– and thus, the travel that allows me to experience it up close – is the sheer palpability of it. There are times and places when and where I swear, I can sense the lives of those who trod centuries – even millennia – before me. It is during those moments that I feel the most compelled to write about history. Partly to bring to life and to honor the lives of such amazing – or amazingly ordinary – people, and partly because I feel at peace when I am homed in on my subject. In the zone.

It was in this spirit that I removed my laptop from my carry-on, with the intent of beginning Chapter One of my Greatest Endeavor, once we were airborne.

But first, I had another technological task to perform. And it involved extermination!

CHAPTER 2

"THERE! PROBLEM SOLVED!" I announced with satisfaction.

Keith was intent upon poking the screen in front of him, scrolling at warp speed through the movie selection. Pity the person sitting directly ahead; it must feel akin to having a crazed chicken pecking at your seat-back. "What?" he asked absently. "What problem?"

"My shoes!" Surely he'd noticed that I was still wearing Minnie Mouse's. Or did that now seem like the norm for me? Men. "Heathrow's Reserve and Collect – I just ordered a pair of seagrass flip-flops. They're all I'll need until I can get my bag, and they'll be ready for pick-up when we arrive. Voila! Problem solved."

With that, we turned our attention to our assigned flight attendant and her bored miming of the safety instructions. She already looked tired, and we hadn't even left the ground yet. It would be a long flight for someone – most likely to include us, as in the row behind us were two young parents and a very fidgety girl of about three, called Pippa. (British family; no doubt fans of Princess Catherine.) It was already after 8:00 PM, and Pippa's parents were trying to get her to settle down – to no avail. This battle continued through takeoff, and once we were safely at cruising altitude, the parents gave in and let her out of her seat-belt. She must have been hopping on and off her perch, because my seat-back was jostled every other beat. I also sensed that she was occasionally on the floor, as the airline-issued pillow and blanket that I had wedged between my seat and the window were mysteriously moving inch by inch. I chose to ignore it, and decided to postpone my writing, as I could see that the meal service was now crawling its way down the aisle. No point in setting up my little office, only to have it immediately displaced by that artery-clogging tray of white roll and butter, crackers with polyurethane cheese, gluey pasta with ketchup masquerading as marinara, limp greens and a packet of fake dressing, and a Metamucil brownie. No, I would wait until dinner was over.

Eventually, it was. Better yet, not a peep was to be heard from behind us. I turned around and stole a look between our seats – then did a double-take. Swiveling forward, I glanced at the floor in front of my own seat for confirmation. Yep. One of my Minnie slippers – which I had temporarily shed as soon as we took off – was missing. Though not really, because it was now clutched firmly in the arms of the sleeping Pippa. Gawd! Now what was I going to do?

"Keith!" Crickets. Earphones on, and entranced by the movie he was watching, I had to poke him a couple of times. "Hon!"

"What?!"

I gestured with my thumb. "Look behind you."

He gave me a slightly startled look, then turned around and peered between the seats. "What am I looking at?"

"Look again! Doesn't that kid's stuffed animal look familiar? What am I going to do? For one thing, I need to use the restroom. I am not walking on that disgusting floor with only one shoe!" Ugh.

He now saw the dilemma – contributing, "You don't have a shoe. You have a slipper."

"Potato – potahto. The point is, I now have only one!"

Keith sighed. Then he did what he always does: he went into problem-solving superhero mode. Unfortunately, he doesn't always consult me first. While he was figuring it out, I was busy digging around in my tote, looking for hand sanitizer (life support on a plane) – so I didn't notice that he'd stood up and was rummaging through my bag in the overhead. I also didn't hear him mutter, "Well, that explains it." By which he meant, as he later translated to me, his discovery explained why I needed so much cabin baggage. Soon he nudged me, a look of accomplishment on his face – and my errant Mouse slipper in his hand. "There!"

He motioned for me to look behind us.

I looked. With horror. Little Pippa was still sound asleep – with a stuffed cat in her arms. A cat that Keith had retrieved from my bag, without bothering to ask me first *why* I had a cat in my bag. Especially since he knows I am not a fan of cats! Well, this cat was now definitely out of the bag, in more ways than one. What Hubby didn't realize – ditto for Pippa nor her unsuspecting parents – was that carefully sewn inside of the stuffed cat was a real cat. A dead one. At least, its ashes. Right before we'd left on our trip, our elderly neighbor, Frank, had asked a favor. Having heard that we were heading to London, he wondered: would I please take the ashes of Dickens, his beloved, recently departed feline, to the one resting place in the world that would give peace to both Dickens and Frank? And where would that be? Why, Westminster Abbey, of course – right at the head of Charles Dickens' grave itself. Frank was a huge fan of Dickens – the writer – thus the moniker for his cat. To boot, Dickens himself was a cat lover – so much so, that upon the death of his own cherished feline Bob, he trotted off to a taxidermist and had one of Bob's paws stuffed and adhered to the handle of an ivory letter opener. What could be more normal than that? (Cat people!) Most importantly, how could I deny sweet widower Frank his simple request?

"Keith!" I hissed. "What have you done?"

I quickly explained the situation, and I wanted to smack him when he shifted into Brit mode with, "Now, this IS a sticky wicket."

"Yeah," I continued, "it's sticky alright – and you'd better 'get wicket' and retrieve that damn cat!" Normally, I'm nicer to my husband (well, most of the time. Okay, almost most of the time), but this time my patience was already thin, and was about to run out. It was late; we'd already had other mishaps; and right now I needed the restroom (stupid airline Merlot). And I had no human shoes.

Putting my screaming bladder on the back burner for the moment, I went into default mode: what would Lucy Ricardo do? Well, she wouldn't have confided in Ricky, for starters. Too late for that.

I poked Keith again. Twice, to get his attention away from the screen. Good grief! How is it that men can be in the middle of a crisis, and still divert to anything projected in front of them that moves and flashes? "I've got it!"

He removed an earbud. "What?"

I repeated myself.

"Great," came his reply. "Well, I'm sure it involves me, so what's the plan?"

"Of course it involves you! You're the one who gave away a cat that doesn't belong to you in the first place!" I let the various facets of that little bit of illogic sink in, before soldiering on. "All you need to do is offer a replacement. Just explain to the parents that you were unaware that the stuffed cat— Oh, just forget it for the moment. I have GOT to use the restroom before we go any further with this debacle."

Switching gears, I ventured, "Are you going to the restroom by any chance?" Well, he knew what that meant. I am fortunate to have a husband who will go into airplane lavatories before me and essentially wipe down the interior so that I don't have to use it directly after God-knows-what strange male might have been in there before me and left it in a disgusting state. After many flights with this little courtesy – the trick is to beat anyone else who may inadvertently get in line before me, so timing is crucial – I once followed Keith directly into the lavatory as planned, only to find that he had made a little origami bunny out of toilet paper for me (the man is creative in the can), and left it on the lid of the toilet. Said bunny even had a loop on it, should I want to wear it on my finger…. This was code that the seat had been cleaned; it was nice. Kind of like finding a mint on your hotel pillow.

Anyway, this was one of those times when just as I unbuckled and stepped into the aisle to await my moment, I saw a big burly guy beat me to it. Keith came out, and Burly Guy went in. Drat! I sat back down, defeated. Now I would go to Plan B: wait and hope for a woman to go in next, then I would rush the lavatory door as she exited.

After what seemed like half an hour (again, men!), Burly Guy exited and headed back to his seat, which was across the aisle from the family behind us. His traveling companion appeared to be his girlfriend, a bubbly blond in pink Spandex. My eyes were trained on the restroom, waiting for a female – any female – to emerge, when suddenly there came an ear-splitting shriek.

"OMG! OF COURSE I'LL MARRY YOU!"

From that moment, everything happened fast. Little Pippa awoke with a startled scream and threw the stuffed cat into the air – which landed on Keith's tray table, spilling Coke all over his lap. Score! Problem solved for us.

We turned our attention to the source of the shriek: Burly Guy's girlfriend – now fianceé – was standing in the aisle, proudly showing off her new engagement ring for everyone to see. It was an origami toilet paper bunny – a perfect size six.

I finally had my chance to use the lavatory; a flight attendant came along to clean up the spilled Coke from Keith's lap (we'll do that, thank you); and after setting myself up with a nice iced tea, I got out my laptop and began to write the first words of Chapter One, as we soared high above the inky black Atlantic at 600 mph.

It was a dark and stormy night…. Corny and cliché, I thought, but let's see where it goes.

Life would soon imitate art.

CHAPTER 3

*B*UMP.

"What the hell was that?!"

Before Keith could answer me, there was another large jolt to the plane – this one threatening to upend our drinks, both of which were sitting on his tray table, as my laptop was open and occupying mine. I was one paragraph into writing my first chapter, after two hours of attempting to produce. Writer's block, fueled by too many distractions, coupled with the late hour (it was after midnight, our time) and the turbulence we were beginning to encounter – and now my mind was suddenly on Red Alert. I generally hate turbulence, and had done my usual due diligence by checking the Turbulence Forecast for the Atlantic, before leaving New York. It showed a few squiggly red amoeba along our path, but nothing major. As well, I had my trusty copy of *Cockpit Confidential* on my eReader – and I knew exactly where to find the calming passages assuring me that turbulence would not likely bring down a plane. For double measure, I also called to mind the Jello Analogy I'd once discovered online, designed to explain to children why turbulence would not cause a plane to fall out of the sky. Thus, I dutifully imagined a small plastic airplane suspended in a bowl of Jello; tapping on the sides and bottom of the bowl would cause the plane to bounce around, but it simply would not fall. Check.

Meanwhile, crickets from Keith.

"Jello. Jello. Jello," I quietly chanted, my eyes shut tight. Breathe in, breathe out….

"You want Jello *now*? Why?" This, Keith managed to hear despite his earphones.

"No! Aren't you concerned about this turbulence?"

"Not particularly," replied my husband, "and you shouldn't be, either." His attention returned to his screen. Bond was escaping his enemies with the help of a jet-pack, which clearly took precedence over our own flight safety.

At that point, the captain came on the PA. "Sorry about the bumps, folks. Our friends up ahead have advised us to expect a light to moderate chop. Hopefully, that will be it for the rest of the flight. As always, please keep your seat-belts fastened unless you absolutely need to get up and move about the cabin for some reason."

No problem, sir. My seat-belt would not be coming off for any reason.

In no time, I needed the restroom again. Damn! I debated waiting it out for as long as possible, weighing the odds of the turbulence increasing versus decreasing in the coming half hour or so. I knew that the captain's reference to 'our friends up ahead' meant that the cockpit was getting real-time reports from other aircraft ahead of us on the flight path, as to what they were encountering. I also knew that pilots relied additionally on weather charts and radar returns. That second source concerned me because I was painfully aware that there is no radar coverage over much of the North Atlantic. Hundreds of planes are simultaneously on eastbound transatlantic flights that depart between 6:00 PM and 8:00 PM every evening, and many of them utilize the jet stream to shave time off of their travel – which concentrates all of these planes into a relatively small area. Oceanic travel requires a 10-minute separation if planes are following the same path, and a 15-minute separation if planes are crossing one another. *Well, here's hoping that everyone stays in their lane*, I thought. That knowledge to ponder, along with the ongoing bumps, definitely killed my writing concentration.

I closed my laptop, stowed my tray table, and opened my copy of *Minerva*. A half-hour into an article about how vibrantly painted frescoes lit up the dark and claustrophobic rooms of Roman houses in Pompeii, things seemed to smooth out in the skies around us. Looking out the window, I saw a full moon, with dense cloud cover below us, and the effect was amazing. As far as the eye could see, there was a landscape of white fluff, brilliantly illuminated by the lunar glow. Ahhh. I was finally starting to feel at peace, and was looking ahead to our days in Britain. Land of the Celts, the Romans, the Vikings, the Tudors, the Harrods....

"THE PIG? Did you just call our daughter a pig?"

Good grief! Now what was going on behind me? I turned in my seat to look, just as Keith stepped into the aisle to head to the lavatory. In a classic move of mispronunciation like only my husband can perform, I heard him say to little Pippa's father, "You're lucky that Peppa was able to sleep through that turbulence. I heard her snoring away like she was makin' bacon!"

Whaaaa?? He not only insulted the family, essentially referring to their child as Peppa Pig, but he mixed metaphors in a way that bordered on handcuffs awaiting us at the gate.

"Keith!" I hissed, beckoning him to sit back down. "What are you doing?"

"What?" Accompanied by that innocent look all husbands have when they've just committed an act of complete insanity, yet truly have no idea.

"You basically called their daughter a cartoon pig! Then you implied she was involved in something hideously under-aged!" I cringed.

"What in the world are you talking about? I did not!" Classic.

"Oh, yes you did!" I took a moment to elaborate, and he finally got my point.

"Oh."

"Yeah!" Geez. "Could we just finish this flight in one piece, please? Without further incident?" Granted, this was rich coming from me, because I am not without folly myself. But there was no point in reminding Keith of that.

The rest of the flight was a long series of stops and starts, turbulence-wise. Every time things seemed to smooth out, there was another round of bumps and jolts. I completely abandoned all thoughts of writing or any serious reading and caved into watching seven episodes of *Big Bang Theory*. Whatever gets you through the night.

⊡

It was 8:00 AM in London (3:00 AM, our time) when we stumbled off the plane at Heathrow, bleary-eyed. We had a long walk toward Immigration, traversing numerous hallways, and an equally long line when we got there. We needed toothpicks to hold our eyes open, by the time our turn came.

As an agent stamped my passport, he commented on my name. "Another Princess Catherine," he said, with equal parts friendliness and eye-roll.

"Pardon? Oh, yes – I guess so," I replied. "Although, I actually go by Cath."

"Cath? Well, if you're heading to Cardiff while you're here, you might want to alter that a bit. You know – the legend and all."

I was too tired for this. "Legend?"

"Yes." The agent disregarded the queue of impatient travelers behind us, and gave me a quick history lesson. "Cath Palug was a monstrous cat in Welsh legend, given birth to by the pig Henwen of Cornwall. The cat was later said to haunt the Isle of Anglesey and was supposed to have killed 180 warriors. Some even said that it killed King Arthur!"

"Oh. I see…." What else could I say? And what was with the affiliation between cats, pigs, and me on this trip, already? Egads.

Shuffling past Immigration – I, still sporting Minnie Mouse's fluffy yellow shoes – we went through Customs. Smooth enough. We were both hungry, having eschewed an airline breakfast of sour yogurt and a packet of sticky granola, and Keith's goal was to head straight to the first Costa or Caffe Nero that we came to. But I had a different plan.

"Heathrow Reserve and Collect! Got to find it. I'm not taking another unnecessary step until I have shed these ridiculous mouse shoes for the flip-flops I ordered." By now the rodent slippers had accumulated enough flotsam and jetsam to basically walk on their own. Ugh.

Among the terminal's many high-end shops was a large kiosk-type store, labeled Reserve and Collect. I approached a clerk, who pulled up my order on her pad and disappeared into the back. In no time, she returned with a box – which seemed a tad larger than what I would have expected. "Here you are, Ms Keith. I hope that you enjoy them. Your receipt is inside."

I opened the box. Well, they were definitely a step up from Minnie's clodhoppers.

"Whose are those?" asked my husband.

"Mine…. They're not my Seagrass Flip-Flops for 9.00 pounds, that's for sure!" According to the receipt – showing that my credit card had already been charged – they were Burberry Stiletto-heel Leather Sandals, for

650.00 pounds. In Black. Minnie would have traded up in a second.

"Excuse me," I said, getting the clerk's attention. "There's been a mistake. These aren't the shoes I ordered. I need to exchange them, please."

"I'm sorry ma'am, but these *are* the shoes that you ordered. It's right here on the order form." She further explained that there were no exchanges allowed at that particular site, as beyond the displays, all items in stock were reserved for other customers.

I looked at Keith and shrugged. I don't wear stilettos, I rarely wear heels, and I almost never spend over $100 on shoes. What was I going to do with these towering monuments to torturous fashion – which I was now stuck paying for, to boot?

"What are you doing?" asked my incredulous husband, as he looked down at my feet.

"I'm wearing them – at least until I can acquire something else. Maybe from a shop by our next gate…" Right. That's what started this mess in the first place, back in Tampa.

"There's no time for that," insisted Keith. "I'm starving, and by the time we grab a bite, it will be time to board for Inverness. Let's go!"

With that, we headed off to the Costa that we'd located in the terminal's directory. Keith dragged our four bags: two piled on two. I wobbled along on stilettos that I would definitely wear only once – yet which cost us more than our four pieces of luggage combined.

I was now towering two inches above my husband. "Hey!" I said, from my vantage point. "I see the Costa about 100 yards ahead!"

One of the twin Minnies smiled back at me from the pocket of my bag, as Keith rolled her ahead. She was riding in style.

❖

Our flight to Inverness was a short but wild ride, due to high winds. And the plane seemed pretty old and rickety, too. However, I was so exhausted by then, that I decided it didn't really matter to me if it crashed or not. Right into Loch Ness. With the Loch Ness Monster lurking nearby. Nope ~ didn't care. How pathetic is that?

The next I knew, we were landing, disembarking, retrieving our bags, and sleep-walking toward the exit, where my sister and her fiancé would be waiting. As tired as I was, I was still thrilled to see several males in kilts. We were truly in Scotland!

"There they are!" said Keith, pointing ahead to a waving Sophie and Ewan.

As we joined up for hugs all around, Sophie looked up at me – something that rarely happens, as we're basically the same height. Then she looked down. "What in the world are you wearing on your feet?" she asked. "You never wear heels."

Ewan glanced down thoughtfully, no doubt wondering if he could get Sophie to wear something similar. No chance! Men.

I explained the shoe debacle to her. Keith glanced at Ewan, who gave him a small smile of sympathy – and if I could read minds, I'm sure it would have been evident that Sophie's intended hoped it wasn't genetic.

"Anyway," I continued, "I'm not taking another step until I've changed out of these overpriced foot-binders." Pausing to sift through my luggage for a pair of flats, I did just that. Finally! Shoes that belonged on a human.

Soon, Sophie and Ewan had loaded us and our bags into their car, and driven us to Inverness's city center for lunch at their favorite restaurant on the banks of the River Ness: The Marigold Seed. As tired as we were, we really enjoyed getting our first glimpse of Scotland during the ride in.

Once inside, I was struck by how much this charming eatery reminded me of a favorite restaurant of ours in Nassau: Cafe Matisse. Both were quaint, laid out similarly, and featured brick walls covered in prints by Henri Matisse.

After ordering, I began to feel chatty in the way that one does when sleep deprivation shifts into a weird sort of overdrive. I decided to ask the owner of the restaurant, who had stopped by our table to check on us, if he were aware that there was a restaurant in the Bahamas that mirrored his own. I smiled in what I hoped was a friendly way, but he just looked at me oddly, and gave me a vague, "No, I'm not." As he retreated, Sophie handed me a little cosmetic mirror from her purse. I looked at her questioningly, then assessed myself with it. One front tooth was completely eclipsed by a piece of spinach. The Ugly Americans had arrived.

CHAPTER 4

POKED AT KEITH, whose head lolled to and fro, in the backseat of Ewan's Skoda, where we were riding. "Hon! You're missing everything!"

The Scottish countryside whizzed by: beautiful rolling green hills, dotted with fluffy white sheep and hazy purple heather. We were on our way to Ewan's little village (now Sophie's home, as well) on the North Sea, and while I was in desperate need of a nap, I also didn't want to miss any of the scenery.

"I've learned so much about sheep since living here," began my sister. That she had. She was so enamored of them that she'd convinced Ewan to let her keep two orphaned lambs – previously belonging to a nearby farmer friend – to raise as her own: little Hamish and Megan. "Ham and Megs," she went on, "have taught me a lot."

My husband opened one eye. "Ham and Eggs?"

"No! Ham and *Megs*. Sheesh! Why does everyone keep asking that?"

Why, indeed. Now it was Keith's turn to give a sympathetic eye – the only one open – to Ewan.

"Anyway," continued Sophie, "You should see it here in the springtime. The fields are alive with bouncy little lambs everywhere. It's like they're on pogo sticks! And, I can't tell you the times that we've had to stop the car and flip over an upside-down sheep."

Now my husband had both eyes open. "What? What do you mean?"

"It's referred to as a 'cast' position, and it's fatal. It happens if a sheep lies on its side, then accidentally rolls onto its back. It can especially occur before shearing, when the wool is heavy – a pregnant ewe being most susceptible. After a few hours on its back, stomach gasses begin to build up, and the poor sheep dies."

We pondered this for a moment.

Sophie went on. "That's not all. Lambing is especially risky. Complications result in a 14% mortality rate for lambs in general, and the rate of ewes that die during lambing can be as high as 13%, depending upon various factors."

"So what happened to little Ham's and Meg's mother?" I asked. "Did she die during lamb-birth?"

"Nope. For whatever reason, she rejected her lambs. Wouldn't or couldn't nurse them."

The woolly orphans couldn't have found a better adoptive home. For now, they were snug inside a little shed in Sophie and Ewan's garden, fitted especially to meet their needs. Once they were old enough, the farmer friend was going to allow the human parents to build a special little lamb abode in his field. There, Sophie could visit and fuss over them at some point each day. Win-win for everyone.

We continued on our way, with me scanning the landscape as it flew by. "There!" I suddenly said. "Look up that hill, to the left. I think I see an upside-down sheep!"

Three heads turned in unison. "Where?" asked Ewan. "I don't see anything."

Sophie and Keith concurred.

"No, I'm sure of it," I insisted. "See – almost to the horizon? Shouldn't we go up and help the poor thing?"

Ewan and Sophie were dubious, but Sophie was not one to let an animal suffer in any way, so she told Ewan to go ahead. He shrugged, drove several more yards, and made a sharp turn off the road, onto a rutted, overgrown path. In no time, our car was rocketing up a steep incline, pitching this way and that as we hit the occasional small rock protruding from the ground. Hanging onto the seat-back in front of me, I glanced at Keith. He was wide awake now, and with each bump of the Skoda, his head came perilously close to ramming the roof above him. My sister was unfazed; clearly, she had adapted to this sort of detour.

Several teeth-rattling minutes later, we came upon an obstacle in our path: a large stream that could only be traversed by foot. As in, using moss-covered rocks as stepping stones. Unfortunately, the belly-up sheep was on the other side, now obscured from view by a small hill.

"Hmmm. What will you guys do?" I asked.

The men looked at me sideways.

"What do you mean, what will 'we' do?" inquired my husband.

"Well, isn't this more of a man-thing? Surely you don't expect Sophie and I to forge this roaring river?"

Sophie pointed out that it was hardly a 'roaring river' – but she conceded that without her wellies she wasn't going to be much help, and thus urged Ewan to go ahead without her. "Maybe Keith can help you," she added hopefully.

Keith was incredulous. "I don't exactly have wellies on, either!"

To which Ewan assured, "No worries, freen. It sounds daft, but it's not. No need for any fantoosh footwear; I've got a stick in the boot that you can haud onto, to help make your way over the stones. I doot that you'll fall, but try not to shoogle it when you walk. Keep it steady. We just need to get frae one side to the other – then back. The main thing is to not fleg the poor yowe – assuming it's not a tup – especially if it's peelie-wally. Poor thing's already tapsalteerie – that's stressful enough."

In the backseat, Keith mouthed, "*What?*"

To which I mouthed back, "*Just go!*" And I gave him a helpful shove out the car door.

Now Ewan and Keith were stepping their way across the stream – Keith tip-toeing, in effort to stay dry. I'm sure I saw a couple of plies and a pirouette in there. Meanwhile, Sophie and I discussed her new life in Scotland, and how she was liking it.

"But how on earth do you understand Ewan?" I asked. "So far, I've been able to decipher a couple of his more obvious words – but *shoogle, peelie-wally,* and *tapsalteerie?* I was totally lost."

Sophie laughed. "Oh, you mean 'shake', 'sickly', and 'upside-down'? You get used to it. When I first moved here, it was a challenge. Now, it's second nature."

My sister exhibited her mastery of the lingo several minutes later, when she glanced toward our approaching men. "Crivvens!" she exclaimed.

My poor husband was soaking wet from head to toe, and Ewan's wool flat cap was equally soggy.

"What happened?!" I inquired, disregarding the obvious.

To which Keith curtly informed me that apparently the boat shoes he was wearing were meant for gripping slippery decks, not slimy rocks.

Ewan presented a woolen blanket from the boot of the car, which my shivering husband wrapped around himself for the rest of the drive to their village.

Once we were back rolling along the roadway, Sophie asked, "So how was the poor sheep? Is everything right again?"

"I don't know about any sheep," answered my husband, "but the abandoned mattress with all of its stuffing sticking out is just fine."

🧰

Twenty minutes later, we pulled up to an old stone farmhouse, with a whisky distillery conveniently located on the property.

"We're here!" announced Sophie.

I was confused. "We're where? I thought we were headed for our inn." I stifled a yawn; Keith and I were both in need of shut-eye – and showers.

"This is it," my sister informed me.

The Finefish B&B sat in the middle of a working sheep and cattle farm, and upon closer inspection, it was pretty attractive, with its grey sandstone exterior, and fiery red trim and doors. In the front garden, I could see a couple of roosters strutting around; their crimson combs coordinated nicely with the farmhouse's colors. Check. This could work.

After unloading our bags from Ewan's car, we approached the house's entry door, and Sophie knocked. Once, twice, three times. No answer. As Ewan pulled out his phone to call the owner – Mrs Anderson, whom he'd known for years – the proprietress opened the heavy, creaking door. She was friendly, and apologized for the delay, explaining that she'd had to deal with the stalled delivery of a new mattress; apparently the original one fell off of a truck somewhere en route. (The four of us gazed skyward.) Introductions were made, and she ushered us inside, politely ignoring Keith's damp attire.

We immediately found ourselves in a small, dimly lit stone chamber, illuminated by a single black iron sconce flickering on the west wall. To the left of the sconce was a spiral staircase, also of solid stone. Mrs Anderson motioned for us to follow her up the steps, cautioning that they were smooth from over 150 years of wear, thus some spots were a bit treacherous. Ewan and Keith bore the brunt of the baggage load, while Sophie and I followed behind, chatting about tomorrow's wedding. This light conversation was crucial for me – it served as a welcome distraction, because enclosed spiral staircases tend to give me claustrophobia, as well as sometimes triggering an inconvenient case of vertigo. Fortunately, this staircase was wide enough for two people to easily stand on the same step, so it wasn't too unnerving. In no time, we were at the top, and our hostess unlocked the door to our room.

"And here we are, freens. I've turned the heater on in the loo for you, and there are extra blankets in the cupboard." This was good, because even though it was summer, it was still plenty cold in the Highlands.

Mrs Anderson handed us a little card. "Breakfast is served in the dining room during two sittings. We can accommodate eight people at a time, so please fill this out with your time preference and your course selections. You can leave it on the red table by the entryway." She then pulled something from her pocket. "And this is for the front door; we lock it after 8:00 in the evening, so you will need it to get back inside after that." With that, she left us with an ancient-looking iron key. It reminded me of something I'd once seen in a museum: a 16th-century set of keys that were found in Kinross-shire, thought to have been used by Mary Queen of Scots when she made her escape from captivity in Lochleven Castle, in 1568.

"So, what time shall we pick you two up for dinner?" asked Sophie, as she and Ewan prepared to leave. "I know you want a shower and a nap first. As for dining...

there's not much in our little town. But, there's a good fish-and-chips take-away nearby. Keith, I know that's one of your favorites!"

My husband heartily agreed. We then chose a rendez-vous time, and my sister and her fiancé left. Now it was time to survey our tiny room, do a cursory unpacking, shower, and collapse on our bed.

The first mistake: collapsing on our bed. They don't call it 'bedrock' for nothing, and I think ours was made of it. (Beds in Europe haven't changed much since my first trip over, during the 1970s. In fact, I don't think that beds there have changed much since the 970s. Regardless of hotel stars earned, there's one commonality: granite slabs are for sleeping upon.)

"Ow!" said my husband – hitting his head on the headboard, as his spine fossilized into the mattress. "How are we supposed to sleep on this?"

"Don't complain," I answered from the minuscule bathroom. This was followed by an expletive as I gripped what I thought was a handrail while stepping out of the doll-sized shower, but was in fact a very-heated towel bar. (These were a common feature abroad, and I should have known better.)

Gawd, these would be a long two nights.

⛭

We were famished, and The Chippy was perfect. It was a simple little fish shop, offering eat-in and take-away, and we chose a seat by the window, overlooking the North

Sea. The view was beautifully desolate, and while it was cold and windy outside, we were perfectly comfortable at our little table inside, with its cozy brass lantern centerpiece surrounded by sprigs of heather.

Keith was in heaven with his first taste of true British fish-and-chips (since his Navy days, that was – when his submarine briefly surfaced in Plymouth, England, and he consumed an oil-drenched version wrapped in newspaper, dockside). The typical side dish that comes with this meal – 'mushy peas' – was not a favorite of his, however. I personally don't think they're that bad. Essentially, the dish consists of dried marrowfat peas which are first soaked overnight in water and baking soda, then rinsed, then gathered into a saucepan to be covered with water, then boiled and simmered until they become mush. Season with salt and pepper, and *voila!* Mushy peas. It's a lot of work for a lowly pea, but who am I to judge? Anyway, I took a few bites of this green side, and it made me feel very British for the moment.

After dinner, Sophie and Ewan drove us around a bit. Just outside of their small village, which contained a short, winding main street lined with quaint cottages, shops, and businesses – most either sandstone or whitewashed – we encountered more countryside. Scores of sheep and cattle grazed among the hills, and we saw an interesting breed of the latter that we certainly didn't have at home: the Highland cow, with its long horns and long brown, shaggy coat. We also glimpsed something even more amazing: a Red deer. These majestic animals are the largest land mammals in Britain, and mature stags can grow antlers that reach over three feet in length.

"During the mating season – September to November – the Red stag has a roar that is otherworldly," Sophie told us. "It's also called a 'bellow' and can be heard for up to two miles. It actually sounds a bit like a lion."

"Wow!" I said. That was something to think about. Even though it was off-season, it sure would be great to hear a stag roar.

We continued on our drive a bit until everyone agreed that it was time to call it a night. Sophie and Ewan had a big day tomorrow – their wedding was to be that evening! And I was hoping to crack open my laptop for an hour or so before bedtime, and get some writing in.

We said our goodbyes on the graveled driveway of our B&B, and Keith and I went in and headed up to our room. Once inside, I settled down at the little desk by the window – which overlooked the sea in the distance – a perfect spot to write. Keith stretched out on the bed, with a brochure for Loch Ness, which we planned on touring the day after the wedding.

"What was that?" I asked, alarmed. I'd written only three sentences and was already distracted.

"What was what?"

"Don't you hear that? I think it's a Red stag!"

"Cath," sighed my husband. "It can't be a Red stag. This is way off-season."

"But listen…. There it is again!"

This time, Keith heard it, too. A low, rumbling growl. I opened the casement windows of our third-floor room and stuck my head out – noting the white trellis that ran from the window to the ground. The breeze from the sea was cold and salty. I didn't see my quarry, so I urged Keith to go downstairs and have a look around outside.

"Don't forget the key," I advised, as it was now 8:30 PM. Even though it was getting late, there was still plenty of daylight, since it wouldn't be dark until about 10:00 PM. Scotland in the summertime!

After Keith left, I returned to my writing. Not five minutes later, I heard a loud yell – I was pretty sure it was my husband's – and a frantic pounding from outside the entry door, which echoed up the stone stairway to our room.

I raced downstairs, and yanked open the door. Keith nearly bowled me over as he rushed inside.

"Close the door!" he gasped. Confused, I did so – but not before glancing outside first. Not ten feet away stood a large, male lion – with an iron key dangling from its mouth.

Again, with the cats?!

CHAPTER 5

THE NEXT MORNING at breakfast – whipped up by Mrs Anderson, and consisting of eggs, 'streaky bacon', beans, tattie scones, fried tomatoes, coffee, and toast served efficiently in a little British toast rack – there was much discussion about what was now known as 'Keith's lion'. The other guests naturally wondered what led him to venture outdoors, defenseless, to investigate a lion's roar.

My husband gave me a side-eye. "It's a long story."

"Yes," I concurred, "but all's well that ends well. Who would have thought that an Asiatic lion would escape while being transferred from the Edinburgh Zoo, and make its way right here to our front door? It's good that Keith had the presence of mind to give it his key, as a distraction."

"I didn't *give* it the key," my husband corrected, "I *threw* the key at it, in an effort to fend it off."

A few of the male guests snickered. One scrawny little man noted that a small iron key was hardly a strong defense against a wild lion. That drew a laugh from his companions.

"*Cheeky little bugger,*" muttered my husband.

Scrawny had a wife – Brawny. She stood up and shook a bulbous fist toward Keith. "What did you call my guidman?!"

Keith looked at me for translation.

"*Husband?*" I mouthed.

To which he mouthed back, "*Poor guy.*"

Apparently Brawny was a skilled lip-reader, because she yelled, "This will teach you to eas-urram my man!" No translation was needed for that, because she followed up by throwing a soft-boiled egg squarely at my husband. It splatted above his right eye, and yellow yolk ran down his cheek – just as Sophie and Ewan walked in to meet us.

Ewan rushed to Keith's defense. "What the…?"

"It's nothing," grumbled my husband. "Let's just leave."

Ewan looked to me for a second opinion, and I nodded. The four of us headed for the dining room exit. Poor Mrs Anderson was on our heels, apologizing profusely for her other guests' behavior. She promised they would be asked to leave and forfeit their upcoming night.

With that, we trotted up to our room before heading out, so that Keith could clean up a bit.

Sophie and Ewan waited for us in their Skoda. They'd be taking us to pick up a rental car so that we could sightsee on our own, while they took care of last-minute wedding details. Tonight was the big night! Even Scrawny and Brawny couldn't ruin the mood.

Decked out in his jaunty tweed backup cap – matching Ewan's – Keith was smiling once we got into the car. So was Ewan. However, they were both looking in the same direction out their windows, and as I followed their gaze, we were all treated to the blast of a big ***REV!*** – coming from the direction of Scrawny and wife's vehicle. This was accompanied by the sight of a gooey egg mess rocketing out of their exhaust pipe. Heavy, thick smoke followed. No doubt, a costly trip to a repair garage would, too.

Don't mess with the Flat Cap Twins.

Ewan had arranged the rental car for us.

"Is this...Avis?" My husband was dubious, as we pulled into a muddy yard, with nothing in sight but a ramshackle little shed. Nearby, a tractor was parked – with a Border Collie sitting in the driver's seat.

"It's Fly!" Sophie jumped out of the car. "Here, boy!"

The dog leaped from his perch and ran to my sister, tail wagging in glee. As the two of them reveled in mutual admiration, Ewan got out of the Skoda and headed for the door to the shed. Keith and I looked at each other and shrugged. Soon, Ewan came strolling back out, accompanied by an elderly farmer with a set of keys in his hands.

"So, you're the Yanks who've come all this way for a wedding! Well, nice to know ya." He extended his hand. "I'm Stuart, and I guess you've already met Fly.

Give me a moment, and I'll bring your car around to the yard." With that, the little man stepped lively and disappeared behind the shed, with Fly close on his heels. Ewan followed.

Out of earshot of her fiancé, Sophie explained. "I hope you weren't expecting an actual rental car agency. There's nothing like that anywhere near this village; the closest thing would be in Inverness. Fingers crossed that you're at least getting a Vauxhall or a Skoda. Some of the vehicles around here are…." My sister trailed off mid-sentence, her jaw dropping in unison with ours.

Careening around the side of the mucky yard was something akin to a car – Stuart at the helm, Ewan jogging alongside, and Fly riding in the backseat. It came to an abrupt, sputtering halt, and Stuart exited. Fly did not. Behind them, Ewan stopped and gave us an apologetic shrug.

"Here you go, folks," said the farmer, proudly handing us the key to our carriage. "You got lucky, because from what I hear, this is the last car available for miles around. Tourist time in the Highlands, you know."

'Lucky' was not a word I would have used to describe what I knew Keith was thinking. Rather than being the recipients of a Skoda or a Vauxhall, we had been presented with a bright blue Reliant Robin. This car had only three wheels – the front wheel being the one that controlled the steering. And, it was made of plastic (okay, fiberglass). This automotive marvel proved popular with Northern miners in the 1970s – plus, a person only needed a motorbike license to drive it.

"What the…?" began my husband. Catching my *Be Polite* look, he amended the direction he was going. "Okay, remember the episode of *Top Gear* when a Reliant Robin was used in an attempt to modify it into a reusable Space Shuttle? It crashed to the ground and promptly exploded! It was officially referred to as the 'largest non-commercial rocket launch in European history'. Later, host and expert Jeremy Clarkson drove one 14 miles from Sheffield to Rotherham. He deemed it, 'not funny; a complete menace'." Keith concluded with, "And we're supposed to drive this as our rental car?"

"Yes, dear." I smiled through clenched teeth. "It will be fine."

Stuart looked from Keith to me, to see who would prevail. Sophie and Ewan stared at the ground. Fly barked from the backseat.

I tried another tactic. "Hon. It's only for the day. We just need to drive to Dunrobin Castle, then south a bit to Inverness and Loch Ness, and then back for the wedding tonight." I banked on the appeal of one of his favorite British characters. "Besides, it's kind of cute – like something Mr Bean would drive. And you like Mr Bean, remember?" I could see that the thought of channeling Mr Bean held some appeal. Bond…Bean…my husband was nothing if not versatile.

"Okay," Hubby conceded. "Fine. Let's get going then, before we're really pressed for time." He looked at Stuart. "Please call your dog out of the backseat?"

"Oh," replied Stuart, "Fly stays with the car."

"What?!" Now it was my turn to be incredulous. I loved my past Shih Tzus – the adorable little fluff balls! – but that was where my affinity for animals started and stopped. There was no way I was driving around with a smelly, panting sheepdog in the backseat – and I voiced this to Keith.

Fly apparently understood me, as he gave a low rumble.

"Well, now you've offended him," informed Stuart.

I gave Keith my *Do Something!* look.

My husband gave me the palms-up – and I'm sure there was a hint of vindication in there. "It'll be fine. It's only for the day, remember?"

Peeling out of the yard on three wheels – literally – we headed for nearby Dunrobin Castle. Keith, me, and Fly – who had settled down nicely in the backseat. Apparently, the dog loved a good road trip, and Stuart had assured us that he'd be fine waiting in the car wherever we went. The weather was cool but not cold, plus we could leave the window down.

"You mean, all the way down? Won't he escape?" I'd asked.

"Well, yes and no," Stuart had replied. "Fly knows his way around these parts. I've known him to go off on an adventure or two of his own when we're out and about, but he has an uncanny way of knowing to be back in the car before I am. Just remember to offer him water along the way."

We'd assured him that we would.

We were approaching the castle – Keith having quickly adapted to the steering wheel on the right side of the car, and to driving on the left-hand side of the road, to boot. In fact, he was a little bit cocky about it. He also adjusted smoothly to driving such an odd little vehicle in general. Once you learn to ride a tricycle….

He tipped his wool cap to me. "Nothing to it, ma'am."

I rolled my eyes. "Let's not be too overly confident, Jeeves."

Once parked, we climbed out of the clown car, told Fly we'd be back within the hour, and asked him to please not go anywhere. The dog gave us a wide-eyed innocent look that said, '*Who, me?*'

Dunrobin Castle is one of Scotland's Great Houses. As we walked up its beautiful tree-lined, gravel drive, the effect was truly majestic; the castle appeared similar to a French chateau. Known for its fantastic gardens, the estate dates back to the 1300s; was home to the Dukes of Sutherland; and is currently occupied by descendants, the Earls of Sutherland. It boasts a large collection of hunting trophies, as well as other curiosities from around the world. Naturally, it's rumored to be haunted, and the entrance hall features a grand staircase and portraits – all with a *Hogwarts* feel.

The castle also features another attraction, which my husband was determined to see.

"Hurry up, Cath. The falconry display starts soon!"

After dashing through parts of the castle to be revisited after the show, we found seats among the crowd that had already gathered outdoors. Following a brief but fascinating education on the subject, the demonstration began.

WHOOSH! And then another, *WHOOSH! WHOOSH!*

"What the hell was that?!" I ducked for cover as a large falcon – just moments earlier wearing a diabolical little red leather Kamikaze training helmet – whizzed by our heads. Now, I love birds – in art – but I do *not* like them flying around my head.

WHOOSH! It was back again.

Keith was totally engrossed, oblivious to my near-panic.

"Hon!" I tried again, "I can't do this. You know I don't do aviaries. This is an open air aviary!" At this point, I was looking for some sort of protection – any port in a storm – and I yanked my husband's cap off of his head, using it to cover my own.

WHOOSH!

Now it was Keith's turn. "What the…?" He reached for the top of his head – specifically, his uncovered hair.

"Don't touch it!" I barked, gagging at the same time.

Sitting atop Hubby's head like a beanie was a glob of raw entrails. Some sort of treat for a job well done, that even the falcon didn't want.

Scurrying away from the crowd, we found an open area of grass off to the side, where Keith bent over and furiously shook his head, until the glob hit the ground. *WHOOSH!* Before we could get a better look – thank God – a peregrine swooped down and picked it up. *Gag.*

"You're welcome!" my husband snapped at the bird, starting to look a little green himself.

"Hon, we've got to wash your hair!" I said, my mind already searching for where in the world this was going to happen.

"Right! How?"

Frantically scanning the grounds, I saw a green hose attached to one of the maintenance sheds tucked around the property. "Over there," I pointed. And off we went – fortunately, no one was in sight to stop us.

"Bend over," I commanded, queasy all over again, seeing the residue in his hair.

I turned on the spigot and aimed a blast of icy water at his head.

"Wait! That's cold — and you're getting my collar all wet! How am I going to dry off?" My husband was shivering now, and I went into thinking mode again.

"Hold on," I said, dashing around the corner of the shed.

In no time, I was back. "Here! Use this."

Keith stared at me like I was nuts. "What is that? Are you nuts?"

"It's all I could find. Just cover your head, and let's go." I handed him what appeared to be a raggedy old pair of men's Long Johns – in faded red.

"Fine. So much for being able to tour the rest of the castle," he grumbled.

With that, he wrapped his wet head, and we walked toward the exit – Keith looking like a sultan with bunny ears, as the legs of the garment were hardened with grime and sticking out on each side.

"Wait! Let me get a picture," I said – the glare I received causing me to reconsider.

Trudging through the gravelly car park, our kiddie car now coming into view, I squinted as I looked at the back window. There was Fly, sitting up like a dutiful passenger in his seat, patiently looking straight ahead.

My husband took in the same view, craning his neck forward. "Who's that sitting next to our dog?"

"He's not 'our' dog" – I looked again – "and I don't know!"

A few steps closer, and we realized that we were either seeing double, or that we now had two Border Collies in our back seat – each gazing forward and ready to roll.

"What the…? Where did that one come from?!" Keith was at a loss for further words.

I pulled out my cell phone and called Sophie.

Upon hearing of the situation, she told me to hold tight, and that she would have Stuart call me back to advise us.

A few moments later, my phone rang.

"Uh huh. Uh huh. Uh huh. Okay. If you're sure. Uh, thank you, Stuart." I hung up.

Keith looked at me expectantly.

I shrugged. "It's Judy. Fly's girlfriend. She's coming to Loch Ness with us."

At that, we got into our three-wheeler and drove off – Keith's faded red bunny ears flapping in the breeze.

CHAPTER 6

*H*ONNNNNK! HONK! HONK! HONNNNNK!

"Keith! What are you doing?"

A line of cars had formed behind us on the A9, the longest road of its kind in the country; a major north-south route that has been called the 'spine of Scotland'. We were on our way to Inverness – specifically Loch Ness, where we'd booked a short boat tour. Our little three-wheeled car was suddenly swerving, and Fly and his main squeeze Judy were hunkered down in the backseat, the whites of their eyes showing.

"What do you mean, 'What am I doing'? I'm trying to keep the lunatic behind me from running us off of the road!"

There was a reason the lunatic behind us appeared angry: he was driving with a pair of faded red Long Johns plastered to his windshield. They had flown off of Keith's head and out the window, a half mile back.

"Well, criminently! Don't get us killed! Just pull over and let him go past." I turned around to look out the back window, and saw a grizzled, angry face peering through the crotch of his windshield dressing.

"Pull over where?" implored my husband.

He had a point. There was little shoulder to the road, and the deep, cold waters of the Moray Firth – an inlet of the great North Sea – were on the other side. (Home to around 900 harbor seals, and up to 1300 grey seals in the summer, I'd been scanning the water hopefully – but hadn't seen any yet.) Pulling over was not an option.

I continued my vigil out the back window, and fortunately, it was only a matter of time before the Long Johns flew off the irritated driver's windshield, over a fence, and into a nearby field. With that – and a momentary cessation of oncoming traffic in the opposite lane – the menacing driver sped around us, shouting something at Keith as he sped by. I doubt it was a friendly *Haste ye back*.

A half hour from Loch Ness, Fly and Judy started romping around in the backseat of our car. This was no easy feat, as it was a small space. One of them had discovered a short piece of dirty old rope, and they were playing tug-of-war with it.

"Stop it, you two," I said lamely. Right. If anything, that spurred them further, and soon there was a flurry of two tails and eight paws behind us. Occasionally one or the other would bark. And slobber was starting to fly. In no time, a large drop of something landed on my wrist.

"Keith!" I said, flinging my hand. "Aaaackkk! Do something with those two!" To further my point, I wiped the drool on the nearest thing I could find: the knee of my husband's jeans.

"Fly! Judy!" Keith barked – no pun intended. "Knock it off! Do I have to pull over and stop this car?"

I swear, they understood. They stopped immediately, Fly gave an apologetic whimper, and they both laid down in their own seats – remaining that way until we pulled into the Loch Ness tourist center. (Why do kids always listen to the father, but not the mother? Good grief.)

Once parked in the small, crowded lot, and fixing a fresh bowl of water for Fly and Judy (Stuart kept an assortment of bowls and other vessels in the boot of the car; presumably Fly and his friends were frequent passengers), we reminded the dogs of the rule: "Don't go anywhere." Judy was asleep, and Fly's eyes were closed – but he did lift one eyelid and look at us as if to say, "Sure. Right."

We headed off past the assorted little visitor shops and displays – all of which featured the Loch Ness Monster for sale in various forms – and across the street to the dock on the loch.

Approaching the tour point that we were ticketed for, a sign told us that the vessel we were going on was actually a small research boat.

We climbed aboard the red-hulled *Nessie Quest*, joining our weathered little captain, his one-man crew, and three other passengers. Before heading out, the captain went over a few safety rules, as well as a brief history of Nessie, of the loch itself, and of the imposing Urquhart Castle ruins that are situated high on a beautiful green headland overlooking Urquhart Bay, on the banks of the loch.

"The waters off Urquhart Castle have produced the largest number of Nessie sightings," began Captain Murdo Wight. "The castle itself, which you will see on your right as we head out, dates back to the 11th century – although the well-preserved ruins that you see today date largely from the late 16th century. In 1692, the castle was reduced to its present state when it was blown up to prevent Jacobite revolutionaries from making use of it."

I made a mental note of these facts – they would make an interesting addition to my book in progress. If I ever got past page one, that was. Sigh.

Captain Murdo took a sip of coffee from his battered tin cup. "As for Loch Ness itself, it's extremely long and narrow. Running 24 miles in length, it contains Britain's greatest volume of fresh water. Depths of over 800 feet have been plumbed, and its murkiness is due to the peat-richness of it. Poor visibility, plus an average water temperature of five degrees Celsius [59 degrees Fahrenheit], mean that divers and submersibles lose daylight just a few meters below the surface."

At this point, we tourists collectively looked over the side, into the deep abyss. Naturally, that included an intense scan from all, hoping to spot the elusive monster.

"Now Nessie," continued the captain, "made very few appearances in the 1400 years following her first recorded sighting by the Irish monk, St Columba.

Then, in the 1930s, there were several reported sightings, and a controversial photo presumably of the monster was published in a London newspaper. Since then, despite several hoaxes, there has been enough inexplicable evidence to spark the interest of science. There still is."

Left to ponder this knowledge as we cruised around the misty lake – foreboding clouds hanging low, adding to the moody atmosphere – I suddenly remembered the treat that our loony neighbor Osman had asked me to deliver to Nessie. Reaching into the outer pocket of my water-resistant Tumi bag – khaki, so that it coordinated with everything, of course – I pulled out the little snack and tossed it over the rail of the boat.

Instantly, there was an enormous ruckus in the water below, and the handful of passengers – as well as the crewman, and Keith – rushed over to view the eruption.

My husband looked at me, then down at the churning mess. "Did you just toss something into the water?"

"Ach, what on earth was that?" echoed the crewman.

By now, scores of thrashing eels were competing for the lone treat, gnashing at one another in the process. Little did they know it was hardly worth it.

"Chocolate salami," I replied sheepishly. "You know: the Romanian biscuit-type thing made with broken cookies, Turkish delight, almonds, and cocoa." Didn't everyone know what chocolate salami was? Sheesh.

Captain Murdo joined our group, and he wasn't happy. "And ma'am, you thought that the eels of Loch Ness should be fed this concoction...*why?*"

"Not the eels, sir," I explained. I hadn't even known that Loch Ness had eels. "It was for Nessie."

Several pairs of disbelieving eyes looked at me – not the least of which were my husband's.

I continued, "See, we have this neighbor from Romania…."

"Never mind," the captain cut in. "Apparently, I neglected to mention one of the main rules on the loch: *Don't throw anything into it!*" He stomped back to the wheel.

I apologized, everyone dispersed, and I thought that was the end of it.

Moments later, one of the women on the boat screamed.

Keith gave me his *Does this involve you?* look, to which I gave an innocent palms-up.

Following the other passengers to the scene of the melee off the stern of the boat, we saw the problem: the screaming woman's polka-dotted canvas tote was resting open on the deck, its contents clearly visible: sunglasses, a small umbrella, two bottles of water, and the slimy head of an eel – its mouth gaping – clearly a casualty in the Chocolate Sausage feeding frenzy.

Off the boat and back at our car, Keith opened the passenger door for me. Looking inside, I immediately noticed something wrong with the picture.

"Fly and Judy are gone," I announced.

"Well, that's just great," declared my husband, looking at his watch. "It's almost two o'clock, I'm starving and would like a bite of lunch, we have to be at the church before six, and now we have two AWOL dogs."

"No worries." I pulled out my phone and called Sophie.

Within a minute or two, I received a call from Stuart.

"Uh huh, uh huh, uh huh. I see. Thank you, Stuart." I hung up.

Keith looked at me expectantly.

"Stuart says not to worry. Fly and Judy have certain hitchhiking points that they use to make their way back home." I shrugged. Don't people teach their kids the dangers of anything anymore?

Next, we took a moment to pop into one of the little eateries at the Visitor Center, hoping for a quick bite. As usual, I nabbed a table in the crowded dining area, while my husband went to the counter to order. He'd asked me what I'd wanted; my only stipulation was one that he knew well: iced tea. This was a bit of a challenge in Britain, as in all this land of tea lovers, there was nothing available but a pot of hot. So we'd established a routine of asking for two things: a pot of tea, and a glass of ice. Invariably, we were met with three things: a stare of incomprehension, an eventual a pot of steaming hot tea, and a clear glass harboring two tiny ice cubes marooned at the bottom. This was always followed by my apologetic request for more ice; eventually we learned to ask for a glass of ice 'full, FULL' – complete with a dramatic interpretation of what such a glass with adequate ice might actually look like.

"Here." Keith unceremoniously plopped two plates of foreign matter on our table. "It was all they had left. Extra-busy tourist day, they said."

By now, I was hungry – my trusty sidekick, a Fun Size pack of Peanut M&Ms to stave off famine, now long spent. I sized up the odd-looking item – a large Idaho potato-like offering – and cut into it. Hmm. Some sort of ground beef inside of a vegetable, I decided.

I took a bite.

"Aaackk! What IS this?" This was bad. Very bad. This mouthful had to go somewhere – and it definitely wasn't going down. Frantically looking around for an adequate place to deposit it – the flimsy paper napkin with a smiling Nessie logo wouldn't do – I waved my hands at Keith, code for *Do Something!* (A standard code in our marriage that he was well versed in.)

Ever the problem-solver, my husband glanced around, and grabbed the only thing he could find: an abandoned kids' green Croc from under the table next to us. Perfect. It served the purpose, and it was a fitting color.

Upon his return to the table, after having thrown away the evidence for me, I asked my husband what on earth that muck was – which, by the way, he'd been eating without a glimmer of revulsion.

"Haggis," he replied, forkful poised.

"*Haggis! HAGGIS?* Do you know what that even is?! Eeeew!" I was gobsmacked. "Well, I'll tell you. It's a so-called 'pudding' containing sheep's heart, liver, and lungs. It's usually minced, with onion, oatmeal, suet, spices, and salt, then mixed with stock – and stuffed into and cooked inside of THAT." I pointed at the encasement holding this concoction, for emphasis. "THAT," I continued, "is a sheep's stomach! Eeeew, eeeew, EEEEW."

Unfazed, Keith thought for a moment. "Well, I've had worse," he declared, taking another bite. "Remember, I grew up in east Texas."

He had a point.

⚏

Arriving back in our village by 4:30 PM – the drive was uneventful and canine free – we parked the car at the Finefish B&B. I exited and dashed ahead through the red front door. It was now starting to drizzle, and my shoes were a bit wet.

WHUMP! Two bounding steps up the ancient stone stairway, and I was flat on the ground.

Keith walked in, and dropped our bags in order to help. "What happened?!"

I grimaced. "Crap! Double crap! I think I twisted my ankle." This was not good, as I was the matron of honor in my sister's wedding. How was I going to walk gracefully down the aisle in less than two hours, a vision of loveliness in pale pink chiffon?

After helping me upstairs to our room, my husband located some ice, and we set about trying to wrap my ankle. There wasn't any real first aid available on such short notice, so we improvised.

"Well, that looks just great," I huffed, surveying the look. It would have to do, as it was now time to get dressed and head for the Church of Scotland, where the nuptials were to take place.

Once we were ready – I in my pink dress, and Keith in a trim navy suit – I hobbled down the stone stairs with Hubby's assistance, we entered our three-wheeled carriage, and we were off.

The church stood under a now-sunny sky: a beautiful historic building of grey sandstone and wooden beams, with an impressive pipe organ inside its chancel.

Guests were starting to arrive. All of the males wore kilts, from ages 0 to 90 – proudly displaying their individual family tartans (skillfully hiding other items; yes, it's true: most Scottish males do not wear underwear beneath their kilts). Female guests wore pastel dresses or suits, their outfits complete with obligatory fascinators atop their heads; these feathery, flowery hats would make any cockatoo – or the Queen – proud. Some were quite impressive.

Most of the wedding guests were friends and family of Ewan, but Sophie had people there from the US as well, including her bridesmaid, Patty – and Sophie's entire Scottish Highland Dance Group, from our hometown in Florida. This group was something that my sister had joined before making her move to Scotland, and they'd remained close. Like Sophie – and pretty much every Scottish citizen from young to old – they knew the traditional dances well, and took them seriously.

I stopped to talk with Patty, and we went off together to find the bride.

Keith disappeared; I assumed that he was attending to last minute details, as he had the honor of walking my sister down the aisle.

Finding Sophie ready and glowing, Patty and I left her in her small dressing room, and headed out to the red-carpeted aisle, to await the beginning of our march.

Soon, the organ music began, and Ewan's little niece Penny, the flower girl, started down the aisle. Beside her was an adorable toddler – Ewan's nephew and ring bearer, Jamie – in a tiny kilt and full regalia. Next up was Patty; she stepped out in time to the music – and then it was my turn. Before my first foot hit the ground – with a twisted ankle, I stepped carefully – the music stopped, and instead there was a loud, high-pitched blast behind me.

WAHHH wah WAAHHH wah WAAAHHH!

Too bad that no one warned me to expect a bagpiper to be on my tail, because it was definitely startling. Enough so that I jumped a bit, dislodging the makeshift bandage around my injured ankle – which was in fact, one of Keith's neckties. Up until now, it was fairly well hidden under my dress (if one didn't look too closely), but now it was trailing behind me like a burgundy and white striped snake. Nonetheless, I regained my composure, and continued my hobble down the aisle, taking my place beside Patty.

The bagpiper halted, then began a new tune.

Sophie and my husband appeared at the end of the aisle, ready for the march to the altar. All eyes were on the bride – except for mine, which were on my husband. Who was now wearing a kilt. And he was clearly loving it, because he looked very pleased with himself, very 'one of the clan'. Men!

Regaining my composure for a second time, I watched as halfway down the aisle trek, guests began pointing and snickering behind Sophie and Keith. Following their gaze, I was shocked to see Fly and Judy strolling side by side as though it were a double wedding – and I was even more shocked to see that Fly was carrying something in his mouth. Once at the altar, the dog trotted over to my husband, and dropped the object at his feet.

Everyone looked down to inspect what turned out to be a clear zip-lock bag – with a pair of men's under-wear inside.

I raised an eyebrow at Keith.

He winked at me, then mouthed, *"Commando."*

The wedding dinner, and the dance afterward, were a lot of fun.

Dinner included roast beef or local salmon, several other culinary treats, and a traditional wedding cake similar to a fruitcake (albeit, a good one) with fondant icing. Scottish favorites with intriguing names were offered: Clootie Dumplings, Cocky Leeky Soup, Scotch Woodcock, Sweet Mutton Hotpot and Dumplings, Stovies, Cullen Skink, and of course, Scotch Eggs.

The dance was lively – if a bit awkward for me, as I'm a terrible dancer, and I was at a further disadvantage with my wobbly ankle and lack of Scottish dance skills. Nonetheless, I was dragged out to the dance floor by Ewan's brother John – who I am sure regretted it immediately, once he saw how inept I was. He gallantly tried to coach me, to no avail.

Deciding to sit the rest of the dances out, and happy to be an observer (Keith concurred; it was much more fun from the sidelines, as we have four left feet between us), there was still no peace for me. Eunice, one of the women from the visiting Scottish Dance club who was sitting at our table, heckled me relentlessly about not getting out there and kicking up my ghillies, so to speak. I have no idea why she even cared, but an end was put to it once and for all when she left her seat for a moment to hit the dance floor.

The pesky woman returned to find a zip-lock bag on her chair. Judy was sitting at attention next to it, with a rose from the bride's bouquet in her teeth, and a gleam in her eye.

Late that night, we returned to our B&B, after lots of hugs and well wishes for Sophie and our new brother-in-law Ewan. They were heading off to the Orkney Islands in the morning for their honeymoon, and we would be leaving for the next leg of our adventure: London!

Exiting our tiny car and approaching the entry door to Finefish, Keith found he didn't have our key.

"I must have left it in my pants pocket," he lamented. His pants – as well as the rest of his suit – were still at the church. Great. Sophie would have to ship them home to us.

I asked the obvious. "Well, how are we going to get in? It's cold and dark out here, and the nearest house – farm or otherwise – is at least five miles away."

"No worries!" assured my husband, his bravado likely spurred on by his one glass of whisky at the wedding (we're both lightweights). He disappeared around the corner of the farmhouse, where our window was located on the third floor.

I had a sudden flash of what he was planning. "Keith, don't…."

A solid thud and a loud yelp later, my husband was lying tangled in the now-broken trellis that he'd tried to climb.

"Are you okay?" I rushed to his side. "It's a good thing that rose bush broke your fall!"

"Yeah." He winced, as he removed a thorn. "So glad I decided to go commando."

CHAPTER 7

"DO YOU REALLY think that you have time for that?"

Keith and I were waiting at the Inverness Airport for our short flight to London, it was early morning, and a flight delay had just been announced. I'd decided to make good use of the time, and work on my book-in-progress. By this point, I actually had two whole pages written. I guessed that made me an official writer, and I was anxious to proceed.

"Yes!" I replied. "Anything I can get down will be a plus. I'm on a roll."

"And what's your topic – this time?"

My supportive husband had been hearing me lament my lack of authorship for a few years now, and during my many starts and stops, I'd changed topics frequently. The problem was, I couldn't seem to settle on one subject within my genre – historical non-fiction – because I was interested in so *many* areas of history. Specifically, I loved ancient Egypt and ancient Rome, but I also found the medieval era fascinating – plus, a lot of other periods intrigued me. Help! I was basically the fly that couldn't decide where to land, so it just sat on the window, watching the parade of successful writers go by.

I smacked the table holding my laptop, for emphasis. "Well, I'll be a fly no more! I have an idea!"

Keith raised an eyebrow. He'd long since given up attempting to decipher my logic, and resigned himself to hoping for the best – and that it didn't involve him.

I continued. "I think I've hit upon something that will allow me to change subjects with each chapter, in a way that will still bring cohesiveness to my book."

"Go on…."

"Oscar Wilde – the Irish playwright and author – once said: 'Life imitates art, far more than art imitates life.' However, the opposite often applies, and my book could explore the life and times of the contemporary world, relative to the individual works of art being featured. Rather than being a book on art history, this would be about the historical world surrounding the art."

"It's good…but I have a better idea," suggested Keith. "Have you ever thought of writing humorous fiction? Your main character could be an aspiring writer and historian, whose attempts are hilariously thwarted at every turn. It could be funny!" Men. Where do they get such lame ideas?

"No, thanks," I huffed. "I think I'd prefer to write something a little more cerebral."

After landing in London, we took a black cab to a boutique hotel on Nevern Square, in the Earls Court district, not far from Kensington Palace. The restored red-brick Georgian townhouse was situated across the street from Nevern Square Garden, and the whole area was very 'Mary Poppins' – complete with the iconic Victorian, black wrought iron fencing found throughout the city. I loved it!

My husband had another focus.

"Why are there so many stairs in Britain?" Keith observed, dragging our bags gingerly up the slick, white marble entry steps where the driver had left us in a light rain.

Once inside the small lobby, we went to the check-in desk. Waiting for someone to appear, I looked around. I loved the decor! It was a beautiful mix of European and Oriental influences, and there was a lot of carved teak furniture – including a Taj Mahal-looking birdcage complete with two budgies in residence. Not my personal style, but it was captivating.

I pointed at the brochure I'd picked up. "Look at these room names: Saanvi Suite; Eshana Suite, and so forth…. They sound so exotic! I wonder which one will be ours." While I knew that the hotel had twenty rooms, and that each one was different, I presumed they were all on a par with each other.

Before my husband could answer, an Indian gentleman appeared at the desk.

"Hello. How may I help you?" inquired Name, according to the name on his name tag.

"Good morning," replied Hubby. "My wife and I would like to check in, please. The name is Keith Keith."

Name looked down at his registry, then at his computer. "I'm sorry, but we have no reservation under that name."

"But you must!" I interjected. "I booked it online months ago. I have an email receipt right here." I handed him the printout.

Name glanced at my receipt, then at his computer again. "Ahhh, I see the problem now. Because you neglected to give us a surname, we were unable to confirm it for you."

I pointed to my email. "But there's a surname right there: *Keith*."

Uh-oh, here we go again.

"No ma'am, you're confused. Keith is not your surname. It is your husband's first name," insisted Name, now growing bored with the whole exchange.

"I am NOT confused. My husband's name is Keith Keith! Look at his passport!"

At this point, Keith had the document out and ready. He knew the routine.

"Well," sniffed Name. "That is one odd name situation, if I ever saw one."

My husband had heard enough. "Hold on, Name. *You're* telling *me* that *I* have an odd name? Your name is NAME, for crying out loud!"

Name pulled himself up to his full 5'3" height. "I'll have you know, sir, that Name is a very common uncommon Indian name! It is of Sanskrit origin, and it means 'supreme'!" With that, he picked up the desk phone and called his manager.

"Uh huh, uh huh, uh huh. I see. Thank you." Name hung up the receiver, then addressed us. "We're giving you our special Garden Room." He handed us a room key, pointed toward the elevator, and warned, "You may find that two trips are needed. You have a lot of bags there."

We did?

We walked the five steps to the shiny brass elevator door, and when it opened, we could see Name's point.

My husband turned to me. "Okay, we can do this one of three ways. Either I go up with two bags, check out the room, then you come up with the remaining two bags; or you go up first with two bags, then I'll follow with the other two."

"What's the third way?"

"We tell that snooty Name to get his derrière over here and transport our bags in whatever 'supreme' manner he is accustomed to."

I selected option One, and Keith went up first.

In no time, he was back. "Up isn't up."

"What do you mean, 'Up isn't up?' What else can it be?" This can't be good, I thought.

"It's down. As in, half-down. Apparently, 'Garden Room' is synonymous with 'subterranean closet'. We're not taking it. They'll have to give us something else."

I waited by the large teak birdcage, while Keith went back to the desk to parley.

"Here, birdie, birdie, birdie," I said to neither one in particular.

Feathery heads together in some sort of budgie-huddle, they stopped their soft chattering and looked at me. The larger of the two – I'd just noticed a little plaque featuring their names and pictures; they were Kiwi and Houdini – flew to a perch, near the side where I'd leaned in close to admire both the birds and the intricacies of the carved cage. The wool scarf that I wore around my neck was intriguing to Houdini, and in no time, he had a piece of its tan yarn in his beak. And the yarn was woven into the scarf's label.

"Hey!" I said. "Let go!"

Houdini was having none of it. There quickly became a discreet tug of war – discreet that was, until a thread from my now-fraying accessory became entangled in the nearby brass latch to the cage's exit, during a fierce yank. In a blur, the little wooden door popped open, and a rush of green flew past my face. (Birds! Again!) Little Kiwi was no fool; she saw her opening, too, plus a fragment of scarf – and took both.

Keith's head whipped around as Houdini, then Kiwi, zoomed past the desk where he and Name were engaged in heavy negotiations.

Name's head swiveled, too. "Were those my birds that just flew by?" His voice was raised in alarm.

"Uhm, yes – I'm very sorry. You see…. "

"Sorry? SORRY? Those birds are of royal Indian descent!" Looking out the open door to the street, Name amended, "*Were* of...!"

Houdini and Kiwi had flown straight outdoors. Within seconds, there was the honking of horns and screeching of tires.

Keith and I stood frozen – with a good view of the scene unfolding outside.

Name ran out the front door and down the marble steps, over the sidewalk and into the street. The light drizzle was now a heavier rain, and someone was huddled down in front of a red Mini Cooper, holding a black umbrella over the two avian...victims.

Gawd. I hoped they weren't victims!

Keith's dropped jaw returned to its proper position. "What on earth happened?"

I explained the little incident.

"Well, I hope these two blue-blooded birds make it, or we could have an international incident on our hands. Crikey!"

Several tense minutes passed, before Name returned indoors – cupping the two delicate fugitives in his hands. He set them gently in their cage, then turned to us, perplexed.

"Talk about luck," he said, presenting a fragment of something for our inspection. "The only thing that saved these two little beauties was this odd scrap of scarf." He shook his head. "The woman who would have otherwise hit them said she didn't see any birds, but she slammed on her brakes when this Burberry label fluttered past her windscreen. She took it as a sign; apparently she was on her way to Burberry's in Knightsbridge, to break off a date with one of their executives. Now she's changed her mind. She said 'plaid trumps all' – whatever that means."

Name and my husband exchanged stymied glances. For the moment, the two men were simpatico.

"See?" I gestured toward Houdini and Kiwi, who were once again chirping happily in their regal cage. "No harm, no 'fowl' – so to speak."

The upshot of our accommodation situation was that there were no other rooms available for the first night of our stay. We were relegated to the partially buried Garden Room for one night, with the promise that for subsequent nights we would be upgraded to the Eshana Suite.

"The Eshana Suite." I said. "That sounds luxurious!"

"Could be…." My husband waggled his eyebrows at me. "It's an Indian word for 'desire'."

"Right. Well, don't get your *aasha* up," I advised.

"What does that mean?"

"Hopes," I explained, with an eye-roll. Men!

We tag-teamed the elevator with our bags, down a half-level.

Once the brass doors opened, I saw the problem.

Stepping out onto a cramped landing, there was an immediate turn to the right, followed by six steps down – steps which ran below a very low, sloped ceiling.

"Watch your head," advised Keith.

I bumped my head. "Thanks. What the heck is the deal down here?"

Surveying the area – which took about two seconds – it appeared that we were alone in the burrow. Just one room existed – plus a small utility closet that held two antiquated vacuums. A little plaque on our door announced *Garden Room*.

We unlocked the door, but progressed no further. The bed, as it turned out, protruded by about a foot into what should have been the door's clearance.

"Well, this is ridiculous," grumbled my husband. "How are we supposed to get our bags – not to mention, ourselves – into this tiny box?"

"Move over so I can get a look." I squeezed past. "Hmm. Well, look how cool the furniture is! Look at all of this wood!" Beautifully carved teak pieces were crammed everywhere: a four-poster bed, an armoire, a small desk and chair – it was definitely elegant, if tight. "Come on," I encouraged, "it will be fine for one night. Let's just bring our bags in, and then head out for the day. We're in London! Time's a-wasting!"

Going in first, climbing over the bed to do so, Keith stood on the other side of the pint-sized room. "Here. I have an idea." He grasped the edge of the bed's frame – which was heavy – and began to pull. "If we can just move it enough to get the door open all the way…."

CRACK!

"What was that?!" I called from the doorway.

"Well, it wasn't my back, if that's what you're concerned about," he puffed.

"I'm more worried about the expensive piece of furniture!" I replied, instantly rethinking my priority…. "Now what are we going to do?"

"Do you have any wood glue in your bag?" asked my husband.

"Wood glue! Why on earth would I have wood glue? Plus, that's your territory, not mine." Geez. "The best I can offer is paper tape."

"Paper tape? Why did you bring paper tape?"

"Because. Everyone knows that if you tape your foot in areas that might otherwise get killer blisters from lots of walking, you're as good as gold. Runners do it all the time."

"Well,   hand it over, Wilma Rudolph. I need to try and fix this."

Ten minutes later, our bed had received first aid, our bags were situated in the room, and we were headed out for our first day in London.

It was almost noon, and we had a Red Double-Decker sightseeing bus to catch!

CHAPTER 8

"MIND THE GAP!" I said.

"What are you talking about?" My husband glanced down as he took a step. "Mind what gap?"

We had left our hotel, and were walking up the sidewalk toward the Earl's Court station, which was the nearest Tube, aka Underground. In other words, London's subway system. From there, we would ride to St James Park, where we'd disembark and walk the short distance to The Albert, a historic pub, for lunch. Afterward, we would catch one of the double-decker tour buses – which would not only give us the lay of the land, but would allow us to 'hop-on/hop-off' at various sites. Perfect!

"You'll see. It's something I remember about the Tube, from my trip here ages ago. There's a constant recording running for many of the trains, depending upon the station – announced in a very proper British voice! – reminding passengers to step on and off carefully, since there's a large gap between the platforms and the trains. It originated in 1968," I added.

"Ahh," replied Keith. "Well, mind the rat."

I rolled my eyes. "Gap. GAP."

"No...*rat*." My husband gestured downward.

"Aaaackkk!" Sure enough, a large dead, bloated rat was lying on the sidewalk in front of us, just where I was about to step. "When were you going to point that out?"

"I just did," came the reply. "At any rate, there's our station up ahead. Let's hoof it.

🧳

Having successfully navigated the Oyster card (ticket) purchase, the turnstiles, and the ancient glass lift to the platform level (did this tiny elevator date back to the station's opening in the late 1800s?), we were finally on the train and moving.

Before reaching our St James Park stop, there were several other stops, including historic Victoria Station, famed since the 19th century for its quick connections to seaside resorts such as Brighton. Also, this was the station that allowed a quick transfer to Sloane Square.

I sighed. "I would have made a good Sloane Ranger."

"How would you have made a good Lone Ranger?"

"Sloane. *Sloane*." Geez! Sometimes the communication gap between my husband and me was exhausting. "Princess Diana was a Sloane Ranger, for example. Basically, it's a young upper- or middle-upper class woman with a home in both London and in the country.

She wears pricey but casual country clothes." I googled the topic, to further make my point. "It says here, 'The Sloane girl will spend large amounts to look scruffy. She strongly avoids looking like she's made an effort. This is how she differs from generally rich people.' "

I pondered that charade for a moment. Well, at any rate, I wanted to buy something 'Sloane', if time permitted.

My husband suspected as much. "Moving on," he redirected, "our stop is coming up. It's crowded on here, and these train doors don't stay open for long. You'd better hand me one of your bags, so that we can move quickly." He did a double-take. 'Wait. Why do you have two bags? Isn't your purse enough? What's in the tote?"

"Dickens is in the tote. And don't say another word to me about it," I advised. "I can't let Frank down. Once we find Charles Dickens's grave inside of Westminster Abbey, we're good."

Before he could reply, an overhead announcement indicated our upcoming stop, in a very smooth British monotone: "St James Pahrrk…."

As the train came to a halt and the doors opened, Keith gave a resigned sigh and relieved me of the tote carrying the felicitous feline. We disembarked.

Trekking toward the pub on Victoria St, I gave my husband a brief history lesson. "The Albert was built in 1862, named in tribute to Queen Victoria's husband, Prince Albert—"

"Right!" Keith interjected. "Prince Albert in a can! I used to play that phone game as a kid…."

I rolled my eyes. "Yes. Anyway, according to the pub's website, it survived The Blitz during World War II, with its Victorian features remaining virtually untouched: the ornate ceilings, the hand-etched frosted glass windows, and the iron balconies inside. Amazing! And another cool thing: it still has a Parliamentary Division Bell."

"What did that do?"

"Well, the clanging of a division bell was a noise intended to alert any MPs (Members of Parliament) that it was time to put down their food and spirits, and return to the House of Commons to vote. At one time, about 400 bells existed in pubs and restaurants in Westminster, because of its proximity to Parliament."

"Ahh. Well, here we are." My husband opened the pub's door for me.

After ordering fish-and-chips at the beautiful old mahogany bar, we took seats at one of the round wooden tables nearby.

Keith went back to the bar to retrieve our drinks, which naturally included my pot of Earl Grey and a glass of however much ice we could procure.

He placed my iced tea formula before me. "Be careful pouring that."

"Got it." Except, I didn't – because as soon as I poured the scalding liquid into the tall glass with its two lonely ice cubes at the bottom, the glass shattered and there was a cascade of hot tea running across the table and over the edge. I jumped up to avoid being soaked – and burned.

I shouted to Keith, "Move Dickens out of the way!"

I meant, of course, the tote – but as my husband fumbled around under the table for my bag (yes, from the sticky pub floor; there was nowhere else for it), a woman at the next table misunderstood and assumed that we were looking for our dog. Dogs under pub tables in Britain were ubiquitous.

"Oh, the poor thing!" the lady exclaimed. "Here, pooch, pooch, pooch," she began.

Soon, other pub guests were doing the same.

My husband stood up, explaining to the Samaritans, "No, no – it's fine. You don't understand! It's only a dead cat."

A collective look of disgust shot our way.

"Americans!" sniffed our neighbor to her companion, in a stage whisper.

We wiped up our mess with the barkeep's well-worn rag, and our fish-and-chips arrived. Heads down, we tried to enjoy our meal while avoiding the curious glances around us – and any further debacle.

⊞

Walking down the sidewalk after lunch, we located one of the red tour buses that matched our reserved tickets. Attempting to board, we were told by the impatient driver that while yes, this was one of their stops, and yes, it was a hop-on/hop-off situation, it did not, in fact, apply to us. Since we were just beginning our journey for the day, we would have to walk several blocks farther to one of the approved embarkation points.

I was already doubting the sufficiency of Wilma Rudolph's blister tape – but off we went.

Twenty minutes and a first blister later, we were at the correct spot and on our bus. Keith wanted to sit upstairs on the breezy open deck, but I argued not.

"My hair!" I thought I stated the obvious.

"What's wrong with your hair? It's fine," came my husband's usual response.

"I know. That's the problem. It IS fine." followed my usual retort. It was true. My hair was the bane of my existence.

Knowing from experience that he couldn't win, Keith found two seats on the lower deck, and we adjusted our individual tour headphones to English. First stop: Westminster Abbey! I told Dickens to hang tight.

🧳

Approaching the Abbey, I filled Keith in on its history. "According to an article in *Smithsonian Magazine*, the abbey is much older than Germany, much older than Italy, a little older than France, and not much younger than England. It was founded around 960 as a Benedictine monastery, and Edward the Confessor – the Anglo-Saxon king who was later made a saint – had a Romanesque church constructed on the site beside his palace. It was consecrated on December 28, 1065 – Hey! My birthday!"

"Yes," observed my husband, "give or take 900 years."

"Anyway," I continued, "the king was too ill to attend the consecration, dying only a few days later. He was buried in the Abbey. His successor, Harold Godwinson, ruled for a few months until his defeat and death at the Battle of Hastings. Enter the Norman victor, William the Conqueror – who made sure to have his coronation in the Abbey, attempting to legitimize an association with Edward. Ever since then, the Abbey has been famed as both a royal burial place and a crowning place. Sort of a 'church of bones and thrones', as the article puts it."

I went on with my history lesson. "So every monarch since William the Conqueror has been crowned in the Abbey, with the exception of Edward V (one of the two young prince brothers who mysteriously died while imprisoned together in the Tower of London) and Edward VIII (who abdicated), who were never crowned. The ancient Coronation Chair – in steady use since 1308 – can still be seen." I added, "I can't wait to see that!"

Keith interrupted my tutorial. "Well, the Abbey website said that there are around 3300 burials in the church, plus many more memorials. And, there are over 600 monuments and wall tablets. We'd better shake a leg if we want to see it all."

"Right. The interior is enormous, covering 32,000 square feet – and the grounds include ancient cloisters, plus three gardens. That's a lot to cover."

My husband thought for a moment. "So who all is buried here? And who was buried last?"

"Actually, thousands of renowned dead! Royals, nobles, writers [I had a moment of wistfulness], musicians, scientists, politicians – the greatest of Brits! The last burial was of Stephen Hawking."

Keith was impressed with the scientist bringing up the rear.

Entering the Abbey, we were awestruck by the sheer enormity of it, in addition to feeling a profound reverence for its eternal dwellers. And, it was not lost on us that most recently, Prince William and Princess Catherine had been married there – and that decades earlier, Princess Diana's funeral had taken place within the same hallowed walls.

Abbey map in hand, we set out to find various tombs: Keith, myself, and Dickens the Cat.

"Where – and how – are you going to place *that?*" inquired my husband, pointing at the small copper canister barely visible in my tote. Fortunately, it had passed through security without question – ditto for the then-empty vessel's transatlantic ride in my suitcase, days earlier. (The cat's ashes were not in it, because I wanted to keep them close – in case of lost baggage.)

"I'm not sure," I mused. "I guess I'll figure it out when we get to Charles Dickens's tomb. I imagine that I will simply set the little coffin in a discreet place, and leave it there, wishing for the best." I gave a hopeful shrug, aiming for his concurrence, but his expression was closed – which I knew translated to, 'I want no part of this.'

"At any rate," I continued, "we have other graves to visit first, before we get to Poets' Corner. Dickens will be in good company, by the way. In addition to his namesake, he will rest for all eternity alongside the likes of Shakespeare, Jane Austen, the Bronte sisters, Chaucer, Lord Tennyson, and Rudyard Kipling, among many others. But for now, let's see who's coming up first."

Beginning on one side of the glorious Abbey, we first came to the Shrine of Edward the Confessor, and the nearby tombs of both Edward I and Henry III. Moving on, we found the single tomb housing both Elizabeth I (formidable red-headed queen; daughter of King Henry VIII and his second queen, Anne Boleyn) and her half-sister Mary I (also a Tudor queen; daughter of King Henry VIII and his first queen, Catherine of Aragon).

Sharing real estate with the above royal tombs were Henry VII and his wife, Elizabeth of York; and the long-suffering Mary Queen of Scots. This Mary lost her head under the order of Elizabeth I; they were cousins, and Mary was a threat to Elizabeth's seat on the throne – partly because she was a legitimate heir due to her descending from Henry II, and partly because she was a Catholic – and this made her a focal point for plots against the Protestant Queen Elizabeth I.

Next up was the ancient Coronation Chair.

"What do you think it's made of?"

"It looks like oak," said Keith.

It was. The royal chair was made by order of Edward I to enclose the famous Stone of Scone, which he brought from Scotland to the Abbey in 1296. It was originally painted and decorated with patterns of birds, foliage, and animals on a gilt ground, with a figure of a king, his feet resting on a lion, painted on the back. Centuries of wear and tear have reduced its artistic glory, and during the 18th and 19th centuries much graffiti appeared on the back of the chair, as Westminster schoolboys and visitors carved their names on it. Later, a 1914 bomb attack thought to be organized by the Suffragettes actually knocked a small corner off of it.

"Women!" proclaimed my husband.

Okay, I'll give him that one.

Proceeding through the Abbey, I halted suddenly.

"Wait!" I said in a hushed voice. "We need to go into stealth mode now. Poets' Corner is right here." Fortunately, there were no tourists in this particular alcove at the moment, and the nearest guard, known as a Beadle, was several yards away and looking in the opposite direction.

Scanning the various upright tombs and large statuary in the dimly lit, beautiful stone area, I couldn't seem to locate a monument to the famed writer. I was thinking, the bigger the better, as it would be much easier to just tuck little Dickens's coffin into an adjacent cubbyhole, where it likely would never be discovered – or at least, not for a while. I was at a loss, and looked for Keith, for assistance.

He was standing a few yards away from me, shaking his head, and pointing to the floor. What was that supposed to mean?

I walked over to him. "What is that supposed to mean?"

"Look down," he said.

I did – and gasped. "Holy smokes! Now what are we going to do?" While many of the tombs in this area were large, intricate, and most importantly, upright

– Charles Dickens had apparently opted for the floor model – meaning he chose to spend eternity lying under it, with his tomb merely a simple engraved stone slab lying flush with the ground. This was his wish, expressed in his will.

"I don't know what *you're* going to do," clarified my husband, "but leave me out of it." With that, he walked off to the side of the alcove, and tried to remain inconspicuous, among the many stone niches.

"Well, I can't let Frank down. I need to think. Think, think, think!" I muttered to myself.   Scanning the area, I spotted a small, brass floor grating not far from the author's tomb. I had no idea where it led, but I assumed that it was an opening of little consequence; Europe was full of those. It probably went to a simple, run-of-the-mill dungeon.

Kneeling down – and noticing my chicken husband peering around Shakespeare – I glanced about surreptitiously, making sure there was no one else in sight. What luck! There wasn't.

Unscrewing the little lid from Dickens-the-cat's copper coffin, I deftly removed the small plastic bag of ashes, opened it, and sprinkled the powdered feline through the grating. *There!* I thought. *Mission accomplished!*
CLANG! CLANG! CLANG!

In less time than it took to think, *It was the best of times, it was the worst of times,* I was afraid that the latter lay ahead for us. The alarm continued its cacophony, sending tourists and guards every which way. I skittered over to Keith, and we made our hasty retreat.

Once safely outside – amid a swirl of arriving London police officers ("Look!" I said to my husband, "Real Bobbies!" To which he replied something about my being certifiable) – I asked what he thought was beneath the floor, through the grating, that could have possibly warranted such an uproar over a few cat's ashes.

"I have no idea," replied my husband.

Before we could speculate any further, a police officer came out and addressed the crowd who had evacuated the site.

"Ladies and gentleman, we believe that it is now safe to resume your visit to the Abbey. Something appeared to trigger an alarm below the Poets' Corner, but we found nothing amiss." The officer then shrugged. "Probably just a stray cat."

CHAPTER 9

"NO MORE CATS, okay?" pleaded my husband.
I couldn't agree more: *no more cats!*

We were back on the red double-decker bus, headed to the next stop on our (okay, my) list: Harrods. One of the most famous department stores in the world, I had been there once before, as a teen – and loved it.

"Wait till you see it," I told Keith. "It's wonderful!"

He rolled his eyes. "It's a department store. How special can it be?"

I ignored his cynicism.

"Let me give you a little history of Harrods," I began, consulting Britannica.com on my phone. "It was originally founded in 1849 by Henry Charles Harrod – as a grocery store. By the late 1800s, it had expanded with many new departments, and customer service was set to provide every possible need, including what was boasted as 'the best circulating library in London'."

I pondered that last feature for a moment. A library within a department store…it doesn't get any better than that!

I went on. "Using the store's services, customers could buy theater tickets, make travel reservations, and arrange funerals."

"I'll bet people were just dying to go there," quipped my husband.

Undeterred, I continued. "Over the years, Harrods – note: there is no apostrophe before the *S* [as if my hubby cared] – placed cash desks around the store to take customers' payments. Up until then, most large retailers used mechanical devices or employee runners to move customers' money between counters and a central cash station.

Fast forward to present day: the current Harrods building was constructed in 1905, and houses 300 departments, 20 restaurants, a bank, and a beauty salon. Although its Food Hall still sells myriad gourmet food items, the general emphasis is on high-fashion clothing. Known for its impressive customer service, it's considered the best department store in Britain. In 1985 it was bought by Mohamed Al-Fayed – you know: Dodi Al-Fayed's father. Dodi was the Egyptian man that Princess Diana was seeing when they were killed in that horrible car crash in Paris."

"Right," replied my husband, at the conclusion of the lesson.

Looking out the bus window, I saw that we were turning onto Brompton Road in Knightsbridge, home of the flagship store. Spotting Harrods' iconic architecture ahead, I took in its enormity: spanning an entire block, it covered 1.1 million square feet. Equally recognizable was the row of flags displayed on flagpoles jutting out along the storefront. Over the years, flags there have ranged from patriotic, such as the Union Jack; to flags of the world; to specialty flags commemorating the Queen's birthday; to sales flags and product-specific flags; and so on. I couldn't wait to go inside!

We hopped off the red bus, strolled up the busy sidewalk, and went in through one of the many Harrods entrances along the street.

The interior was very posh! And packed with customers – attire indicating that they were from all over the world, which felt very exotic.

Floors began with Lower Ground (LG), and Ground (G), then continued upward from One to Six.

"Remember, One is not the ground floor," said Keith, aware that my sense of direction is challenged in pretty much every way possible.

Our first destination was the Harrods Gift Shop on the LG – a large department with everything 'Harrods logo' imaginable. Items ranged from numerous tote and bag styles, to stuffed animals, to all sorts of small accessories; from teapots, to china cups, to chocolates and biscuits; from Paddington Bear, to Beefeater bears, to Union Jack Bears – and everything in between. And Westies! The cottony white Harrods signature terrier was featured everywhere.

"I miss having a dog," I said wistfully. "Maybe someday.... Hey! Let's buy a Harrods souvenir leash – then we'll be prepared, just in case." I had a small collection of cute doggy items at home, which I was stockpiling for the 'perfect time'.

Sighing, my husband followed me to the store's very frou frou pet section. Luxurious pet beds; crown-shaped water bowls with a 'jewel' nesting at the bottom; silver-plated food bowls; alpaca dog sweaters; pricey collars – that sort of thing. I did find a reasonably priced leash in hunter green with the gold *Harrods* insignia printed along its length. Success!

Leaving the department, I spotted a ball of fur out of the corner of my eye. Halting and whipping my head around, I saw a small Shih Tzu sitting all by itself on the floor, beneath a low shelf of boucle dog beds.

"Look!" I tugged Keith's arm and pointed downward.

Just as my husband spotted it, this mostly-black-with-a-bit-of-tan specimen of cuteness gave him the lopsided, one-toothed grin that Shih Tzus are known for.

"He's smiling at us!" I said.

"Hon...." began my husband.

"No, seriously. He is! I wonder where his owner is."

We scanned the area, but there was no sign of anyone looking for a dog. Furthermore, the pup didn't appear fazed by the fact that it was on its own. How curious!

"Yes, well, moving on," redirected my husband. "It's dinner time, I'm hungry, and the Food Hall lists several good restaurants within its Dining Hall. Let's go."

Walking toward the bank of lifts, something brushed against my ankle. I stopped and glanced down. "Look!" I said to Keith. "It's Barrett! He's following us."

"What do you mean, 'Barrett is following us'? And who's Barrett?"

"He is!" I pointed at the still-grinning pup. "Don't you think he looks like a Barrett?"

"No. I think he looks like someone's dog who is probably straying farther and farther from his owner. [By now, it was evident that he was a 'he'.] We need to keep moving, and let him find his own people."

Now at the lift, its elegant doors opened. It was a vision of opulence, all shiny gold and deep blue marble, with Art Deco accents and brass studs, under a velvety dark ceiling. It was like entering a glamorous vintage steamer trunk as we stepped inside – all three of us: Keith, myself, and Barrett.

The doors closed and my husband hit 'G' on the button panel. Looking down in surprise, he asked, "What's he doing in here with us?"

"Well clearly," I stated, "*we* are his people. You know, maybe this is meant to be. We've been saying for a while now that a dog might be nice—"

"Cath. No. Have you lost your mind? For one thing, we're on the wrong side of the ocean to be picking up a new pet – especially one who probably belongs to someone else! Plus, we have a few more days left on this trip; how would we manage the logistics of toting a dog around? AND, speaking of logistics, we have no idea what's involved in bringing a dog out of the UK and into the US. No! I can't see how this could possibly work."

"But I already have a leash," I argued – albeit, a stretch. "And, I can consult Sophie as to what the laws are. She and Ewan are close friends with the vet in their village, who could advise us on the proper channels."

The lift doors opened, and the three of us stepped off.

Walking toward the Food Hall – Barrett in tow – I presented a plan.

"How about this? Naturally, a dog can't dine here with us. We'll go in and eat, and if he's still waiting outside of the Dining Hall when we exit, we'll then go to Customer Service and inquire as to whether anyone has put out an APB on him."

"An APB?" ventured my weary husband.

"Yes. An All Pups Bulletin. Isn't that obvious?" Sheesh.

We were seated in a lovely half-booth inside Kerridge's Fish-and-Chips; just as gorgeous as the rest of the store. Scanning the menu, we ordered fish-and-chips for Keith – his second of the day – and a salad for me, plus a pot of Earl Grey and a glass of ice (the plan being to cool the tea a bit before the twain should meet).

"Would you like the mushy peas with your fish-and-chips?" our server asked pleasantly.

"No thank you—" began my husband.

I silently interrupted with what I hoped was my clear but subtle signal to always take the proffered item that he didn't want, as *I* might want it. I attempted to establish this years ago, yet he never failed to drop the ball. This case was no exception.

"Take the mushy peas, Hon," I advised sweetly.

"I don't care for mushy peas."

Less sweetly I urged, "I'll take them, then."

Still not getting it, Keith insisted, "No, I prefer the fish-and-chips alone."

Our server's head bobbed back and forth between her weird American patrons; she clearly wondered who was going to win this little match.

I smiled charmingly, and said nothing more.

As soon as our server walked away, I hissed, "Next time, just take the mushy peas. TAKE THE MUSHY PEAS."

"But I don't *like* mushy peas." Gawd. Men.

⊞

Upon finishing our dinner – which naturally involved further discussion about Barrett, and my rosy future plans for him – we left our table and walked across the black and white marble floor toward the exit, back into the Food Hall.

"There he is!" I said to Keith.

Sure enough, Barrett had waited patiently for us, right next to a display of the most delectable little cakes and sweets imaginable. The minute he saw us, he smiled.

Before he could catch himself, my husband was smiling back at him.

"See! I saw that! You're as taken by him as I am." I said in triumph.

Keith knelt down, and Barrett made a little leap right into his arms. Sold!

"Okay," sighed my hubby. "Which way is Customer Service?"

Distracted by the sugary display, I engaged the confectioner first. "I'll take two of the white chocolate truffles, please." Truffle fix now in hand, we carried on.

Soon, the three of us were back in a lift, Keith carrying Barrett. Upon exiting, we located the correct department, found a representative, and explained our quest.

"Ah, yes," said the employee, whose name tag read Andreas. "We are quite familiar with this little scamp. Sad story, really. About a week ago, he showed up in our Shoe Heaven department. How he reached the 5th floor, we don't know. At any rate, we were unable to locate his owner, so one of our employees did a little research through her own veterinarian. The dog had been micro-chipped, and it turned out that his elderly owner – a gentleman who used to shop here on a weekly basis – had passed away unexpectedly, leaving no relatives behind to care for his pet. At any rate, no one here has offered to adopt him, so tomorrow morning he will be taken to a shelter."

"Or not!" I exclaimed. "We would love to have him. We just need time to get the logistics in order – transporting a dog from the UK to the US, and such. Is there any way that someone here can care for him until we arrange everything? We'll leave London in just a couple of days, making a short stop in Edinburgh, before heading for home." I paused. "I do understand it's a lot to ask."

"Actually, I know an entire department of employees who will be thrilled with this outcome. They've all grown quite fond of the little chap, and will be happy to see him go to a good home. An American one, no less!" Andreas turned wistful. "I visited Disney World once…."

Leaving Barrett safely in Andreas's care – followed by whoever else would be his temporary guardian for a couple more days – we'd promised to contact the clerk the next day with further details as to when we would retrieve the pup.

We'd then taken the Tube back to the Earl's Court station, alighted, and were now walking toward the lift that would take us up to street level. From there, we would walk the few blocks back to our hotel on Nevern Square. We were exhausted! It had been a long day, and we looked forward to cappuccinos in the hotel's cozy bar.

Arriving at the small lift – with two walls of clear glass on opposite sides – there was already a couple in it. No problem. Room for us as well, according to a posted sign that clearly stated, MAXIMUM 4 PERSONS.

Just as we were about to step inside, a man carrying a suitcase zoomed past us and into the lift, taking our place. I was willing to wait for the next lift, but Keith was not about to be usurped by this encroacher.

"Go! Go! Go!" urged my husband – his Fear of Not Being First Disorder triggered – and stupidly, I complied.

Once inside, the doors snapped shut.

BLARE! BLARE! BLARE!

Following this deafening alarm came an immediate announcement over the PA system – broadcast both inside and outside of the lift. "*The lift is overloaded. The lift is overloaded.*" No kidding.

The door would NOT open, and now a second voice came over the PA, that of a maintenance worker reiterating the obvious: "You've overloaded the lift." The disembodied voice continued, "Someone will be there in seven minutes to assist."

Seven minutes! At this point, I wanted to kill Keith. I really did. It was instantly hot and stuffy, and the vent indicator said OFF. A crowd was forming outside of our glass fishbowl (*Don't you people have a damn train to catch??*), and after what felt like an eternity of enduring this humiliation — not to mention, mild panic as our air supply seemed to dwindle – an actual maintenance man appeared. Henry, according to his badge.

Sizing up our little ship of fools, Henry yelled to us through the glass doors, "You've overloaded! [Duh. Was there an echo in this place?] The sign says only four people – you have five! I'll have to go and get a proper tool to hand-crank you down." With that, he disappeared.

"Hand-crank us down!" I glared at Keith. "We're only two inches off of the ground!"

"Yes, but we're not aligned—" began my husband.

"Don't start with a lecture on mechanics!" I snapped.

I turned to the other couple (but not the interloper with the suitcase) and apologized for our predicament. Blissfully soon after, Henry reappeared, tools in hand. CRANK. CRANK. CRANK.

It took seven more minutes to move two inches, but finally we were down, and the door opened. By now

I had a unibrow for Keith – and I wasn't feeling too charitable toward the spectators who'd been glued to our debacle, either. Refusing eye contact with any of them – Hubby included – I took off with the latter in my wake, hoping to regain my civility before reaching our hotel a few blocks away. My feet were killing me, and I really wanted to just get there, sit down, and enjoy a coffee – and maybe the white chocolate truffles I was still carrying from Harrods. Why was it taking so long to spot Nevern Square?

"Where are you going?" my husband asked, finally breaking the wall of silence I'd erected in effort to not otherwise explode.

"What do you mean? To our hotel, obviously!"

"Well, you're going in the completely opposite direction. Apparently you didn't notice that the station has two exits, depending upon the direction one's train is coming from. The entrance/exit closest to our hotel is the one that we took this morning – because we were leaving Earl's Court. Coming back *into* the station put us on the opposite side."

"Great!" I said. "Well, we now have no choice but to hail a cab, because I'm not walking one step more than I have to."

We waited about five minutes, before a black cab pulled up, and a passenger stepped out. It was a young woman in a Max Mara camel coat, and she was wearing a Harrods name badge. Besides her tote, she was carrying a bundle in her arms.

Woof!

I knew that bark!

"Look!" I said to Keith, "It's Barrett!"

My husband, and the woman, were equally surprised. For some reason, I wasn't. We quickly explained who we were to this employee who was to be Barrett's foster mom for a couple more days, then we all decided to share a pot of tea together at a nearby cafe.

Once inside, I said to the owner, "A table for three, please."

WOOF!

"Make that four," sighed my husband – but with a smile.

CHAPTER 10

WAKING UP THE next morning in the 'Garden Room', I crawled over my still-sleeping husband – my only way out of the bed in this tiny, cramped space – determined to be first in the shower.

The bathroom was equally small, but its beautiful red marble walls and floor made up for what it lacked in size. A charming little toiletries chest carved in teak, about the size of a shoe-box, sat in a deep marble niche.

Opening the chest, I found an assortment of Evelyn & Crabtree bottles and soaps – and a large, colorful spider! My general knowledge of arachnids told me that most spiders in Britain were harmless, so I took a moment to study the intriguing color pattern of yellow, white, and black stripes on its back. Googling it quickly on my phone, I determined that it was a Wasp Spider, and it was the perfect find for the historian in me, because apparently it produces an unusual egg-mass – shaped like a Grecian urn. Awesome!

Scooping my treasure into a small empty bottle, I poked a tiny hole in the lid for air, then proceeded with my shower. My plan was to show the spider to Keith once we were out and about, then set it free in a grassy area. Until then, it would be fine in my purse.

"G'morning, mate!" This I heard, as I exited the bathroom in my robe. It was followed by a loud banging outside of the barely-open window over our bed, which was elevated so that the sill was roughly at our eye-level. The small sunken 'garden area' outside was a few cement steps down from the street, and the common purpose of this little foliage-free space was to hold rubbish bins (aka trash cans).

"What the…?" was Keith's startled reply, as he gazed upward to find a binman peering in our window.

The worker gave a cheery wave and retreated up the stairs.

"This room!" grumbled my husband. "There'd better be a big improvement for our coming nights. Eshana or Saanvi had better be worth the wait."

"Well, there are other rooms, too, so let's hope for the best. Meanwhile, hurry up and take your shower. I'm starving!"

Once I heard the water running, I got out my laptop and composed a few paragraphs for the opening chapter of my book. Now that I had settled on a theme, I was looking especially forward to one of our destinations for the day: the National Portrait Gallery. Surely there would be a painting that would spark my interest, as the anchor for Chapter One's historical foray!

We strolled past the Taj Mahal birdcage in the hotel lobby (Houdini and Kiwi went on instant alert, giving me hopeful expressions and eyeballing their little door, each time we walked by) and entered the breakfast room – just past a narrow, mirrored bar. It was a small but airy atrium, with shiny white marble floors and a vaulted glass ceiling, supported by gorgeous wood beams from which crystal globe chandeliers hung. One wall was lined with casement glass doors, which overlooked a very peaceful, very green courtyard – a lush byproduct of England's near-continual rain – complete with small stone statues and black wrought iron benches. A round, quartzite buffet in the center of the room offered a variety of fruits, meats, cheeses, and pastries.

After choosing bamboo-style mahogany seats at a glass table along the wall, Keith went to the bar to retrieve little French Duralex glasses of juice from a tray. A server brought us coffee.

A few tables away, there was a young woman on her phone – very 'Bronx' – chatting loudly. It was annoying (not to mention, a faux pas in more-reserved Britain)...and I debated saying something to her. It had the potential to be a long conversation, so as I walked past on my way to the buffet, I stopped, smiled, and politely gave her the 'shhh' sign. She nodded and smiled back. Mission accomplished.

Once at the buffet, I found no plates whatsoever, but off to the side and around a corner was a teak sideboard – featuring various dry cereals and a pitcher of milk

– where I spotted low, recessed shelves holding stacks of white dishes shoved a few inches back. What a ridiculous, odd place for guests to have to contort and reach!

Basically standing on my head, I pulled out a plate. It was 'clean' – but not. I pulled out a second plate, which promptly slipped out of my fingers and crashed on the marble floor – not breaking, but instead making a loud WACKETA WACKETA WACKETA sound as it spun itself out before its final swan song on the black and white squares.

The host rushed over to assess the damage, and the irony was not lost on me of having admonished Phone Lady, only seconds before making my own racket.

A server pointed stiffly at an equally hidden shelf near the main buffet. "No ma'am – your plates are over there."

I glanced at our table, where my husband was suppressing a grin.

On my way back, past Phone Lady – now off of her device – I stopped and made a sheepish comment about karma. She laughed and agreed – adding that she had enjoyed relaying the incident to her friend on the other end.

Back at our table, Keith declared that he 'just knew' the crash was mine.

I told him of the chummy outcome between Phone Lady and myself – but my bubble was soon burst.

"Maybe, but you didn't hear what she said to her friend on the phone: 'Some lady just told me I was too loud. I guess all old people have sensitive hearing.' "

Great! Apparently, 49 was the new 60.

"Our first stop has to be Sloane Square," I told my husband, as we walked toward the Earl's Court Tube station. "I want to shop at Mungo & Maud! Barrett will need a few little things. Just small stuff."

Keith sighed. "Okay, but then we really need to make our way to the Tower of London. Especially if you're still hoping to visit the Portrait Gallery this afternoon." He changed course. "Speaking of Barrett, I hope that Ewan has good news as to the ease of bringing a dog out of the country."

As if on cue, my phone rang. It was Sophie.

"Uh huh, uh huh, uh huh. Great!" I said. "Thanks Sophie! And thank Ewan for us!"

Once on the train, I informed Keith. "Well, it *is* good news. All we need is proper health documentation from the vet that Barrett's already seen, and he's good to go. Hmm…." I added, now thinking of the logistics. "We'd better pick up a pet carrier, a harness, some travel bowls, food, a toy—"

"Yay…. More to carry at the airport." My husband rolled his eyes. "Meanwhile, we need to let his temporary nanny know that we'll retrieve him in a day or two. And, we'll need to call the vet first, to make sure his papers are ready."

"Right. You do that," I directed. "That's the easy part. I have some serious shopping to do!"

The doors opened and we headed for our next train, which would take us to Sloane Square.

✧

Walking up pretty Elizabeth Street – a quirky, flower-filled area lined with boutiques and cafes – we spotted Mungo & Maud Dog & Cat Outfitters. It looked very chichi, and as my husband observed, "I doubt if mutts shop here."

"According to their website," I said, "their collection has a creative and understated edge, using an innate sense of color and a strong use of natural materials, including hand-stitched leather collars, minimalist cotton beds, and 'amusing accessories for the most discerning of dogs and cats'. I like the sound of that!"

"I'll bet the prices aren't so 'amusing'," mused Keith.

Ignoring the skeptic, I led the way inside. My husband was correct. The prices were not amusing. A leather dog bed costing over 1600 pounds – nearly $2000 – was nothing to chuckle about. But the merchandise was lovely, so I chose a small, posh toy for Barrett and called it a morning, pricey dog stuff-wise.

"I wonder if London has PetSmart," I sighed.

✧

Back on the road again, so to speak, we made our way via the Tube to the stop nearest the Tower of London. While walking between stations, we had come upon a reasonably-priced pet store, where I'd purchased a soft-sided pet carrier for Barrett to use on the plane. When Keith had protested that buying it at that moment would mean having to lug an extra item around for the day, I'd countered, "Au contraire! It will double as the perfect shopping tote!"

So off we went to Tower Hill – a blue and white gingham doggy carrier slung over Hubby's shoulder. "Let me get a picture!" I'd said, snapping one before he could protest.

Reaching the sprawling Tower of London, my mind immediately drifted back in time. Among other things, this was Henry VIII territory! While it was my second visit here, the impact was still the same. Having served throughout history as a castle, a secure fortress, a royal palace, and an infamous prison, a visitor could spend days here and still not see everything.

We stood in line with our passes. "I wish I were Anne Boleyn," I said wistfully.

"Seriously, Cath?" asked my incredulous husband. "Which part of her life appeals to you the most: having to procreate with an elephantine man with perpetually oozing wounds, or having your head lopped off and caught in a picnic basket?"

He had a point.

"Well, what I mean is, how amazing would it be to play such a prominent role in history? And being the mother of Queen Elizabeth I...that alone is mind-boggling." Albeit, it's not as though Anne lived to see her daughter ascend the throne, given that the child was only three at the time of her mother's unconventional death.

"Yes, well, we're in now, so where to first?" redirected Keith.

"I'm thinking lunch. The New Armouries Cafe is right across from the White Tower, so that would be a good place to start."

We entered the medieval eatery; fitting the castle, it was all wood beam and stone inside. It was somewhat crowded, so we did our usual routine: I snagged a table, while Hubby went through the cafeteria-style line and purchased our food. Returning to the table with a tray, he began to unload the fare – bottles of water, fish-and-chips (my husband is going to turn into a cod), and a pasty.

"What's that?" I said, pointing to the pasty – which is a Cornish meat pie; essentially like an apple turnover, only with an unappealing mash of meat, potatoes, and veggies in lieu of a delicious apple pie filling.

"It's a pasty," replied my husband – pronouncing it incorrectly and thus demoting it to a stripper's accessory.

"Pasty! PAHHHSTY. Short 'a'," I corrected. "I know what it is! But what happened to my Coronation Chicken Sandwich?" Coronation Chicken was the Brits' equivalent to our chicken salad – only better.

"They were out." Of course they were. It's one of the few foods in England that you order because you actually *want* it.

Lunch past, I was anxious for our first stop within the Tower walls. "Hurry up!" I urged my husband. He was fiddling with a zipper on the gingham doggy carrier; for some reason, the side entrance was flawed and tended to flap open.

I enlightened Keith as we scuttled across the green. "The Chapel of St Peter ad Vincula is the burial place of both Anne Boleyn and Catherine Howard. Of Henry's six queens, these were the two who lost their heads. It's also the locale of the bones of other luminaries: St Thomas More; George Boleyn; Jane Boleyn; Thomas Cromwell; Margaret Pole; and Lady Jane Grey – to name a few."

West of the White Tower, before the chapel, we came upon the scaffold site on Tower Green, and the memorial recently created in memory of the victims who were beheaded there (technically, the execution site was several yards away). It was very poignant: a sculpted glass pillow resting atop two large, engraved discs at different levels. Around the edge of the lower disc of polished black stone, an inscription read:

Gentle visitor pause a while, where you stand death cut away the light of many days. Here jewelled names were broken from the vivid thread of life. May they rest in peace while we walk the generations around their strife and courage, under these restless skies.

Circling the rim of the upper disc, smaller and of greenish glass, an inscription lists the names of ten of the souls who were executed there, along with the dates.

It was definitely humbling.

After pausing to reflect, I glanced behind us toward the chapel. "Let's go! There's a Beefeater who's about to lead a group inside."

Beefeaters – aka Yeoman Warders – are an interesting lot. Earlier, we had stopped at a small pub outside of the Tower grounds for tea; sitting solo at a table next to us was an off-duty Beefeater, still in uniform. He was very friendly and quite happy to answer a few questions – and of course he was drinking gin! We learned that it's no easy feat to join his esteemed ranks. Minimum requirements include that an applicant have at least 22 years of service in Her (or His) Majesty's Armed Forces, and must have been awarded the 'Long Service and Good Conduct' medal. Beyond that, a good memory, a passion for history, and a love for London are key.

Joining the tail end of the small tour group, we entered the hallowed chapel. I immediately set my sights on the altar; specifically to the left, where I knew that the bones of Anne Boleyn were found during restoration, centuries after their burial. I quickly took out my cell phone to snap a few photos.

Just as quickly, a stern Beefeater appeared in front of me. "Ma'am, did you just take a PICTURE?"

I reflexively fibbed that no – I was *about* to, but I didn't. Photos were strictly forbidden in the chapel, and I knew that, but for some reason I lost my head in the moment....

The guard informed me that it was a good thing I hadn't taken a photo, as he would then be obligated to confiscate my phone.

Keith sidled up to me, after the guard walked away. "The Tower of London is perhaps the *last* place you want to tangle with the law."

Agreed.

Moving on through fascinating sites such as the Crown Jewels (housing 23,578 gems); the Bloody Tower (locale of the imprisonment and assumed murder of the Little Princes: Edward V and his younger brother Richard, in 1483); the White Tower (the most famous castle keep in the world and home to the Royal Armouries); and the Medieval Palace (built in the 13th century as a temporary Motel 6 for medieval monarchs), we then headed toward two of my favorites on the Tower grounds: the Traitors' Gate, and the Ravens' Lodgings.

"Look at how creepy this gate is!" I said to Keith. "And the waters beneath it seem so dark and foreboding."

The Tower complex strategically sits on the River Thames; most important structures throughout history were built on or near waterways, due to ease of transportation. The Traitors' Gate is associated with treason, and thus some of the most important events in England's history took place there. Specifically, prisoners were often brought by water to meet their fate at the Tower, entering directly through this low, dark stone and iron passage. As well, the bodies of executed prisoners were ferried out of the Tower through this gate, on boats that would take them to their final resting places.

I shuddered to think of Queen Anne Boleyn traversing this passage of horror, although historical accounts differ as to whether she was brought to her imprisonment by boat or by land.

Leaving this somber spot, we headed toward our last stop on the grounds: the South Lawn, home of the six famous Tower Ravens.

I checked the brochure. "Legend has it that Charles II believed that if the ravens were ever to leave the Tower, the fortress and the kingdom would fall. There's even a Ravenmaster who keeps a close eye on them!" We had seen them roaming free on the different greens, and learned that these jet black avians presided over four different territories within the Tower's walls. Intelligent, with unique personalities, this group – known individually as Jubilee, Harris, Poppy, Edgar, Georgie, Branwen, and Rex – could even play games and solve problems. They were also capable of mimicking sounds.

Taking a short break, we sat on a bench near the green where the ebony birds were strolling about and snacking on seeds that had been left on the ground. This was pleasant enough to watch, but I had no desire to view them during their actual feeding times: twice a day, they dine on mice, chicks, rats, and other assorted raw meats and disgusting treats. UGH. Thinking about where their beaks had been, I advised Keith to pick up our gingham doggy carrier that was resting on the ground, as they were hopping in the general vicinity. I didn't want Barrett to contract any medieval bird diseases!

After agreeing that we were done with the Tower of London for the day, we left the grounds and walked toward the Tower Hill Tube station. Our next stop would be the National Portrait Gallery, on Trafalgar Square. I couldn't wait to discover what – or whom – the anchor topic of my book's first chapter would be!

"I can't take one more step with this flap constantly popping open!" complained my husband, fishing around in his pocket for a remedy for the errant doggy carrier door. Coming up with a small zip tie – why he had one, I do not know (men!) – he fastened the two zippered ends together.

"There!" proclaimed MacGyver a bit too loudly, as we moved on.

Finding a seat on the Tube train to Trafalgar, we were each lost in thought.

Suddenly, from the pet carrier resting on the seat between us, a voice came. "THERE!" it said clearly.

We simultaneously whipped our heads down to investigate.

Keith said, "WHAT THE…?"

Peering out at us from inside the blue gingham abode was a shiny black raven – a clear look of accomplishment in its beady little eyes.

CHAPTER 11

"KEITH!" I HISSED in a hushed tone, trying not to alert the other Tube passengers to our stowaway. "Why on earth did you take a raven from the Tower of London?"

"I didn't *take* a raven!" My husband was exasperated. "It must have hopped in while the carrier was sitting on the ground where the birds were snacking. What are we going to do now?"

"Well, we can't keep it off the grounds, that's for sure! Besides theft, it could begin the fall of London."

At that, I received an incredulous look. (He had those down pat.)

I thought for a moment. "I have an idea...."

Incredulity turned to trepidation.

"We'll casually get off at our stop, and as long as Edgar—"

"Edgar? How do you know it's 'Edgar'?" interrupted Keith.

"It has to be Edgar. Look at those beady eyes! All Edgars have beady eyes," I explained. "Remember Poe?"

"Go on…." prompted my wary husband.

"As long as Edgar doesn't say anything else to draw attention, we can turn him loose at Trafalgar Square with the horde of pigeons who hang out there. It's only two miles from the Tower of London; he can fly back home in no time," I said.

"And what if he doesn't know the way back?"

Exasperated at Keith's missing the obvious, I enlightened him. "He can 'home' his way back."

"*Home* his way back? He's a raven, not a pigeon!"

"Yes," I agreed. "But I'm sure there's a pigeon in the group who will instruct him."

Having wished Edgar a surreptitious farewell before one of the four enormous Trafalgar Square bronze lions – a huge pigeon Woodstock if I ever saw one – we hoped for the best for him and for London.

We then climbed the National Portrait Gallery steps, located on the Square. Once inside, we headed straight for the 2nd floor, where the Tudors and the Stuarts – two of my favorite eras – were featured.

"Here's Elizabeth I's coronation portrait!" I said in awe. "Can you believe that she was only 26 years old at the time? The last Tudor monarch, she reigned for 45 years."

We studied the painting.

"Well, with that chalky white skin, she looks 126," observed my husband.

I rolled my eyes. "Yes. Well, there was a reason for her odd makeup. In 1562, she contracted smallpox and was confined to her bed at Hampton Court Palace due to contagiousness from the deadly, viral disease with no cure. A rash formed on her skin, which turned into ugly, weepy blisters before drying and leaving scars. (Ick.) Before her illness, she had a reputation for perfect, fair skin. To conceal the scars, the queen used a heavy white face paint known as Venetian Ceruse – its main ingredient being the mineral cerussite; a white, lead-containing ore. Mixed with vinegar, the ore was used to create the cover-up – and some historians believe that lead poisoning could have caused her eventual death."

"Well, it's easy to see why she never found a king," concluded my husband.

"No…that wasn't it— Never mind." Men.

Moving on, we came to the portrait of King Charles I.

I began my history lesson. "So this particular Charles had it rough. After succeeding his father James I in 1625 as King of both England and Scotland, he butted heads – no pun intended – with Parliament, one too many times. The result was the English Civil War – and the beheading of Charles in 1649." I added, "Charles was a Stuart, whereas Elizabeth was a Tudor."

"Duly noted," noted my husband. "Where to next? We have lots to cover and we still want to ride the London Eye before dinner."

"Right! Well, I'd like to see some lithographs before we leave."

After viewing several more portraits on three separate levels, we came to the section with the prints. Upon spotting John Doyle's *A Venerable Spider and a Buzzing*, I was reminded of the treasure I wanted to show to Keith.

"Reach into my backpack and grab the little bottle at the bottom for me, please. I can't get to it, while the bag is on me." I'd transferred my purse contents into the bag earlier.

He complied.

"OUCH! What the hell was that?" My hubby yanked his hand – with its rapidly reddening thumb – out of my bag. "Something bit me!"

"Uh-oh…it must have gotten loose…." I muttered.

"*What* has gotten loose?"

"Just this cute little spider I found in our hotel bathroom," I explained. "It's a Wasp spider; don't worry, its bite is harmless to humans." By now I had taken the bag off my back. Peering inside, I could see the colorful arachnid sitting on my tortoise shell hairbrush.

"Well, I hope so," snapped Keith, "because my thumb says otherwise. Let's lose that thing."

Taking the brush with its passenger carefully out of my bag, I carried it to an open window in the gallery. I gently flicked the spider outside, intending for it to rest on the sill. I must have flicked a little too hard, because it went airborne instead.

A woman's shriek from below indicated a safe landing.

"Hey!" remembered my husband. "Did you choose a painting to write about?"

We were across the street from the gallery, at St Martin-in-the-Fields – where a church has stood one way or another since medieval times, beginning in 1222. In 1542, Henry VIII built a new church on the spot, and the current church was built in its place in 1726. Currently, we were underground in its crypt – specifically in the Café in the Crypt. We were about to order Cream Tea, as an afternoon treat.

"I did!" I replied. "I chose a popular one for my opening chapter: Vincent Van Gogh's 'Sunflowers'. There are five versions of that work displayed in galleries and museums worldwide – luckily, one is here. According to specifics, Van Gogh created the paintings to decorate his house in Arles, in preparation for a visit from his friend and fellow artist Paul Gauguin. I plan to explore the history of Arles – and France in general – at the time of his paintings." I thought for a moment. "You know, I think another trip to Provence should be in our near future."

"Right," answered Keith. "For now, let's focus on our time here in London, then Edinburgh, and then transferring Barrett smoothly out of the country." He looked past me. "Meanwhile, here comes our tea."

"*Cream* tea," I corrected. "There's a difference, you know!"

There are all kinds of 'teas' in Britain. Cream Tea – an odd misnomer to a non-Brit – refers collectively to a pot of tea, plus a scone with 'clotted cream' and jam. Clotted cream, while sounding rather repulsive, is actually pretty good. Also called Devonshire clotted cream or Cornish clotted cream, it has the consistency of softened cream cheese but tastes more like high-quality unsalted butter. Then there's High Tea – an afternoon meal, consisting of a pot of tea; little tea sandwiches such as cucumber, smoked salmon, and 'egg mayonnaise'; scones; and little finger cakes and pastries. Excellent! Finally, there's Royal Tea, which is more excellent because it's basically High Tea – plus a glass of champagne.

Slathering our scones, we munched away while sipping tea and scanning the crypt. Early brick vaulted ceilings were intact, and historic tombstones lined the uneven stone floor.

I picked up the brochure. "Did you know that the original burial ground for this church – the 1720s version – covered the spot where the National Portrait Gallery now stands, and held over 70,000 bodies? Apparently, there were thousands more in this crypt, and by the Victorian era, London was in desperate need of burial space – prompting St Martin's to clear out this area in 1859." I paused. "One account describes how the naturalist Frank Buckland entered the crypt in an effort to find a specific coffin, in order to have it reinterred at Westminster Abbey; holding a lantern to a vault, he found 'thousands upon thousands of jumbled and broken coffins, crammed everywhere as if deposited by a tsunami'. Wow," I concluded.

"Yeah," offered my husband. "That's one needle in a haystack that I wouldn't want to be looking for."

Switching gears, he pointed to the pen in my hand. "What are you writing on that menu card?"

"Shhh! Hold on," I said, scribbling furiously on the colorful laminated paper. I was now eavesdropping on a couple at the table one tomb away from us…and picking up valuable information for use in my first chapter. I had nothing else to write on (in retrospect, I could have used the Notes feature on my phone, as I often did – but I didn't), and I had to act quickly. The man was telling his partner about an art historian in London who specialized in Van Gogh – specifically Van Gogh's ear, and what likely happened to it after its unfortunate separation from his head. He had just confirmed the historian's contact information aloud, and I hoped to make good use of it, perhaps in the form of getting an interview.

"There!" I tucked the valuable menu-turned-note card into the outer pocket of my small backpack, and took a last sip of tea. "This yellow card could be gold. Now, off to the London Eye!"

I gazed downward. "This is awesome!"

Now 443-feet in the air and at the top of its rotation, our large glass pod (28-person capacity) on the London Eye, aka the Millennium Wheel, had reached its highest point. Located on the River Thames, the 30-minute ride on the world's largest cantilevered observation wheel afforded us a bird's-eye view of Buckingham Palace, Big Ben, and the Shard, among other London landmarks. And, because it was a clear day, we could also see Windsor Castle, 25 miles in the distance.

Opening an outer pocket on my backpack, I felt around for my phone – and noticed something was conspicuously absent. "Oh, no! My note card is missing!"

"What note card?" asked Keith.

"*What note card?* The one with the key to Van Gogh's wayward ear, of course!"

I frantically scanned the floor around me. Then I looked at the glass pod's two sliding doors.

"Oh, NO! Look!"

Trapped at the bottom, between the floor and the right-hand door, was the corner of what was clearly my menu card from the crypt in St Martin's. Nose to the glass, I could barely see the bulk of my valuable note, flapping like a beating wing in the breeze. Before I could decide what to do, the situation was out of my hands.

The bright yellow card broke loose – and fluttered aimlessly toward the earth, swirling this way and that, before finally drifting out of sight.

"Well, there it goes," announced my unhelpful husband.

"Not necessarily!" I declared. "Keep watching in the direction it was going. If it lands on the river bank, instead of in the water, we may be able to retrieve it."

"Cath," sighed Keith. "When would that be – and how?"

I was undeterred. "Just keep watching. If we can spot where it lands, we can go back tomorrow afternoon, during our boat ride on the river. It's a hop-on-hop-off tour; we can get off at the nearest point, and go down to the bank." I added for good measure, "We'll have Barrett with us by then; he might enjoy a little river stroll, too!"

Keith was dubious. "Sure. What are the odds of—"

"THERE!" Squinting, I pointed through our pod's glass toward the distant river bank, as we neared the ground. "I think I see it!" Sure enough, a bright yellow scrap of paper was wedged under what appeared to be a jagged rock protruding from the sand. "I'm glad that I used a Sharpie for my notes. You know how it rains here."

On terra firma again, we walked to nearby Marriott County Hall – a nice hotel on the South Bank of the Thames – for a steak dinner, and a lovely view from our table of the London Eye, and the Houses of Parliament.

After dinner, we strolled over the Westminster Bridge, enjoying the night lights of London. From there, we took a black cab back to our hotel on Nevern Square.

Keith gave me a side-eye, as we approached the front desk. "I hope our new room is an improvement over last night's," he said.

"Uh, oh," I whispered. "Name's on duty again. Be nice!"

My husband greeted the clerk. "Good evening. We'd like to have the key to our new room for tonight and tomorrow night, please."

"Ah, yes. You're back," said Name drolly. "We're giving you our penthouse. Your luggage has already been transferred. I hope that you enjoy the rest of your stay." He handed us a brass key, and was off.

"Penthouse!" I said to Keith. "I didn't know they had one. This should be nice!" I had visions of a spacious boudoir clothed in exotic silks, with bejeweled lamps casting a soft glow over gorgeous carved teak furnishings.

Exiting the tiny elevator on the top floor, we found our room – the only one on this level.

"Hurry up – open the door!" I urged Keith.

He turned the key in the lock and the door swung open.

"What the…?" was my husband's response. "This is an ATTIC! Penthouse, my a—"

"It can't be! Let me see." I pushed my way past him and through the door. Yep, it was an attic. A small 'double' bed, one lamp, a small dresser, and one luggage rack. And a shiny white robot standing by the open window.

"What is this thing?" I asked Keith, pointing at R2D2. "And why is it so hot in here?"

"That 'thing' is our air-conditioner," replied my husband. "I can't believe they call this a room! This is NOT acceptable."

"But what can we do at this hour? It's past 11:00 PM. We'll have to suck it up for tonight, at least." Shimmying around the bed, I moved to the window and looked out. There was a small fire escape, then nothing but the street below.

After much debate that resolved absolutely nothing – the MO for us – we resigned ourselves to spending the night in this matchbox, and began getting ready for bed.

"Please turn that thing on," I implored, as I headed for the bathroom. "It's stifling in here!"

From the minuscule lavatory – even a spider would have had difficulty setting up housekeeping – I heard a loud *clunk*, followed by a *CLANG, CLANG, CLANG* that seemed to get fainter.

"What was that?" I called out to Keith. "Are you okay?"

"I'm fine," came his reply. "But R2D2 will never be the same. His head and right arm just took an unfortunate dive off the fire escape."

It was going to be a long, hot night.

CHAPTER 12

"UH…WHY THE CLEOPATRA look?" inquired my husband.

"I'm not channeling the Egyptians, if that's what you're thinking – but thanks." Well, maybe I was.

We were on the Tube again, heading for the British Museum. While not quite donning henna and kohl, I was wearing a black vee-necked tee, a white skirt with a black elephant batik print on it, cute gladiator sandals, and my favorite cloisonné pendant – which happened to feature an Egyptian queen on its face. (I had visited Egypt long before I met Keith, and bought it in a museum gift shop.)

I continued. "Although, I can almost prove that I'm related to Cleopatra. I have Macedonian ancestry. Alexander the Great was from Macedonia, and technically, Cleopatra was not Egyptian – she was the last of the Macedonian Greek dynasty that ruled Egypt from Alexander's death in 323 BC to about 30 BC. Since

Cleopatra descended from Alexander, I would guess I have, too. It only makes sense!"

Keith rolled his eyes. "Right. I believe you've mentioned that before."

We exited the Tube station in the Bloomsbury district, and walked along Great Russell Street toward the British Museum's magnificent main entrance.

I began my history lesson. "Did you know that this is the oldest public museum in the world? It was established by Parliament in 1753; before that, museums were typically private collections of either kings or regular individuals, or belonged to the Church or universities. It has never been an art museum, but rather a museum about humanity. It contains over seven million artifacts from around the world – spanning almost two million years!"

My husband unfolded his museum map as we traversed the entrance and proceeded to the Great Court at the center of the ground floor. "A lot to see, then. Where to first?"

"The Rosetta Stone, of course! When I visited ages ago, I was so anxious to get into the Egyptian Room that I blew right past it, without even noticing. Not this time." I vowed.

Surrounded by glass on all sides, the Rosetta Stone is one of the first exhibits encountered when turning left off the Great Court and entering the Egyptian Sculpture Gallery. As described in the book *Treasures of the British Museum*, the immense significance of the irregularly shaped slab of pink and grey granite-like stone lies in the three bands of inscriptions in two languages carved upon it. At the top are fourteen lines of Egyptian hieroglyphic script; in the middle, there are thirty-two lines of a cursive form of this script known as 'demotic'; and at the bottom, there are fifty-four lines of Ancient Greek. At the time of its discovery in 1799, while Greek was widely known, the other two scripts had been lost for many centuries. The Rosetta Stone – carved in 196 BC, and found in the Egyptian Nile town of Rashid (known to Europeans as Rosetta) – was the key to deciphering ancient Egyptian script.

I reached into my round wicker purse. "Speaking of stones, I forgot to show you this."

"Cath…."

"I know, I know! Don't worry; you *know* that I don't deface history by pulling stones directly out of it. I only pick up small pieces that are already lying on the ground *near* ancient structures. Stuff that has conveniently fallen off. Anyway," I continued, "this little gem is from the Tower of London – a piece of the White Tower, I think."

I handed Hubby a small fragment of what appeared to be Kentish ragstone. "According to my sources, this type of stone, along with Caen and Quarr limestones from France, and Reigate freestone from the upper Greensand, were used by William the 1st in its construction. This would have been the first stone type to be brought by cart. Fascinating!"

"Yes," said my husband, returning his attention to the Rosetta Stone. "Well, don't get any ideas about *this* stone."

"Oh, I wouldn't," I assured. "It's firmly encased!"

Good thing.

Moving through the Egyptian Gallery and exploring its immense stone sculptures, we stopped at a colossal bust of Ramesses the Great. As one of the largest pieces of Egyptian sculpture in the British Museum, it weighs over seven tons.

"How in the world do you think they moved these statues?" I asked Keith.

"Well, the literature says that when this particular piece arrived at the Museum in the 1830s, a hole had to be made in the gallery wall, and it was brought in using rope and wooden scaffolding. If moving it becomes necessary now, it can be done from above using steel gantries and slings. It can also be moved from below, using large timbers to 'rock' or lower the statue to ground level, where it's then placed on heavy-duty wheels or rollers. It takes hours to move the piece even a few centimeters!"

"Hmm…. If they ever have to move Ramesses, I'd like to be standing nearby," I mused. "Think of the little stone fragments that could fly off in the fray."

Spending the next couple of hours in the British Museum, we covered such highlights as the Sloane astrolabe; a stone chopper from Tanzania – the oldest object in the museum; the magnificent Parthenon sculptures; and the Sutton Hoo ship burial treasures. We also explored the

Oxus Treasure; the Mosaic of Christ – the earliest image of Christ in Britain; the Assyrian Lion Hunt reliefs; and the Code of Hammurabi.

We viewed scores of other famous artifacts, including the Ashurbanipal Library Project, which was truly awesome.

"This is the granddaddy of all libraries!" I said. Beyond that, I was momentarily speechless as I gazed upon shelves of prehistoric books: a partial collection from over 30,000 clay tablets and fragments inscribed with cuneiform – a type of writing used in Mesopotamia (ancient Iraq). They looked like typical reading material on modern-day library shelves – only the books were made of hardened clay! Very surreal to the historian in me.

"Interesting. These tablets were discovered in the ruins of the city of Nineveh – now northern Iraq," read Keith, from the information plaques. "The city was once the capital of the Assyrian empire, ruled by Ashurbanipal from circa 669 to 631 BC. Nineveh was consumed by fire around 612 BC; it most likely baked the clay tablets even further, making them among the best-preserved documents from thousands of ancient Mesopotamian history pieces. Incredible!"

"Yes," I added, "and these allow the Assyrians' story to be told in their own words. These stone documents follow court intrigues, secret intelligence reports, the steps of rituals, the words of hymns and prayers, and the details of medical handbooks. What a find!"

I pondered all of this for a moment. "You know what they say: 'Say it, forget it; write it, regret it.'"

My husband was about to reply when I switched gears. "There's one more thing that I absolutely can't miss. The Vindolanda Tablets. They're here now! Let's grab lunch, then head over." Roman Britain – particularly, Emperor Hadrian's Roman Britain – is one of my favorite subjects.

I kind of have a thing for Hadrian….

After climbing the curved staircase to the Great Court Restaurant, located in a circular area under the huge latticed-glass roof of the museum, we were seated next to an older couple who were dining in companionable silence.

"Look!" I whispered to Keith. "It's 'Lionel and Jean Hardcastle'!" Lionel and Jean were two beloved fictional characters from the British TV series, *As Time Goes By*, and we were both big fans. The role of Jean was played by Judi Dench. "They're making me think of Barrett."

"How so?"

"Well, Judi Dench is a lover of Shih Tzus. She had two whom she mentioned in one of her books – called Minnie and Henry."

At this point, the gentleman seated next to us weighed in. "Ah! Dame Judith Dench. Sorry – I couldn't help but eavesdrop. She's a neighbor of ours, you know."

"Yes," added the man's wife. "She's absolutely lovely! Say – I know this is short notice, but we're having a little candlelight supper at our home tonight, and Judi will be there along with a few other guests. Would you like to join us? You seem like a nice couple of Americans."

Keith and I glanced at each other with startled expressions. What?? Could this be happening? Dinner with Judi Dench, aka Jean Hardcastle, aka M of *James Bond* fame, plus a host of other esteemed film and stage roles?

Before I could gather my wits, my husband spoke for us. "Sure, we'd love to! Thank you!"

The rest of lunch was a blur. We chatted about all sorts of things with our new friends, Alistair and Helen. We told them of our happy situation with Barrett and that we'd be picking him up that afternoon.

Alistair offered, "Well, bring him along! What's a proper English supper without a dog under one's chair?"

Indeed!

After securing the couple's address and bidding them goodbye until later, we finished up our Afternoon Tea – our plush teal chairs coordinating nicely with the elegant green floral-and-bird print on the crockery – and then made our way to the Vindolanda exhibit.

"I've read so much about these tablets, and now they're right in front of me!" I said.

The Vindolanda Tablets are a set of wooden writing tablets from the Roman fort of Vindolanda, which was situated along what would later become Hadrian's Wall, in northern England. Composed of thin slices of wood the size of postcards, they were scribed in cursive Latin using black ink. Most date to around AD 100, during the reign of Trajan (Hadrian's predecessor). This collection of tablets is by far the largest number found anywhere in the Roman Empire, and they provide an amazing insight into life in a Roman auxiliary fort. One of the most famous writings among them is a birthday invitation:

'Claudia Severa to her Lepidina greetings, On the third day before the Ides of September, sister, for the day of the celebration of my birthday, I give you a warm invitation to make sure that you come to us, to make the day more enjoyable for me by your arrival, if you are present. Give my greetings to your Cerialis. My Aelius and my little son send their greetings. I shall expect you sister. Farewell, sister my dearest soul, as I hope to prosper, and hail. To Sulpicia Lepedina, wife of Cerialis, from Severa.'

I sniffled.

"What's the matter?" asked my husband.

"I kind of miss Sophie. You know: sisters and all."

He hesitated. "Well, cheer up, because I have a surprise for you. I wasn't going to say anything yet, but I'll tell you now so that you can happily enjoy your evening with Judi Dench. When we arrive in Edinburgh tomorrow, Sophie and Ewan will meet us there. They're going to spend a couple of days with us. They shortened their honeymoon to make it down!"

I was definitely cheered. "That's great!" I said. "They can meet Barrett, too! Speaking of whom, it's almost time to pick him up. We'd better head back to the hotel and get his things." I thought for a moment. "Do you think we should buy a little life vest for him? You know, the Thames boat tour and all. I wonder if I can find one in blue gingham…."

Having retrieved Barrett's essentials, including his carrier, we took a cab to Harrods to meet up with Charlotte, the salesgirl who had fostered him. Stepping out, we spotted them waiting for us on the sidewalk by one of the store's entrances.

"There's our little guy!" I picked up my step and dashed ahead.

Barrett must have recognized us; his plumed tail wagged excitedly.

When my husband approached, the pup leaped into his arms.

Charlotte laughed, and gave Barrett a final pat. "We're going to miss his furry little face around here! He's been a joy to have. Thank you so much for taking him."

I smiled. "Thank *you*, for holding him for us. Clearly, he's been in good hands." We promised to keep Charlotte and her co-workers posted on how Barrett was doing – complete with photos of the rest of his journey – and with that, we parted ways.

After tending to all of our new pup's doggy needs, we hugged him and tucked him into his gingham carrier – wearing his spiffy new harness and nametag – and headed for the Tube that would take us to our next destination: the short boat tour.

"Remember," I told Keith, as we emerged from Westminster Station, "when we reach the area where my yellow note card fluttered down from the London

Eye, we're getting off. With any luck, it's still lodged beneath that piece of jagged rock in the sand."

"Hon," began the naysayer, "you can't possibly think your note will still be there…."

"It certainly could be!" I looked for concurrence from our new family member, who was peeking through the mesh opening at the end of his carrier. "Right, Barrett?"

Barrett gave the slightest little nod.

We boarded our boat at the Westminster Pier, and settled on the open upper deck, which afforded a good view of the banks of the Thames. Keith took Barrett out of his carrier, and held him on his lap – leash firmly clipped to harness. Cruising along, father and dog-son bonded quickly; Barrett was torn between watching the sights before him, and whipping his fluffy little head around to gaze into Keith's eyes. It was mutual.

I'd been scanning the shoreline for my treasured note card. Shortly before we came to the Tower Pier, I spotted a scrap of yellow anchored under a half-buried oblong rock.

I jabbed Keith with my elbow. "There it is! We need to get off at this next stop."

"Cath…are you sure?"

"Yes. Come on!" I was already out of my seat, and waiting for the boat to fully dock.

Knowing that resistance was futile, Keith stood up with Barrett, and handed me his empty carrier. Shortly after, we disembarked.

The three of us walked the short distance to a river-bank access. Barrett was doing wonderfully on his leash, and Keith and I commented to each other on what an easy dog he seemed to be.

Once down on the sandy bank, we spotted the slender, encrusted rock with its yellow bounty, about 50 feet ahead. Apparently, Barrett spotted it too, because he suddenly slipped his harness and was off like a shot. Keith took chase after him, while I tried to catch up.

We both shouted, "*BARRETT!!*" But of course, the name meant little to him yet.

Reaching the rock that anchored my prize, Barrett stopped short and began barking adamantly. This attracted the attention of the handful of people who were combing the bank – some with metal detectors – including a man with a Nikon, who came over to check out the commotion at my site (as I now thought of it).

The photographer knelt down. "What have you found, little fella?"

Followed by, "Holy smoke!"

At that point the man set aside his camera, and began gently flicking away the sand and dirt surrounding the mystery 'rock' – tossing aside my yellow note (which I quickly scooped up). As he slowly extracted the object from the soil, it became apparent that it was *not* a rock.

For one thing, rocks do not have finger bones – with jewels attached.

The cameraman began furiously snapping photos.

Keith secured Barrett, while everyone stood around the site, speculating as to what the find was.

Or to be more exact, whose bejeweled hand it was.

Barrett just smiled pretty.

CHAPTER 13

A SMALL CROWD HAD gathered around our impromptu archaeology dig on the bank of the Thames. There was exciting debate around 'Barrett's Find', as people were now referring to it.

Before long, a representative of the British Museum showed up – likely called by one of the bystanders. Her name was Annabelle Pargetter, and after a cursory glance at what was presumed to be the skeleton of a small human hand with three finger bones loosely attached – one sporting a gold ring, set with what seemed to be a ruby, an emerald, and a sapphire – this efficient official proceeded to read us our rights under the ancient laws of Treasure Trove.

Our rights! Keith and I looked at each other with alarm.

"It is my duty to inform you," began Annabelle, "that in the year 1114, the *Leges Henrici* was compiled. This stated that in some parts of Europe, the acquisition of 'concealed and ownerless' treasure was in certain circumstances the treasure of the king. The law remained virtually unchanged until 1996, when it became the Treasure Act. This created a new definition of 'Treasure' which applies in England, Wales, and Northern Ireland. (Scottish law has always been different.) Applicable objects must be at least 300 years old, or contain over ten percent silver or gold, or be groups of coins or prehistoric metalwork found together. 'Treasure' found must be offered to the British Museum and other museums; the finder and landowner are rewarded with the full market value if a museum decides to purchase."

I could see the wheels turning in my husband's head, and I was pretty sure I was thinking the same thing. The three-gemmed ring would have to be offered to the museum; clearly, they would have to compensate us, since Barrett found the treasure – and we were now his owners.

What must these jewels be worth?

And what about the hand – whom did it belong to?!

Annabelle must have read my mind. "Now, I will call my staff to come to the site and remove the Treasure." She handed me her business card. "Please email your contact information to my office. Should we decide to purchase this find, we will be sending a check to your dog."

Keith and I exchanged glances. Our dog? Barrett gets the check? These Brits and their hounds. Egads.

WOOF!

Barrett was clearly pleased with this natural order of things.

Before leaving the cordoned-off archaeological site on the Thames, Barrett made one last claim on his treasure: as Annabelle reached out a gloved hand to pick up the skeleton and jewels to prepare for transport, our new pup made a grab for the finger sporting the gems.

There was a collective gasp from the crowd – mine and Keith's being the loudest – as our canine son held antiquity between his teeth. Before we could think what to do, Barrett dropped the bones on the ground; mercifully, it was a short drop.

Annabelle quickly scooped up the bounty and assured us that she would be in touch – not only with a possible offer from the museum, but with an update on whom the ancient hand might have belonged to. The possibilities for the latter were endless!

We'd hastily made our way back to the hotel on Nevern Square, to change for dinner with our new acquaintances, Alistair and Helen – and of course, Judi Dench! Now dressed for the evening – Keith in a pair of khakis and a blue Oxford shirt; I in a royal blue summer maxi dress – my focus turned to Barrett.

"Which of these outfits do you think he should wear?" I asked my husband, holding up two morsels of cuteness.

"Huh? Where did those come from?" was Keith's response.

"Luckily, I thought to start a little wardrobe for him, when we were in the shop where we bought his carrier.

So…which one?" I presented for his perusal two little vests: one in blue and white gingham (to match his carrier), and one in red with little black dogs on it.

"Well, clearly not the Scottie one – he's a Shih Tzu."

"I know that. Duh. But this is a Radley. You know: Radley…Scotties…?" Men.

"I don't follow," said my half-interested husband.

With that, I explained to a deaf ear the history of the Radley London brand and its iconic terrier mascot.

"Never mind," I finally said, fitting the little gingham vest on its furry new owner. "There. Now he coordinates with his parents."

⚏

It was a warm summer evening when our taxi pulled up to our hosts' row house in Holland Park, a borough of Kensington in central London, and near Notting Hill.

"I still can't believe this!" I whispered to Keith, as he paid the driver.

He then set Barrett – harnessed and leashed – on the sidewalk in this quiet tree-lined neighborhood. "This must be it: Number 21." With that, the three of us walked up the steps to the glossy black entry door and rang the brass doorbell.

In no time, the door opened.

"Come in, come in!" beckoned Alistair, ushering us into the foyer. "We're so glad that you could make it! It's a lovely night for a garden party, don't you agree?"

We did.

Following our host from front to back of the main floor of this four-storied Victorian home, we were happy to see that while many of the properties on the street had been remodeled inside (according to real estate information that we'd read), this particular home still wore the dark and cozy markings of its roots.

Alistair's wife Helen joined us as we approached the kitchen, which led to the back garden. After a warm greeting from her, and our complimenting her and her husband's home, she explained, "The Holland Park area derives its name from 'Holland House', which was a large mansion built in 1605, and once owned by Lord Holland. That house in particular was sadly bombed during WWII, and now only some ruins of the ground floor remain. In deference to the area's history, we've chosen to keep our interior as authentic as possible – with certain modern conveniences, of course!"

Looking around, I took note of the warm wood tones; comfortably mismatched china and crockery; and the slouchy-but-inviting chintz pillows – even in the kitchen. So British! Fabrics ranging from silks to wools, and patterns in competing stripes and florals – all in varying greens, reds, and golds – abounded.

Keith was carrying Barrett at this point, and we noticed his little ears perk up as we passed a corner of the room near a huge flagstone fireplace. (Victorian fireplaces were small, so this was a later addition.) Looking down, we saw a sleeping West Highland Terrier; clearly, our dog's presence hadn't fazed it.

Noticing Barrett's response – the British are very in tune with canine nuances! – Helen laughed. "Oh, he must have seen our Beth! She's a sweet old girl; she'll probably join us in the garden for dinner – if she detects the lamb roast, that is."

I shot a glance at Keith. *Oh, no!!* I don't eat lamb – they're way too…cute and woolly – and if that was to be served, what was I going to do? I certainly couldn't offend our hosts!

"Do something!" I whispered in desperation to my husband, as we walked down the back steps and out into the garden. It was now almost dark outside, and the beautiful verdant space – bordered by alternating high brick walls and black wrought iron fencing, all lined with a combination of fragrant rose bushes, thick trimmed hedges, and the occasional fountain – twinkled like a medieval fairyland, due to the little white lights placed tastefully in the weeping willows and acacias throughout the yard.

"What exactly would you like me to do?" came the side-mouthed reply. "Create a diversion when the main course arrives? Perhaps accidentally tip my chair backward, and while I'm on the ground, you pass me the lamb steak, which I'll quickly hand off to Barrett?"

"Oh, would you? Thanks!"

Keith sighed.

Before I could give further thought to avoiding a dining faux pas, we were approached by another couple, who had come to introduce themselves. They were very welcoming; a little younger than our hosts, and anxious to talk Disney World with us – having learned that we were from Florida – as they were planning a trip there soon with their two grandchildren. We chatted amicably with them, answering their questions while Barrett stood beside us on his leash, a model of canine manners. Just as we were winding up the conversation, we heard an exclamation from behind us and felt Barrett dance around in tail-wagging delight.

"Ohhh, who is this very handsome boy? He's absolutely adorable! Hello, Love," said Judi Dench, as she knelt to give our pup her full attention.

Keith and I looked at each other. (There was a lot of that on this day.) *Judi Dench! And she's petting OUR dog!*

My husband extended his hand in greeting, as she stood up. "Hello, Ms Dench. I'm Keith Keith, and this is my wife Cath." He gestured downward. "And this is Barrett. It's so nice to meet you!"

"Please, do call me Judi," she smiled. "And shall I call you Keith, or Keith?" There was mischief in her eyes.

We all chuckled, and my husband replied – for about the zillionth time – "Oh, I prefer Keith."

Now Judi turned to me. "What is it that you do, dear?"

Uhhh. "I'm a writer," I replied – immediately doing a mental forehead thunk. Why had I said that? I was hardly an official writer; I'd only written one page – *one page* – of my book.

"Well, Cath, I'd love to hear about your work! I must ask Helen to seat us next to each other. Plus," she winked conspiratorially, "with Barrett under your chair, I'll have someone to sneak my lamb chop to. Too cute and woolly to eat."

I imagined that Judi Dench and I could become fast friends.

Our wonderful dinner under the stars passed in the blink of an eye. Guests were sipping after-dinner drinks – brandy, port, whisky, coffees – and strolling about the garden.

At one point, glancing through the base of a wrought iron fence section, I spotted the ankles of a woman in sensible shoes walking along the sidewalk, with two men in suits by her side. All three had Corgis on leashes. I didn't think much about it until I glimpsed halfway above the shoes, a Launer London handbag hooked in the crook of the woman's arm. Could it be? Noooo. I shouldn't have had that second glass of Merlot with dinner….

The woman stopped, and peered in through the fence. She called out, "Beth? Beth! Where are you, dear?"

With that, our hosts' dog came bounding out from under Helen's chair and ran to the fence. The Westie and the Corgis wagged and nosed each other in greeting. Barrett wagged from afar.

My jaw dropped and I poked Keith with my elbow. "Look! It's her!"

"Her who?" asked my husband.

"*Her* – the Queen – Her Majesty! See her dogs? See her shoes? See her *purse?*"

"Cath…."

At that moment, everyone at the garden party stood and curtsied or bowed to the figure on the sidewalk.

I poked Keith with my elbow again, and he followed suit.

As did I – my knee cracking.

Looking down at Barrett, I saw that even he had gone down on his two tiny front knees. A proper British dog!

Helen approached her friend – the Queen! – and they chatted briefly through the black iron pickets. Soon, Queen Elizabeth, her Corgis, and her guards continued their stroll.

Our host turned to see our astonished faces.

"Oh!" she laughed. "Her Majesty and I go way back. Didn't you wonder why our dog's name was Beth?"

I couldn't say that I had.

We were preparing to leave the magical evening.

"Custard tart?" Judi Dench asked us.

"Pardon?" I replied, glancing at Keith for enlightenment.

He came up blank.

"I don't know about you, but I'm famished after skipping the lamb course! There's a lovely little café around the corner; their custard tarts are brilliant!" Judi winked. "Care to join me?"

Well, of course, we did!

The next thing I knew, the four of us: Keith, I, Barrett, and Judi Dench (again, I mentally pinched myself) were seated at a cozy table on the sidewalk, sharing custard tarts and tea. By now, we were beginning to feel comfortable with our famous companion. Keith asked her about her long and illustrious career as an actress – one which included the honors of receiving the titles of OBE (Officer of the Order of the British Empire) and DBE (Dame Commander of the Order of the British Empire) from the Queen.

As our late-night tea wound down and it was time to depart, we thanked Judi for a wonderful conversation and mentioned how serendipitous it had been for us to be seated next to Alistair and Helen during lunch at the British Museum. Had it not been for this lovely couple inviting us to their home for such a special evening, we would have never had this chance to meet one of our favorite actresses – nor glimpse the Queen on a walkabout with her Corgis!

"I'm always happy to meet new fans – and to make new friends!" replied Judi.

With that, Barrett stood from his place on the ground between my chair and Judi's. He very gallantly placed one paw on the actress's knee.

"Most especially, the four-legged ones," she added, with a twinkle in her eye.

CHAPTER 14

IT WAS OUR last morning in London – and our previous night had ended with an upgraded room that lived up to its promise. Airy French doors opened onto a spacious garden – a real one full of English beauty.

As my husband put it, "That snooty Name was holding out on us."

Keith, Barrett, and I were having breakfast in the hotel's snug atrium – our opportunistic pup under my chair, patiently awaiting a crumb to fall.

While enjoying British dark roast coffee and chocolate croissants, I glanced at the man seated beside us, reading his morning copy of *The Daily Mail*.

I did a double-take.

I pointed at the newspaper's cover page. "What...? How...? Look!"

My husband looked. Twice. "What the...?"

In living color, taking up half the page, was a close-up photo – of Barrett. More precisely, it was of Barrett holding the bejeweled finger of a skeleton in his teeth. 'Our' skeleton. Looking like a gangster with diamond fillings, he seemed to be grinning, to boot. The extra finger bones dangled like double cigars from his mouth.

"Good grief!" I said. "Remember the guy with the Nikon who was taking shots on the river bank? He must have sold this photo to the paper!"

Quickly googling the accompanying article on my phone, I read the gist. "Ugh. Listen to this," I quoted to Keith, *"American couple allows their dog to excavate our beloved Thames without a permit. The Shih Tzu, who goes by the name of Barrett, certainly appears to have lived up to his moniker's meaning."*

"Oh, swell," replied my husband. "What sort of implications might *that* have?"

I wasn't sure. "I don't think that we should be too worried, because the lady from the British Museum certainly would have advised us otherwise. Right?"

Keith pressed on. "And what was that reference to the meaning of Barrett's name all about?"

Doing another search on my phone, I found the answer immediately. "Well, here's the translation for 'Barrett'...."

"And?" prompted my husband.

" 'Troublesome'."

At that, Barrett looked up at us – smiling his most disarming, lopsided smile.

Now in the lobby and ready to check out of the hotel on Nevern Square, I walked Barrett on his Harrods leash over to the teak birdcage for one last goodbye to Houdini and Kiwi.

Simultaneously, Keith handled the business end with Name – and confirmed that the cab called by the long-suffering desk clerk was on its way.

I leaned in toward the birdcage. "Bye, little birdies."

The two budgie buddies halted their huddled conversation and gave me a quizzical look. Houdini had one eye on Barrett – who had both eyes on the bird pair. There was a brief stare-down between the species.

Just as I was about to pick up Barrett, he gave a loud but friendly *WOOF!* – which startled the birds and caused a great flutter of wings. During the melee in the cage, Houdini's tail feathers poked through one of the wooden bars – just enough to knock over a light porcelain vessel perched on a small stand next to the cage. The vase crashed to the floor, breaking into a million shards, while spilling its contents: about a ton of birdseed. (Who knew that tail feathers were so strong?)

Keith and I were speechless.

Name was the first to react. He ran out from behind his desk – and immediately slipped and fell in the birdseed, which had created a slick mess on the marble floor. I didn't even want to think about the shards of porcelain mixed in – neither their sharpness nor their value.

"I am SO sorry…" I began, as Keith scrambled to help the man up.

Name's eyes were wide. "YOU. PEOPLE. OUT!!" he roared, pointing toward the street.

At that moment, a uniformed driver poked his head through the lobby door. "Someone call for a cab?"

We didn't have to be asked twice.

⛣

Once our bags were loaded into the taxi boot, we climbed into the backseat and were about to close the door.

Suddenly the driver did a double-take at Barrett.

"Blimey! I know that dog!" said the impressed man. He turned to Barrett. "I read about you on the front page today! Brilliant job, clever mate! How would you like to ride up front with me? You can call me Bert."

Barrett wagged his tail in consent.

Keith and I looked at each other and shrugged. Apparently, our new canine had the magic touch – and he was mysteriously recognizable, too.

Due to lively conversation, the 12-mile ride to Heathrow Airport went by quickly. When our driver heard that we were going to Edinburgh, he had all kinds of advice. "Of course, you'll go to Edinburgh Castle and the Palace of Holyrood House. They're located at the top and the bottom of the Royal Mile. And whatever you do, don't miss Mary King's Close!"

"Mary King's Close? What's that?" inquired my husband.

"Oh, it's an experience to behold!" began Bert, handing us a copy of an online article on the subject – entitled

The Little House of Horrors – which he kept on hand for tourists. "Beneath the streets of modern Edinburgh, there's an entire underground village. The Royal Mile has many small alleys called 'closes'. One of these is Mary King's Close – and it's notoriously haunted!"

At that last comment, Barrett's ears perked up – and he gave a little whimper.

Our driver continued the history lesson. "The city of Edinburgh grew up around its impressive castle; by the 17th century it became the most populated city in Scotland. Back then, with little sanitation, the narrow, dirty streets smelled awful. All waste was thrown outside, where it remained on street level. Houses were built vertically; some buildings were 14 stories high! The wealthy were given houses higher up; the poor lived down low, in the muck. A series of alleyways were formed; there were gates to protect the residents from thieves at night. During the 16th and 17th centuries, the population in these closes sometimes reached 21,000!

In the 1750s, the town council wanted to build a covered market, to keep merchants off the streets. The Royal Exchange took seven years to complete, cutting off the tops of many buildings inside Mary King's Close. That close is actually a cluster of several closes connected by small alleys and walkways; it's very much a labyrinth – and it has eight layers! And here's an interesting fact: Mary Queen of Scots spent her last night in Edinburgh in Mary King's Close, in 1567. She had just lost the battle of Carberry Hill – not a real battle, but a series of negotiations – and after that, she was taken to prison in Loch Leven Castle."

"But where does the haunted part come in?" I asked.

Our driver continued. "I'm getting to that. But first, imagine this: back then, oil lamps with fish oil were used. And there was no indoor plumbing. So the stink was awful! People threw their buckets filled with human waste down the street. Allowed to do this twice a day, they called out the French words *gardez l'eau* (mind the water) – but in Scottish it sounded like 'gardyloo'. That, combined with the fact that ceilings were really low, rooms were cramped (whole families shared a room), and people kept their livestock inside the close – well, it must have been a nightmare. And, there were other dangers, too."

"Go on…." prompted Keith.

Barrett wagged his tail in concurrence.

"Murderers, rapists, and thieves also lived in the close. In addition, there were other dangers to public health. For instance, workshops – like the tanner's – where horse urine was used for the leather-making process. Mary King's Close was located next to the Old Nor' Loch, a heavily polluted swamp, used for dumping rubbish. Poisonous bio-gas arose from the quagmire penetrating the walls of the close. This gas caused hallucinations and produced a creepy greenish glow, which was mistaken for ghostly apparitions."

By now, we were seeing signs for Heathrow, but I wanted to hear more about this fascinating place – and wondered if there was more to the ghost stories. "What about the Plague?" I asked. "I know that Edinburgh was affected horribly during this period."

Bert nodded. "In 1644 Mary King – the widowed fabric merchant whom the close was named for – died, and four months later the Plague broke out in Edinburgh. Due to overcrowding, two types of plague spread quickly: Black Death (pneumonic plague) and bubonic plague. When the disease hit, 300 infected residents were sealed within the Close. The victims were given food and ale daily, and 'Plague Doctor' George Rae was left with them for care. He wore a long leather coat and a birdlike beak filled with herbs to protect him against the illness. The doctor saved many lives by cutting away boils and burning the flesh. Awful sounding – but effective. No one expected George Rae to survive, but he did! The Council owed him a large salary for his work; he spent ten years fighting for his money but died without receiving a penny." Our driver thought for a moment. "He was truly a hero."

Keith and I murmured in agreement.

"Since that time, there have been many reports of ghost sightings. But you will have to see for yourself when you visit!" concluded Bert, as we pulled up to the Departures area at the airport.

Getting out of the black cab, we thanked our driver profusely for his friendly and informative chat – and gave him an extra tip.

Bert handed Barrett to us, saying, "Bye, little guy! And happy treasure hunting!"

Barrett wagged his entire back end in response, as we slipped him into his little gingham carrier.

Our cabbie drove off with a friendly wave, and we headed inside Terminal 3 with our bags.

"On to Edinburgh!" I said. "After we stop by Gate 27, that is."

My husband was confused. "Why Gate 27? That's not our gate."

"Doggy facility," I explained.

I swear Barrett winked.

Our flight to Edinburgh was easy. Barrett rode quietly in his carrier, under the seat in front of Keith. He seemed familiar with the routine; perhaps his former life included a lot of travel. Who knew? I made a mental note to contact Charlotte, the Harrods clerk who'd kindly cared for him in the interim, to ask if she had any real background information on him. We knew little of his life with his former person, the elderly man who had passed away – except that the gentleman frequented Harrods, usually with Pup in tow. And, he must have been very good to Barrett, because the dog, in turn, was very loving.

Once we landed in Scotland, we made our way to Arrivals, where Sophie and Ewan were waiting for us.

"Sister!" Sophie and I called out simultaneously, followed by hugs and greetings all around. I was anxious to hear about their short honeymoon to the Orkney Islands.

But first, Sophie had a question for us.

"What is this?!" asked my sister, waving the front section of Scotland's edition of *The Daily Mail* at us. "And aren't you going to introduce us to your famous pooch?"

I made the introductions and explained the root of Barrett's current fame. "It's weird," I said. "People just seem to recognize him. Go figure."

Sophie patted Barrett's head. "Well, once the late owner of the skeleton's hand is determined, you may have a real celebrity on your hands – no pun intended."

"Yes," chimed in Ewan. "Britain is full of mysteries like that, waiting to be solved. Depending upon the bones' identity, Barrett may want to start his own little sleuthing business."

"Right!" added my husband. "We might want to change his name to Toby. Get it? Sherlock Holmes's dog…?"

We got it.

As the four of us (five, counting our furry passenger) rode in a cab to our hotel, we discussed what sightseeing to do. It was early afternoon, so we decided to tour Edinburgh Castle before it closed at 6:00 PM. But first, we needed to check into the Pear Tree Hotel.

"What an odd name for a Scottish hotel," I mused.

"Not really," informed Ewan. "Pear trees are native to central, western, and southern Europe. The farther north you go in Scotland, they do need more shelter, but they can still thrive here. At any rate, my boss recommended this hotel, so here's hoping."

We pulled up to the hotel. Exiting the cab with our bags, we climbed cement steps flanked by black wrought iron railings and matching Grecian urns, overflowing with pretty, red campion flowers. The inviting white trim around the covered entryway, highlighting the deep maroon front door, looked promising.

My husband entered the townhouse, getting the first glimpse. "Does your boss not like you?"

Sophie pushed past Keith. "Let me see!" She saw enough. "Ewan! Mr Blugs recommended THIS? What was he thinking?"

Now it was my turn to step inside. Holding Barrett, I took a quick look around. Yikes. A tiny, dark, octagonal lobby – covered in peeling, green-and-gold striped wallpaper – greeted us. The floor was covered in a musty old carpet – likely once a vibrant, burgundy Oriental print, but now just a sad remnant of better days.

Standing at the small check-in desk was a kind-looking elderly man; when he greeted us with a smile, I noticed he had only one tooth. I instantly felt sorry for him and was hoping that no one would complain – as though it were his fault that the hotel was so shabby.

Sophie motioned us aside, for a quick conference. She was apologetic to Keith and me, while simultaneously giving Ewan the evil eye. Poor Ewan, of course, had no idea that his boss's standards were so…low. We assured him it would be fine since it was only for two nights. With that, we returned to the little man at the desk – whose name tag read Charles – and resumed checking in.

Now it was Charles who was apologetic. "I'm sorry that our elevator isn't working; it's a little ancient, and your rooms are on the third floor. If you'd like, I can help carry your bags up."

Before our husbands could even think about letting the frail man help – we were pretty certain they wouldn't, but didn't want to take any chances – Sophie and I thanked Charles and insisted that we could manage.

The five of us huffed and puffed up three flights of stairs: the men carrying the bulk of the bags, Sophie carrying her and my two totes, and I carrying Barrett plus his carrier full of doggy necessities.

Reaching the third-floor landing, we paused in trepidation before heading to our rooms.

"Crikey!" said Keith, opening our rickety door – a feat which involved jiggling the worn key quite a bit before any success. (Across the hall, we heard similar machinations from Ewan.)

We stepped inside. Once again, we were in a hotel room where the bed took up ninety percent of the space. Only this room had an added touch.

"What in God's name is that?" I pointed at a Port-a-Potty lookalike in the corner of the room, then turned to my husband. "No way! Where's the bathroom? Where's the shower? Where's the health department??"

Barrett looked expectantly at Keith, in solidarity with me.

"Geez," was my husband's reply. "I don't know. Let me check with Ewan— "

At that moment, there was a knock on our door. Sophie's eyebrows were at her hairline, matching mine at that point. We had a flutter of outraged-hen chatter (sometimes it just is what it is), while our husbands went to the lobby to consult Charles.

In no time, they were back.

"Charles says that they're planning to renovate soon; these buildings are old and are not en suite, as such," Ewan informed us. "There is, however, a shower down the hall for each floor of rooms." There were four rooms on each floor.

"No way!" Sophie and I exclaimed in unison. By now, we had the sister act down pretty well. We read each other's minds: *There'd better be a Boots nearby, where we can buy some dry shampoo!* Boots was a pharmacy chain in the UK and we were all quite familiar with it.

Resigned to our fate and deciding to make the best of it, we agreed to freshen up however we could. We'd then meet in the lobby before traveling from the Haymarket district we were staying in, to Edinburgh Castle.

Just as we were parting ways, my cell phone rang.

"Ms Keith?" came the voice on the other end. "This is Annabelle Pargetter from the British Museum. We have examined the artifact that your dog found on the riverbank of the Thames, and we would like to make him an offer."

CHAPTER 15

"THEY'RE PAYING BARRETT for a fool?" asked my confused husband.

"Not fool: *Fool!* Okay, a fool…." I conceded.

Keith, Sophie, and Ewan looked at me expectantly. So did Barrett.

I went on to explain. "According to Annabelle Pargetter, the museum has determined that the skeletal hand very likely belonged to Anne Boleyn's personal fool, Jane!"

Keith mused, "Anne hooked up with Henry VIII – and Jane was the fool…?"

"Yes. Anyway," I continued, "royalty kept fools before and during the Tudor era; they were responsible for much entertainment. Two types of fools chronicled over the years were the 'natural' or 'innocent' fool, and the 'merry' fool. The former would have mental or physical disabilities and not necessarily be in control of their faculties; the latter were entertainers of sound mental health but pretended otherwise for laughs." I added, "Fortunately, they were all treated as precious possessions of the court, which may have helped offset the indignity of the job."

Sophie chimed in. "I remember reading that Anne Boleyn bought a new gown and a green satin cap for her fool, sometime in the 1530s. Maybe she lent Jane some rings, too. And, there is a famous painting of Henry VIII and his family, with the fool Jane in the background."

"Moving on to the present," prompted Ewan, "we're all dying to know what the museum is offering Barrett in exchange for the loot!"

"Well," I began – eight eyes upon me, two of them canine – "for Barrett, they are providing a year's supply of dehydrated duck feet and lamb tracheas." I suppressed a gag as I announced these common British doggy treats.

"And for Barrett's parents...?" Keith ventured.

"They've offered us lifetime tickets on British Airways: two adults, one canine; unlimited High Tea in the British Museum's Great Court Restaurant; and one more thing."

"What's that?" chorused my companions.

"A check for 10,000 pounds – with the stipulation that Barrett's furry face can be used in the museum's brochure."

"Deal!" proclaimed my husband. As an afterthought, he added, "You did remind them that Barrett cannot cash his own check, correct?"

I did a quick redial.

⊡

Before we could head to Edinburgh Castle for the afternoon, Keith and Ewan had to take a couple of quick business calls. Keith-the-water-guy had a large system about to be installed in St Martin, in the Caribbean's Leeward Islands. There was some sort of issue with it – which could require an upcoming trip to the island. Another potential history trip in the works!

Ewan was on a call with Mr Blugs; the shipping forecast for the English Channel was dicey, and a whisky export could be affected.

I was tucked in the corner of the small lobby, making notes for the first chapter of my book. I told Sophie about the conversation I'd eavesdropped on in London, and the contact information I'd scored on the Van Gogh expert whom I hoped to interview one day – the contents of my now-famous yellow note.

At the same time, Sophie was looking up tourist information on the castle, while holding Barrett in her lap.

"Uh, oh," said my sister. "Listen to this: dogs are not permitted at the castle." She looked up. 'What are you going to do?"

Barrett whipped his furry little black and tan head around and gave me an expectant look.

I glanced at Keith and Ewan, still across the lobby on their phones.

"Come with me!" I said.

We scooped up our materials and Barrett, and headed for the door. "Didn't I see a Marks & Spencer just up the street?" I caught Keith's eye, and gave a little wave.

"I think so," said Sophie, "but what good will M&S do for us now?"

"No time to explain. You'll see!"

And we were off.

⊟

A half-hour later, Sophie and I strolled back into The Pear Tree lobby.

"Where were you two—" Keith's jaw dropped mid-sentence, and he pointed at the cargo I was now pushing. "What is THAT?"

"It's a pram – a baby carriage," I said, stating the obvious.

"But WHY? And where's Barrett?"

At the sound of his name, Barrett popped his blue-bonneted little head up enough to see over the edge of the carriage, from his supine position. His cap matched his little jammies – which were covered in yellow ducks – and a pacifier in his mouth completed the picture. I swear he made a sound similar to 'Goo'.

"Meet your new son," I said to my husband. "Now, are we going to make it to the castle in time or not? Let's go!"

⊟

While I pushed our pram up the street toward the bus stop, Keith and Ewan made a concerted effort to stay several paces behind. Once our transportation arrived, however, the hubbies had no choice but to lift our cargo onboard for us.

Barrett was conspiratorially quiet on the bus ride, and only a couple of passengers looked our way, stealing glances through the protective screen zipped over the carriage.

One child said to her mother, "That baby needs a shave."

Our stop for the top of the Royal Mile came blissfully soon. We exited, then climbed up Castle Hill, situated on an enormous rock for strategic advantage.

My husband took in the view. "Wow! I've been reading about this. During the Iron Age a hill fort was built upon this rock. The castle defenses have evolved over hundreds of years, and Mons Meg – one of the greatest medieval cannons ever made – was given to King James here in 1457. And, Edinburgh Castle is the most besieged place in all of Britain."

"That's all true," said Sophie, as we made our way to the entrance. "But the castle was also home to kings and queens for many centuries. And according to its website, Queen Margaret – who was later made a saint – died here in 1093, thus the chapel built in her honor by her son, King David. Fast forward to 1511, when James IV oversaw the completion of the Great Hall. He died shortly afterward at the Battle of Flodden, fighting English forces sent by his brother-in-law, King Henry VIII of England."

"That Henry. His handiwork is everywhere," quipped my husband.

"And," I chimed in, "it says that above the door to the Royal Palace are the gilded initials MAH – for

Mary Queen of Scots and her second husband Henry Stuart, Lord Darnley. Mary gave birth to James VI in the Royal Palace in 1566; he became king of Scotland at just 13 months old and united the crowns of Scotland and England in 1603. Imagine! An infant king – which I know was not uncommon, by the way. Rule, of course, would have been by regent. But still, the idea of a baby king….” I shook my head.

Woof! said the baby in the stroller, one tan eyebrow raised in dissent.

Having successfully breezed through the castle entrance with our 'baby' unquestioned, we were now free to wander about the castle and its grounds. At one point, my husband noted that while we'd been able to give Barrett water in the pram, surely he needed the loo at some point. What to do?

Walking as far from the castle structures as we could, we found a grassy spot near some trees. With Sophie and Ewan on the lookout, I went about taking Barrett out of his little jammies, before Keith snapped his leash to his harness, and carried him to his throne – no pun intended.

Following success, we were just about to put him back into his duck jammies and into the pram, when we heard a stern voice behind us.

A kilted guard stood about three feet away. “Halt! That's a dog. No dogs are allowed on the grounds.”

I shot Sophie and Ewan a glance.

They shrugged apologetically.

Keith stammered, a bead of sweat forming on his forehead. "We're sorry, sir. We had no idea. We'll—"

"Wait!" ordered the guard, peering closer to examine our foiled foil. "That dog! I know him. It's Barrett, right?" Now his demeanor changed, and he was fawning over our contraband. Barrett was loving every minute of it, his question mark of a tail wagging furiously.

"Yes…" I began cautiously, "but how did you know? People seem to recognize him easily, but we're totally perplexed as to how!"

"It's simple," explained the now-friendly guard. "That little bit of tan fur over his eyebrows: the one on the right is shaped like a feather. Tan feathers are a symbol of health, protection, guidance, comfort, and so on. We Brits have a pretty turbulent history; we'll take all of the good we can get!" He patted Barrett on the head and handed us a pass. "This will allow the little fella into any of Britain's national treasures. I'll just need your signatures here," he pointed at a line – and then at a square space below it, "and Barrett's pawtograph here."

The guard produced an ink pad (does this happen often? we wondered), Barrett stuck out his little paw like a pro and made a stamp, and we were off.

♦

Leaving Edinburgh Castle, it was now time for dinner.

Ewan offered, "I have the perfect pub: The Greyfriars Bobby." He then added for clarification, "No apostrophe before the 's', guys."

"Yes!" agreed Sophie. "You know: from the 1912 children's novel – and the later Disney movie – *The Tale of Greyfriars Bobby?*"

Keith and I were vaguely familiar with the book, and Sophie went on to explain the true story, consulting the bar's website. "The pub's name refers to a Skye terrier called Bobby, a police watchdog who belonged to Edinburgh policeman John Gray. Bobby helped his owner guard animal pens on market days in the Grassmarket, and both regularly lunched there. When Gray died in 1858 he was buried in the Greyfriars Kirkyard (Scottish for 'churchyard') next door. For 14 years, his faithful dog kept watch and slept on his master's grave. Bobby's loyalty touched the locals, and on his death in 1872, he was buried along with his master in the Kirkyard. His headstone is still there, and fresh flowers are laid on the grave daily.

"Awww…," we all said in unison.

Barrett gave a plaintive whimper.

"Sounds good, then!" said my husband. He took Barrett out of his baby disguise and set him on the sidewalk, leashed.

Walking down the Royal Mile, we crossed the George IV Bridge to the Grassmarket district. Soon we spotted the large, commemorative bronze statue of the Skye terrier, resting at the corner of the bridge and Candlemaker Row.

Again, the collective, "Awww…."

Behind the statue of Bobby, was Greyfriars Bobby's Bar, which occupies the ground floor of a row of

Georgian rubble-built houses; these join onto the 1722 Candlemakers' Hall.

Ewan mentioned that at one time, Candlemaker Row stood outside of the city boundary, "because no one wanted an entire street of candlemakers with highly flammable materials near the timber houses of the city!"

We entered the cozy pub, taking our seats at a burgundy leather half-circle booth under a large bay window. The glass panes allowed a cheery light, in contrast to the dark mahogany interior. Barrett made himself at home under the table, by Keith's feet – and our pup had a good view of three other dogs who were also under their owners' seats: two Yorkies and a Westie lounged nearby without a care in the world.

I scanned The Greyfriars Bobby's menu, wondering what to order. Haggis, neeps, and tatties? Nope. Fishcakes salad? No. Rump of lamb? Definitely not. Crayfish and Marie Rose sauce? Yes! This, I recognized. I had ordered it when we'd first come to Scotland for the wedding, and it was pretty good. It's fairly common in Britain, and similar to a Shrimp Louis salad in the US.

Keith went with fish-and-chips, while Sophie chose Welsh rarebit, and Ewan opted for the chicken, Wiltshire ham, and leek pie. Barrett had his bowl of water, and some kibble.

All was good, as our server, Molly, approached to take our order.

From under our table came an otherworldly howl. *AWOOOOHOOOOHOOO.*

"What the hell was that?" exclaimed my husband.

We all four looked under the table.

AWOOOOHOOOOHOOO. There it was again. For some reason, Barrett was in a state, and the whole pub was glaring at us for it. Even the other dogs looked appalled.

"Barrett!" I hissed. "Hush! Quiet!"

The howling continued – and it stopped abruptly as Molly skittered away. Soon she was back with our drinks – and Barrett resumed his caterwauling. The ruckus was so jarring, that our server dropped some coins from her tray, and I looked down as she put her foot on one to stop it from rolling away. *My,* I thought, as I noticed her red-soled Louboutins, *she must make some pretty good tips here.* Her shoes were out of sync with her faded black tee-shirt and grimy jeans, but what do I know?

The duration of our dining included Barrett's cacophonous starts and stops every time Molly approached or left our table, and we rushed through our meal, to make a hasty exit.

Leaving an extra-apologetic tip, we scooted out the door and onto the sidewalk. Keith and I were a bit shaken, wondering what sort of devil dog we had acquired.

As if reading our thoughts, Barrett smiled his lopsided smile up at us, sweet as shortbread.

***

Finally back at our hotel for the night, Keith and Barrett went up to our room – Barrett was going to get a quick sponge bath – while Sophie, Ewan, and I lingered in the lobby for a moment, discussing our plans for the morning. First up, we'd decided to tour Mary King's Close – two of us, that was. Sophie and Ewan had done it before, and as Sophie put it, "Once was enough." They offered to kill time on the Royal Mile with Barrett; we all agreed that the Close was no place for a dog.

Climbing the stairs to our rooms, we heard a woman scream. Hastening our steps, we reached the landing in time to see a frazzled Keith standing at the top – but no Barrett. As we tried to make sense of this, an elderly woman stepped out of the bathroom, and into the hallway – wearing what appeared to be a curtain yanked down from a window, and a scowl twice the size of the curtain.

I looked to Keith. "What happened? And where's Barrett?"

In that moment, I had my answer. Barrett came racing down the hallway from around a corner – the lady's yellow bath towel in his mouth. He came to a screeching halt when he saw me, wagging his tail furiously.

Through gritted teeth, my husband explained. "Community loo. Apparently, Barrett wanted to get a jump on his spa treatment."

CHAPTER 16

"ARE YOU SURE you want to do this?" I asked my husband. "It will be tight quarters, you know."

We were walking down the cobblestoned Royal Mile in Edinburgh's Old Town, past ancient churches, pubs, and myriad shops, including those of the weavers' mills (selling beautiful kilts, tartans, and cashmere), on our way to Mary King's Close. The Close was getting... close. We'd left Barrett with Sophie and Ewan for the morning; they would be window shopping and promised to find a Scottish doggy souvenir for our pup. Of course, he was already British, so it may not be significant to him...but I would treasure it!

"Of course I'm sure," replied Keith. "No problem."

Spotting the sign for the Close ahead on the left, he strode on; when I caught up, he opened the door with a flourish. "Madam!" He bowed, gesturing for me to proceed.

We entered the small, dim, black and red lobby, and I sensed my husband's bravado waver. Straight ahead was a tiny elevator with a black door, where we joined our little group of five tourists.

Our guide, Ian (in period costume), told us we'd descend three and a half stories below street level. "We'll have to make two trips down to accommodate everyone." He then added with a laugh, "If anyone suffers from claustrophobia, speak now!"

I raised an eyebrow at my husband.

He nodded the go-ahead.

We stepped into the lift with the guide, comprising the first 'shift'. After an agonizingly slow descent, the lift door creaked open, and we stepped out into total darkness. Ian handed Keith a flashlight (aka torch) and told us to wait here while he went back up for the other three victims. And then he was gone.

"*Wait here!*" I was already feeling creeped out. "Where else would we go?"

Keith shone the flashlight around; its beam was weak, but we began to get a feel for our surroundings. A steep, narrow dirt street lay deep between weathered and crumbling blonde sandstone tenement buildings – some, three stories high at that point – dating back to the early 1600s.

"Right," agreed my husband. He took a few steps forward. "It's not like we're—ACKKK! What the hell did I just step in?!"

At that moment, the lift door opened again, and the rest of our group stepped out.

The guide instructed, "So as I was just saying, watch out for mud down here. It can be a little slick in certain areas, due to the dampness. And centuries of animal dung and blood are mixed in. There's one room in particular – it was the butcher's – where you can still smell the…."

At that point, I blocked out the rest of Ian's history lesson. I was beginning to feel queasy, wondering what possessed us to take this tour – and what was in the mud now covering Keith's shoe.

It was all that London cabbie Bert's fault!

A half hour into the 50-minute adventure, we'd traversed much of the warren that was the Close. A few buildings had been fitted with sparsely placed lanterns on their facades so that it was possible to see down off-limits streets. One area was particularly fascinating: a guard rail allowed visitors to peer over the edge – deep into an abyss that contained buildings and streets several *more* stories below the level we were walking on. It was under excavation, and I could only imagine the vermin running wild – not unlike the days of the Plague. Some of the current rats were probably descendants!

Treading carefully around muddy areas and over uneven, sloping terrain, occasionally we would come to a building where a room had been carefully preserved and staged to reflect the period. Each room was cramped, dark, musty, and had low ceilings.

One such chamber featured a replica of Doctor Rae, the Plague doctor, leaning over a patient in his bed; the doctor was wearing a black cape and the famous raven-beaked mask. The effect was unsettling, and before I had much time to absorb it, the guide moved us on to the next room we would visit: the butcher's. True to the previous mention, there was a very faint odor of blood emanating from the dirt floors and walls. I clamped my hand over my nose and mouth and quickly exited. GAACKKK! It was too much. No wonder Sophie and Ewan opted to remain up in the fresh air with Barrett!

As we neared the end of the tour, there was one more room to visit.

"This was Annie's room, and here is where some supernatural activity has been detected." Ian explained, "In the 1990s, the renowned Japanese psychic, Aiko Gibo, came to visit the Close while making a film about the haunted places of Britain. When she came to this room, she could barely enter because of the pain and unhappiness she could sense. 'I cannot enter this room… it is too strong…there is a child beside me, her little hand is clutching my trouser leg. She was separated from her parents. She wants to go home to her family… her desire haunts this very place strongly,' declared the psychic. Eventually, Gibo crossed the threshold. Once inside the room, she communicated with the young girl's spirit near the fireplace. Her name was Annie; she had lost her favorite doll and was heartbroken. The psychic soon purchased a doll from a local Royal Mile shop and returned to the little girl. The doll apparently brought comfort to the child, and Gibo said that so long as the doll remains, the room will never again be disturbed by her spirit."

We turned our attention to the enormous pile of dolls, toys, and jewelry in a dim corner of the room. From around the globe, visitors have shown their sympathy for Annie, by leaving these items for her spirit. As Ian pointed out, "Even first responders from the New York City Police Department, and numerous police and fire departments across the US, have left their badges as a mark of respect."

Wow. By the end of the tour – which Keith powered through despite the close quarters and his sodden shoe – we were both humbled, educated, and starved for some fresh air. Emerging out onto the street again, we spotted Sophie, Ewan, and Barrett several doors down, in front of a kilt shop.

"Good grief! What's Barrett doing?" asked my husband. We both squinted to get a better look.

Trekking ahead, we heard the skirl of a bagpipe – and spotted our pup at the center of the half-circle of spectators that had formed around the piper. The people laughed and clapped, as Barrett – dressed in a tiny kilt! – danced a little Highland fling on his hind legs. He seemed to be having the time of his life and was right at home with this Scottish tradition. Who knew?

Ewan laughed as we approached. "Your little guy is quite something! I wonder where he acquired his moves?"

"He certainly didn't get it from me," I replied, remembering with chagrin my inferior dance skills on display at my sister's wedding.

Our next destination was at the bottom of the Royal Mile: the Palace of Holyrood House. But first, we stopped for lunch in a pub along the way. Barrett took a seat under the table by Keith's feet; our pup's black fur with its tan – or Dobie – markings looked very dapper against the red plaid carpeted floor. (By now he'd discarded his tiny kilt, so there was no clashing of design.) We'd noticed a lot of plaid carpeting in pubs, inns, and such in Scotland, and asked Ewan about it.

"Actually," began my brother-in-law, "each plaid is somebody's tartan – 'tartan' referring collectively to the distinctive cloth patterns. Patterns are determined by a person's clan – which is linked to their surname. Historically, surnames give not only a sense of identity, but also provide a feeling of solidarity. Possession of a Scottish surname entitles you to wear the tartan of your clan. There are over one hundred great clans, but there are also other ways to wear a tartan if your surname isn't among them. Chances are, you bear the surname of one of the septs; these last names arose within a clan as a result of landless men or outlaws attaching themselves to the clan for protection, rendering service in return. *Sept* derives from the Latin word septum, meaning fence or enclosure, and alludes to the fact that originally land was set aside for these landless followers where they could establish a village of their own. And there's more…."

Keith and I looked at Ewan with admiration. He was a font of Scottish knowledge! Even Barrett tilted his little head and seemed interested.

Ewan continued. "Another way to be allowed to wear a tartan is as a subject of Her Majesty the Queen.

You could wear the Royal Stewart tartan to show your allegiance. Or, if you prefer to avoid politics, you could wear the Caledonia tartan, devised in the nineteenth century to embrace all the people of Scotland. Or, you could wear the Jacobite tartan, allegedly worn by the clanless followers of Bonnie Prince Charlie."

At this point, Sophie added, "There are also occupational tartans designed to be worn by shepherds or ministers of religion. At any rate, few Scotspeople can trace their roots with certainty before the beginning of the 1700s, because parish records rarely exist from an earlier period. Although, there are some clan histories that do go back into antiquity."

I was impressed. "How do you know all of that?"

"Simple: what my husband hasn't imparted, I've gleaned from reading an excellent source: *Clans and Tartans of Scotland*, by James MacKay."

There was an inquiring bark from under the table. We all looked down. Barrett was holding his little kilt in his mouth, having pulled it out of the bag under my chair.

"I think Barrett wants to know whose tartan he's wearing," I translated, pointing at the beautiful woolen weave of red, yellow, and blue.

"It's ours, of course!" said Sophie and Ewan in unison. "MacBean!"

"And," added Sophie, "all clans have a badge. Ours is a demi-cat rampant, with the motto 'Touch not the cat bot [without] a glove.' "

No chance of that from me.

Following lunch and now munching from a bag of Scottish tablet (a tasty treat similar to fudge, but with a grainier and more brittle texture), we reached the Palace of Holyrood House at the end of the Royal Mile. Bringing our pup inside would be no problem since we now had his special pass.

Checking our stroller in the proper area, we proceeded through the entrance – Barrett now on a plaid leash that Sophie surprised us with, which matched his little kilt. Plaid definitely suited him!

"This palace – the official Scottish residence of Queen Elizabeth – can only be visited when she's not in residence. So we're in luck," said Ewan.

Sophie turned to me. "But what you really want to know about, Cath, is Mary Queen of Scots' history here. I'm sure she'll come up in your writings at some point."

She was right. The long-suffering queen with the short and turbulent reign was my main focus, and I had one particular destination within the Palace's neoclassical walls. "How do we get to her private apartments? I want to see the room where Rizzio was murdered!"

"Who was Rizzio?" asked my husband.

"Well, I'll tell you!" I began. "Rizzio was the personal secretary of Mary Queen of Scots. He was killed by the Queen's jealous husband, Lord Darnley. Lord Darnley was actually Mary's cousin, aka Henry Stewart. Both he and Mary were grandchildren of Margaret, the sister of King Henry VIII."

"No inbreeding there," quipped Keith. "Kind of explains why the Royals all look like whippets in their portraits."

I rolled my eyes. "Yes. Anyway, Darnley never cared much for Mary, and sought far more power than she was willing to give. When the Queen was six months pregnant, her husband joined a group of Scottish nobles who broke into her supper room, and dragged her secretary, Rizzio, aside and stabbed him to death – claiming he had undue influence over her foreign policy. Mary naturally believed that Darnley wanted to kill her and her unborn child as well, thus ascending to King of Scots.

After Rizzio's death, the nobles kept Mary and Darnley prisoners in Holyrood Palace. Nearing the end of her pregnancy, she was desperate to escape, and convinced Darnley to help her. They escaped together, and three months later, the future King James VI of Scotland was born. At just 23 years old, Mary had fulfilled one of her main duties: providing a male heir to the throne."

"Did the Queen and her husband live happily ever after?" inquired Keith.

"Nope. The nobles who had plotted with Darnley were infuriated that he helped Mary escape. In February of 1567, his house – Kirk o' Field – was blown up. Darnley's body was found strangled in the garden."

We pondered this for a moment.

Ewan said, "Right. Well, let's head to the room where Rizzio was murdered. I hear that there's still a blood stain on the floor!" Men.

Barrett trotted happily alongside us as we passed through the palace ruins of the Abbey where Mary Queen of Scots was married; viewed an astonishing collection of tapestries; walked under magnificent plasterwork ceilings; and finally approached the northwest tower, where the private apartments were located.

I looked at Keith. "Uh, oh. What am I going to do now?" Straight ahead was the only access to the apartments: a 500-year-old very narrow, steep, spiral stone staircase. Vertigo waiting to happen for me.

"You'll be fine!" dismissed Sophie.

Keith was not as convinced. "It'll be okay…."

I looked ahead of and behind us. Groups of tourists lined both directions; some already climbing, and some waiting for us to get going. In other words, no escape route if I needed one.

Sophie and Ewan barged ahead, and began their ascent. Keith was holding Barrett (his special status badge attached to his collar), and gave me an encouraging nod. Before I knew what was happening, I was shoved onto the first step by a lady behind me. An accident? I didn't think so. I had no choice but to keep moving.

Halfway up the agonizingly slow and suffocating climb, I felt I couldn't breathe.

"I can't breathe!" I said to my husband.

"Sure you can! If you're talking, you're breathing. We're almost there. You can do it."

From that point on, everything was a blur. My feet kept moving, but all I could see were grey spots swimming in front of my eyes. Just as my legs got wobbly, we arrived at the top. We then shuffled through a very low doorway and into the Queen's bedchamber.

"I need to lie down!" I gasped, falling onto the Royal bed.

No sooner had I done so – much to the shock of my family – when I heard an angry voice.

"Ma'am!" boomed a guard. He rushed past the other visitors in the small room, and to my bedside. "Remove your head from the cod at once!"

Eyes popping open, I peered in confusion out of the heavy brocade canopy that surrounded me – while taking a moment to notice the decorative oak ceiling above – and wondered what in the world a fish had to do with anything.

"The cod, ma'am!" The guard pointed at the pillow where my head had landed. As I would soon learn, a 'cod' was a priceless northern English pillow from antiquity. "Kindly remove your head from it! In fact, please remove your entire body from the Queen's bed."

"Yes, sir. I'm sorry, sir," I mumbled sheepishly, as my husband helped me up. By now, the other visitors had thankfully turned their nosey attention toward the Supper Room – the tiny chamber off of the bedchamber – where Rizzio had been slain. Ewan and Sophie had joined them.

"Cath," muttered my husband, "no more shenanigans, please." He switched gears. "Come on! Ewan's motioning that he's found Rizzio's blood spot on the floor!" He handed Barrett to me, and skittered off to investigate.

Barrett looked at me quizzically.

I shrugged. "Let's go see yet another display of British refinement. I'm sure it's not as scandalous as an American woman resting on the late Queen's bed for a moment...." Sheesh!

Leaving the Palace, we trekked back up the Royal Mile. Our last stop for the day was to be St Giles's Cathedral, almost directly across from Mary King's Close.

My husband picked up his stride. "I've been looking forward to this. I understand there's a chapel where James Bond was knighted!" He then clarified, "Well, not exactly James Bond – but Sir Fitzroy MacLean, who was the inspiration for Ian Fleming's Bond character."

"True," said Ewan. "The Cathedral itself was founded by King David I, and has been a working church for almost 900 years. One of the key things that happens inside is the service for Most Ancient and Most Noble Order of the Thistle. In 1911, the Thistle Chapel became home to the Knights of the Thistle, which is an order of chivalry in Scotland dating back to the 17th century."

I was intrigued. "How does that work?"

"Well, the Order itself consists of sixteen members; a new member can only be invested when another member dies. Each of the members is appointed by the ruling British monarch, and when a new knight is installed, the current members put on their green velvet robes and white-plumed hats for a ceremony in the Thistle Chapel."

We came to the magnificent Cathedral. Touring the inside, we learned that the church's early beginnings in 1124 were Romanesque; it later became the center of the Scottish Reformation as John Knox's church; and in present day it serves as a Presbyterian church.

We approached the Thistle Chapel, and Keith picked up Barrett in order to carry him through.

"Wow," said my husband. "This is really something!"

He was right.

The chapel had been designed in the neogothic arts and crafts style, and was renowned for its intricate wood carvings of angels, animals, and flowers. One of the most interesting of the carvings was of three angels playing bagpipes.

A rich, dark area that comprised the vaulted-ceiling holy space included the knights' stalls, which lined the sides of the chapel. Coats of arms of knights past and present also line the walls, and ornate canopies atop the stalls are crowned with the crests of the living members of the Order.

"I wonder where the real James Bond's stall is?" mused my husband, as he strolled past the different stalls, lost in thought.

I had a better question. "Where's Barrett?!" I asked in alarm.

We all four swiveled our heads; no dog to be found.

It wasn't long before a guard approached us. "Ahem!" he began. "Have you lost anything? A dog, perhaps?"

Absurdly, I asked, "What dog?"

The guard was incredulous. "THAT dog!" he said, as he pointed toward one of the knight's stalls.

Much to our shock, there was Barrett – with a small white feather mysteriously perched atop his head, as though awaiting knighthood. He sat proudly in the elevated, elaborately-carved seat of Sir Fitzroy MacLean.

"Well," said Ewan to Keith, "it looks like he's found your man."

CHAPTER 17

"I WANT TO GET away…I want to flyyyy away…."
"Hon." My husband nudged me. "HON!"
"What?" I said too loudly.

I removed my earbuds, my little reverie interrupted. We had just taken off from Edinburgh Airport, on our transatlantic flight home via JFK. Barrett was nicely tucked under the seat in front of us, his blue gingham doggy carrier where Keith's feet were supposed to be. It was an aisle seat, so at least my husband could stretch a little when possible. I was staring out the window, dreaming of our next trip. This trip had been so great! – despite our usual follies – and we were coming home with a new family addition, to boot.

"Well, for one thing, while you're bobbing your head like a demented chicken, other passengers can hear Lenny Kravitz three rows ahead. You need to adjust your volume. Especially given your odd playlist. What all have you got there, anyway?"

"It's not odd," I defended myself, "it's eclectic! For your information, I have two Kravitzes; two Peter Framptons; Blind Faith's *Can't Find My Way Home*; a track from the movie *Rum Diary*; Jelly Roll's *Need a Favor*; Glen Campbell's *Wichita Lineman*; Smokey Robinson's *The Tears of a Clown*; The Rolling Stones *Wild Horses*; Bobby Goldsboro's *Summer* [love, love, love that one...]; Bradley Joseph's *The Glen*; and Michael Franks's *Popsicle Toes*. Which reminds me: I'm cold! Could you get my jacket from the overhead, please?"

My husband sighed and complied.

I shifted gears. "You know, I've been thinking. Barrett seems to travel really well, doesn't he?"

"So far, yes. Why?"

We looked down at Barrett, his small body barely visible through the sturdy mesh door of his carrier. With his fur being mostly black, if it weren't for his little tan eyebrows raised quizzically at us, we'd have been unable to tell if we were looking at his face or the back of his head.

I pressed on. "Well, as much as we travel, it wouldn't be fair to board him every time. There's really no reason that we can't bring him with us, to most places. And, there's a big plus!"

Keith raised an eyebrow. "What's the 'plus'?"

I made my case. "With a lifetime of free tickets on British Airways for us and for Barrett; unlimited High Tea at the British Museum; and a pass for Barrett to all of Britain's National Trust historic buildings and houses

– well, it would be absolutely wasteful not to plan on regular trips to Britain in the future!" I thought for a moment. "Hey! Northern Ireland and Wales are also part of the UK. We should add those to our travel list, too. And, while we're in the area, we may as well see Ireland. Perfect!"

"Cath, travel still isn't free, you know. This flight, for example. We're not on British Airways; they aren't going to be available to us every time."

"Pish, posh!" I said. "We'll still save a fortune."

I hailed a passing flight attendant. "May I have a cup of hot tea, please, when you have a chance? Irish Breakfast, if you have it."

A half hour into our flight, I got out my laptop and added a few paragraphs to Chapter One of my book.

"I've really got *flow*!" I said.

"What's that?" Keith was distracted, tapping away on the entertainment screen in front of him.

"Never mind," I said. "Even Barrett probably knows what 'flow' means."

Barrett had other thoughts. At that moment, he let out an otherworldly howl. *AWOOOOHOOOOHOOO.*

The female flight attendant passing by looked aghast, as did nearby passengers.

"What the…?" exclaimed Keith. Again, we both looked down at our pup; the gaze he returned to us seemed to convey, *What? Everything's good here.*

Shaken, and wondering what else Barrett had in store for this eight-hour flight that had barely begun, we returned to our writing and movie-watching.

About five minutes passed, before a different flight attendant walked by.

Again, the earsplitting lament. *AWOOOOHOOOOHOOO....*

Now my stress level began to climb. When it happened a third time as yet another flight attendant walked by, I went into detective mode. It didn't take me long to connect the dots.

"Egads!" I said to my husband. "It's the flight attendants! They're all wearing Louboutin pumps!"

Keith gave me a blank stare.

"Louboutins. The red soles! Remember the waitress in Edinburgh at Greyfriars Bobby's Pub? She was wearing the same shoes."

"I thought dogs were supposed to be color-blind?" was my husband's unhelpful response.

Good grief. "Well, apparently ours has super-powers, because yet again, his canine shenanigans are above and beyond." I turned in my seat, raising up so that I could see several rows back and down the aisle. "Holy smoke! ALL of the flight attendants are wearing the same Louboutins. That means Barrett will be seeing red – literally and figuratively – every time one walks by!"

"Great," declared my hubby. "What do you propose we do?"

"Beats me," I groused, "but I'd sure like to know why an airline that can foot $800 shoes as part of its female flight attendant's uniform can't cough up more than a mini bag of Cheerio-sized pretzels for its passengers' refreshments."

"Yeah," agreed Keith. He struggled to pull the miniature bag open, only to have it rip in all directions, sending a cascade of doll-pretzels to the floor in front of Barrett.

As one tan paw reached stealthily out from the carrier and drew the fortuitous bounty inward, a flight attendant walked by – in peace. No cacophony erupted from under the seat.

"Excuse me, miss?" said my husband, getting the attention of the next attendant. "Could we have perhaps ten more of these little pretzel bags?"

It was going to be a long flight, and we needed extra insurance.

After landing at JFK, we disembarked and stood in line for Passport Control. I was thinking back to our time in Edinburgh with Sophie and Ewan.

"Did you notice that Ewan's Scottish lingo seemed minimal when we were together again? I could actually understand everything he said! I wonder why the difference, from when we originally met him up in the Highlands?"

"I don't know," replied my husband. "Maybe it had something to do with altitude."

I looked at him incredulously.

Our queue moved at a snail's pace, and we were concerned about missing our connecting flight to Tampa, but we'd finally gotten through and were now walking toward Customs. We came to a fork where you either got in line to *Declare*, or you scurried freely on through *Nothing to Declare.* I veered one way, while my husband headed the other.

Noting my absence beside him, Keith trotted back to me. "Why are you in the *Declare* line?"

"Because!" I explained. "You know we made purchases; we have to declare them."

"No, we don't. That's just for ridiculously expensive stuff, like Rolexes. Or booze. We have neither."

I disagreed, and refused to get out of the queue.

My husband sighed, and having no choice, waited in line with me – Barrett's carrier perched atop his suitcase.

Eventually our turn came.

The customs agent scrutinized Barrett's documents, then began sifting through the pile of small shopping bags I'd presented to him, full of souvenirs. Suddenly he did a double glance inside of one of the bags, then turned it over and dumped out its contents. "What's this?" he asked gruffly.

I felt a bead of sweat form on my forehead, as Keith gave me a subtle but questioning look. Even Barrett seemed to want an answer.

Several small stones and architectural chips had tumbled out of my bag and were now on the counter in front of us.

"Oh, those!" I attempted a casual smile. "They're just some random stones that I picked up on our trip. You see, whenever I trav—"

"Ma'am!" the customs agent cut in sharply. "Do you realize there's a penalty for bringing in Cultural Artifacts or Cultural Property from another country?"

"There is?" I was horrified. Spread out before me were very small pieces of the Tower of London, the Palace of Holyrood House, Buckingham Palace, and Urquhart Castle – to name a few. Granted, I had NOT technically removed them from the actual structures, but admittedly, I had helped a few loose crumbles land on the ground before surreptitiously picking them up…. "I'm so sorry! I had no idea. They're really just random stones that I found on the ground from various park paths and such," I lied – though I am a terrible liar and as a rule don't do it.

My husband turned slightly pale. "Sir, we're truly sorry. Can we just leave the stones here with you? What do we need to do?"

The agent thought for a moment – glancing at the growing line behind us. "Yes, under the circumstances, I'll allow that." He scooped them up into a plastic bag, and pulled out an official form for labeling. "But DON'T DO IT AGAIN."

After thanking him profusely, we were on our way again.

I started to complain to Keith, "Drat! There went my castles and palaces and—"

"Cath!" my husband interrupted. "You heard the man! DON'T DO IT AGAIN. Geez!"

Well, *Geez!* was right. I highly doubted that Europe would miss a little bit of rubble.

⊞

Finally, we were home. After bringing in all of our bags, and checking the house over, Keith showed Barrett around, giving him the tour of his new digs. I went into the kitchen to see what we'd need from the grocery store the next morning.

"AAACKKKK! Call Dan Brown!!" Upon opening the freezer door, I'd been met by the sight of a frozen lizard splayed out like Vitruvian Man. How the stupid thing got in there, I do not know.

Now back in the kitchen, my husband peered over my shoulder. "Yep. Or DaVinci."

I rolled my eyes and slammed the door shut. "Gawd. Sometimes I hate living in Florida."

"Speaking of our home state," began Keith, "I've been thinking. Isn't it about time we owned a boat? I mean, I grew up puttering around lakes in east Texas, and you spent your teen years on your parents' small yacht – so why have we lived here for so long without a seagoing vessel of our own?"

"Seagoing vessel? Are you kidding? You were a teenager piloting a row boat, and I didn't pilot anything; my dad did all the work. All I did was jump from boat to dock, tying lines to cleats."

"I know," continued my hubby, "but it's like riding a bike. You never forget how! I think I'll start looking for something

194

smallish tomorrow – maybe 18-feet or so. Used – so that it's not much of an investment, if we don't like it." He paused for a moment, stroking his trim beard, a gleam in his eye. "But, how could we not like it?!" he asked excitedly.

Right.

Two days later, we'd settled into a routine at home. Barrett was liking his new pad; Keith was back on the job; and I was starting to carve out time in my den for some serious writing – I hoped.

My husband came home from work that evening, with news. "Hon! I've got double news! Can you be packed in less than two weeks and ready to go?"

"Go where? We just got home! I mean, you know I love a trip – but don't we need a breather?"

"This one is shorter. I've got business in St Maarten. Are you in?"

I thought for about two seconds. Of course I was in! Who would pass up a trip to the eastern Caribbean? It was late summer – still off-season for tourists, and the crowds would be down. "Sounds good! What's the other news?"

"We've bought a boat!"

"We have? What do you mean? How did you find a boat so fast? What is it? And where will we keep it?" I was full of questions – and dread.

"A man in Naples is selling it – trailer and all. We need to drive down this weekend and pick it up. It's an

18-footer; barely used. A real beauty, according to the pictures."

Oh, boy. "Pick it up, and bring it where?" I asked. As an afterthought, I added, "And most importantly, what will we name it?" Now I envisioned the various accessories I could have monogrammed: hats, totes, a doggy bandana, Tervis Tumblers…and was starting to warm to the idea.

"No problem with storage. Tom [a co-worker] is letting us use his slip for free; he's sent his boat up north for the season."

"What about when he wants to bring it back down? Then where will we store our boat?"

Keith sighed. "Cath. We'll cross that bridge when we come to it. It will be fine!"

Sure it would. Boat ownership: what could go wrong?

A few days later, we'd retrieved our vessel, had it registered and its name painted on, and were wearing hats with *Caribe La Vie* proudly embroidered on them – Keith's, navy with white; mine, navy with pink. Barrett was wearing a jaunty little nautical bandana, with the initials *CLV* on it. Yes, we were going to live the Caribbean Good Life!

We were towing our boat to the bay, where we would launch. Leaning back in the seat of my husband's truck, I took a sip of iced tea from my *Caribe La Vie* tumbler – pulled from my *Caribe La Vie* tote. Ahhh…this could be the start of some relaxing time at sea….

"Crap!" said my husband succinctly. "Which one do I use?"

Having just turned into the park, we were driving gingerly toward the launch area – pulling what suddenly felt like a ship. There were three spots to choose from – and there were lots of boats coming and going. Clearly, the other captains knew what they were doing – unlike Captain Keith, who was already in over his head.

"I don't know. Just choose one!" I directed – now feeling tense.

My husband picked Door Number Three, and our turn finally came to back the trailer and boat into the water.

I noted, "By the way, I've been telling you for two days now that I needed a run-through as to what I am to do with the lines, and what I am to do with the boat in the water, while you park the truck. You kept telling me it would all be 'fine'. It's not fine!"

It was not fine. By now, we had an audience. The main thing we disagreed on: Keith kept insisting that I only needed to hold the bowline until he returned from parking the truck; I kept asking, *What about the stern line? What will keep the boat from drifting perpendicular to the dock?* Barrett and I looked at him expectantly – our little pup in full doggy life jacket, peering out from the front-carrier I was wearing – but I may as well have been speaking Swahili. No further advice issued forth from the captain.

Once the *Caribe La Vie* was fully in the water, and awkwardly unhitched from the trailer by the hubby, I held the bowline while Keith drove away. In no time, the boat – how many tons of fiberglass? – went *WHOOOP*, and the stern swiftly floated out into the middle of the launch lane (for lack of proper term). I was left holding the line, while my boat blocked other vessels from coming in. At this point, I had a unibrow for my husband, and was also wondering why we'd hastily joined the stupid Power Squadron with its mates and commanders and other Skippers and Gilligans. Gawd.

"What the…?" was the exclamation I heard from Keith, as he approached – now running toward – the dock.

"Surprise!" I hissed. "I told you that I needed a way to hold the stern line, too!"

My husband now conceded.

Meanwhile, another boater came along and helpfully shoved our vessel back our way (and out of his way). With that, it was now time to actually get INTO our boat. The tide was low, and the only way that I could get in was to sit on the dock first – in a pile of dried seagull poop which was conveniently aligned with the stepping-in point – and slide in.

"Man, I hate Florida," I muttered under my breath.

"Cheer up!" said Keith, as he got in the boat behind me and untied the lines. "It will get better from here on out!"

Even Barrett looked dubious at that.

It did not get better from there on out. The winds were now at 15 knots. I'd told my husband earlier that it was too windy for this little venture, but he'd insisted it was 'only five knots' – even though our boat's GPS, our NOAA weather radio, and the app on my phone all sided with me. Thus, once out of the launch area, as we headed into the open waters of the bay, they became very choppy.

"SLOW DOWN!" I yelled to Keith. I hugged Barrett closely with one hand, while hanging on to a rail with the other. To no avail. Captain Ahab determined that the only way to get to the Intercoastal through the waves was to ramp up the speed to a 'planing point'. And to keep up that speed, once in it.

"IT'S THE WATER'S HIGHWAY!" he yelled back.

"WELL, IT'S NOT I-75, FOR GODSAKES!" Geez! It was windy, there was a lot of boat traffic – meaning several wakes to hit just right or be swamped – and I continued to nag him to slow down, which he insisted he couldn't do. Meanwhile, I struggled to stand up and put on a life jacket, without being flung overboard, as we 'planed along' at a 45-degree angle. All while not dropping Barrett.

Finally in, then back out of the Intercoastal and heading into a cove near a marina, we sat in neutral and pivoted in a circle (the best part of the trip), while Captain Crunch tried to read one of the charts. Between watching for other boats not to hit us; reading the markers (and trying to stay on the correct side of them); and constantly reading the depth-finder (to make sure we didn't run aground) – he actually thought I might like to 'take over the boat and practice' there. HELL NO!

"Just head back in!" was my directive. At this point, I was wondering what to do with our *Caribe La Vie* hats;

our *Caribe La Vie* tote and tumblers; and in fact, the stupid *Caribe La Vie* itself.

The bumpy ride back to the Intercoastal was peppered with me alternating between, "SLOW DOWN!" and "DO YOU SEE THAT BOAT COMING TOWARD / IN FRONT OF / BEHIND US?" It felt like an eternity.

Finally, we were back to the launch area, for the dreaded docking and tying up. The docks were full, so we had to idle – and try not to drift into traffic, or block anyone – and wait.

Our turn came.

"Quick!" shouted my husband, pointing to a cleat on the dock as he struggled to keep us from drifting, "Tie the bowline to that!"

Reaching out for the cleat while trying to keep my footing, I noticed that it was covered in rust – and hanging from the dock by one screw. I tried to impart this information to the captain of this failed voyage, but he wasn't getting it.

A little boy of about six or seven, from a boat docked nearby – a big, new boat – scurried over and took our stern line from Keith. Clearly this kid had way more experience than we did, because he deftly tied it to a nearby cleat before his concerned mother ushered him away from the crazy people. Us.

We climbed out of the boat, and Keith went to retrieve the truck and trailer. Barrett and I waited in shame.

Soon, my husband was backing the trailer into the water with my guidance, and then trying to line it up to the boat. This latter move took several attempts (again, with an audience), culminating with Hubby wading waist-deep into the water in his clothing, to hitch, unhitch, and re-hitch the boat numerous times. Once it was stable, he pulled it up and out of the way – and did whatever it is that you do to a motor that takes forever before you can leave.

Barrett and I waited in the truck and played Candy Crush.

The drive home was quiet, because no one wanted to be the first one to say it.

Glancing in the mirror, I finally broke the ice. "My God – it's following us."

⛊

A week had gone by, the *Caribe La Vie* was up for sale, and I was busy packing for St Maarten. I couldn't wait for the sun, the sand, and the history! Plus, this would be Barrett's first trip to a Caribbean island. He'd need a little sun visor….

"You're going to like this, Cath!" announced my husband, as he walked in the door from work that evening. "How would you like a side trip to St Barts while we're there?"

"I'm in!" I said, then had an afterthought. "But how will we get over there? The only options from St Maarten are a notoriously rough ferry ride, or a short flight into one of the 'World's Most Dangerous Airports'. What a choice!" I pondered this for a moment, before answering my own question.

"Never mind. The boat it is. But only if you stay far, FAR away from the wheel."

CHAPTER 18

WHOOOSH!!

"Oh my God, that was AWESOME!" My nose was glued to the window by my seat, as the Boeing 757 we were flying on from Tampa roared into St Maarten's Princess Juliana Airport. The standard approach for this airport was so low over Maho Beach – its landing strip located immediately behind a chain link fence, just across the road from a narrow public beach – that as each incoming jet skimmed the ocean, then the sand, beachgoers could almost reach up and touch the enormous plane's belly. Or so it seemed!

Keith had been to the island before on business. "I told you it would be! Wait until we come back to Maho in a day or so; being directly under these jets as they scream overhead is an incredible experience."

I couldn't wait!

Meanwhile, we had to disembark; go through Immigration with Barrett (and his papers; I carried duplicate copies, just in case); pick up a rattle-trap little rental car (island-common); and drive to the waterfront villa that Keith's colleague generously offered us on his private property – gratis.

Logistics past, we were now in the car – our second one, as the first vehicle assigned to us had a flat tire.

"No, it doesn't," the rental lot kid had lied.

"Yes, it does." My husband poked the squishy rubber – basically a pancake sizzling on the hot pavement – for emphasis.

A small debate ensued, but we'd won, and were now driving along the main road.

"So do I understand correctly?" I asked. "The international airport is in St Maarten, the island's Dutch side – but Alain's home is in St Martin, the island's French side?"

"Correct," answered my husband. "He and his wife Claire built three homes on their property a couple of years ago: one is for Claire's mother when she visits from France; one – ours – is a guest rental; and one is Alain and Claire's private residence."

Having done my research before leaving home, I knew a little bit about this small, interesting land mass located in the eastern Caribbean's Leeward Islands group, with its rare bi-national history of open borders. It was the oldest officially so in the world, since the Treaty of Concordia in 1648. At only 37 square miles, the island is divided between France and the Kingdom of the Netherlands. St Martin, with its capital of Philipsburg, is the slightly larger half – and is considered quieter, with a bigger area of nature sites. St Maarten – with its capital of Marigot – is the busier side, full of shopping, nightlife, casinos, etc. The French side is greener and more forested; the Dutch side is drier. And, Philipsburg is the only national capital in the world located on a beach.

I shifted my thoughts to relaxing along the water. "Did you know that St Maarten has more beaches per its compact surface than anywhere else in the world?"

"Yep. And they're topless, too!" was the hubby's too-enthusiastic reply.

I raised an eyebrow. Hmmm. Well, *I'd* be on the beaches – but he'd be busy working. Best to keep it that way.…

I glanced at Barrett, riding in the backseat, safe in his little seatbelt. He gave Keith a stern look, in solidarity with me. Good boy.

🧳

After an engine-gunning coastal drive up steep inclines, and careening around hairpin turns while circling the island's two nations – the magnificent Atlantic Ocean on the north side, and the dazzling Caribbean Sea on the south side – we climbed the secluded and very perpendicular driveway to Alain's residence. Located in the Terres Basses (French 'lowlands') section of the rolling hills of St Martin's westernmost region, on the very tip of Pointe du Bluff, his property overlooked Nettle Baie (bay), and the ocean beyond.

"Be careful of the slanted stairs ahead," cautioned Keith, trotting through the small jungle ahead of me, bags in hand. Barrett followed on his leash, quite happy to explore the flora and fauna around him. At one point our black pup was surrounded by dozens of tiny white butterflies, resembling confetti. I would later learn they were simply called Florida White or Tropical White butterflies, were found throughout the West Indies, and were extraordinarily swift – able to traverse long distances in a few seconds.

"Will do— EEEEKK! What the hell is on my shoulder? What is it? Get it off of me!" Reaching to fling away whatever had accosted me, my fingers met with a startled ball of slime, which gave me a wide-eye as it whizzed past my face and landed on a bush.

"Oh – I forgot to tell you about the Coqui frogs. They're everywhere here. Wait till you hear them sing after dark. It's amazing!"

"Yeah, I'll look forward to that," I muttered, treading carefully now and swiveling my eyes in every direction. "Anyway, we'd better step it up. What time did Alain say to come for dinner?" Alain and Claire had graciously invited us to their home for our first evening – located on the other side of a long, white stucco wall dividing our two villas; a wall which was covered in beautiful fuchsia-colored bougainvillea – and we needed to freshen up a bit, as well as feed Barrett, who would be staying behind in his cozy carrier in our bedroom. He'd had a long day; we all had.

"Six o'clock for drinks. Then Alain will be grilling something for our dinner. Claire is originally from Marseille; she usually likes to add a bouillabaisse from her childhood. They're both excellent cooks!" added Keith, who'd dined there before.

"Sounds good," I replied, really taking in our villa for the first time. I was immediately impressed. The gleaming-white, minimalist, Mediterranean-style stucco abode sat almost directly on the edge of a cliff, overlooking the water; the only thing between the villa and the heavily-foliaged terrain hovering above the bay was a private swimming pool: a smallish square of very dark blue water set within a rustic, cantilevered deck. Bougainvillea flourished everywhere. It was stunning.

"I'll get the rest of the bags from the car," offered my nice husband, "while you and Barrett look around."

We did. The villa consisted of two beautiful rooms, very much 'indoor/outdoor'. Both areas opened fully, via large glass retractable doors, to a covered, comfortably furnished deck, which then extended to the open pool. At night, or when leaving, there were automated shutters that could be rolled down, entirely covering the glass. (For Caribbean storms, security, etc.)

The main room was a combo living area and open kitchen. Sleek white walls, a white leather sofa, and white modernist accessories created a blank canvas for a few features to really pop. A large three-paned window on the rear wall butted immediately against a vertical rock hillside, giving the effect of a natural work of art 'hanging' on the wall. A French Louis XV armchair, upholstered in a bold, swirling black and white brocade, coordinated perfectly with a black lampshade nearby. A black granite countertop ran along one wall, which topped the white linear kitchen. It was simple and beautiful.

A half-bath of equal beauty stood off the main area: solid white stone, with black towels, and a wall of fuchsia orchids sustained by a skylight.

The bedroom, although adjacent to the living area, could not be accessed from it. The only entry was to go back outdoors and then through a separate, second sliding glass door, linear to the first one.

Stepping inside, Barrett and I walked around the white goose down duvet-covered bed and past minimal white furniture, and peeked into the master bathroom off the back of the room. It was small, and very 'naturalist'. The shower (like many French showers) had no door whatsoever, and it faced directly a large window which butted up against the same vertical cross-section of rocky hillside as the window in the living room. There were about twelve inches between the glass and the rock wall. And in breaking with the all-white theme of the rest of the villa, the walls of the bathroom, and the shower, were bathed in a slurry of grey concrete. It reminded me of my Girl Scout camping days, when we had to create a bathroom, *au natural*. Only Troop 98 didn't have a counter top with a Murano glass vessel sink to wash our hands in. Overall, the effect was edgy and pretty cool.

At this point, Keith walked in with the last of the bags. "What do you think of the villa?" he asked. "Nice, huh?"

"It is! But this window facing the shower kind of creeps me out. What if someone slides in there, between it and the rock wall? There's no privacy!"

"Cath," said my unconcerned husband, "who in the world would do that? There's no one up here except for Alain and Claire, and us. I wouldn't worry about it."

Right. We would see.

Alain arrived to escort us through the 'secret door' that was cut into the stucco wall between our villa and his. It could only be opened from his and Claire's side, and existed so that they could come and go between the two villas without having to first walk down their long driveway and then back up that of ours. It was pitch dark outside, and there were no outside lights whatsoever to illuminate the area. The stars, the moon, the twinkling lights far across Nettle Bay – that was it. The Coqui frogs were singing in chorus at the top of their lungs, and I was torn between enjoying their haunting melody – and feeling uneasy by the knowledge that hundreds (thousands?) of amphibians surrounded us in the darkness at that very moment.

Stepping carefully through the narrow, rocky walkway – behind Alain and in front of Keith – I was suddenly accosted out of nowhere by two black Labrador retrievers (in the blackness of night). It turned out that the dogs were pets of Alain and Claire, and they loped about freely. Of course they were curious about visitors – I understood that (once I recovered from my shock), but I was glad that my expression was obscured by the darkness, because a) I am skittish around big dogs; and b) I was wearing a tropical white and gray-print maxi skirt with a white top, and did not want muddy paw prints as part of my look.

"Allez, ouste!" admonished Alain, shooing the Labs away.

To me, he apologized. "They're Claire's babies…I could take or leave them. Pfft!" This was accompanied by a dismissive hand gesture, and the dogs seemed to shrug as they stalked off – at least, the best I could tell in the moonlight. It occurred to me that we'd want to keep Barrett at a safe distance, until we knew otherwise; I made a mental note of this as we entered our hosts' foyer.

Alain and Claire's home was stunning in a sort of Frank Lloyd Wright way – and very different from our bright white stay next door. Similar to our villa, the entire home was wide open to jungle, cliff, and sea – but the décor was very dark and woody; a lot of russet and such. The main areas were under roof, but essentially a gumball could roll off the dining table, across the terrace, past the large pool, and over the cliff. There were no boundaries between the inside and outside worlds, which is lovely, but not without its drawbacks, as we would soon find out.

"Please, have a seat," Claire gestured casually – a cigarette dangling from her fingertips.

Alain handed us each a large goblet of French red wine.

Soon, the four of us were lounging on leather couches, while Alain plied Keith and me with various hors d'oeuvres. It felt very Roman: us at a triclinium, being fed grapes by the servants…. It's all fun and games until someone consumes something potentially horrid; in this case, it was me with a large mouthful of what seemed to be anchovy paste, proffered on a French Triscuit. I gagged it down, and followed with a large swig of Merlot.

The conversation flowed; Alain and Claire were entertaining in and of themselves. Claire's upbringing in very tough Marseille gave her a rougher edge than Alain, but they were both pros at chain-smoking cigarettes, consuming probably a bottle of wine each (with no apparent affect), and generally conveying a smooth attitude of *C'est la vie! Bien joue! Let them eat cake!* – that sort of thing. I was secretly envying their breezy demeanor – why couldn't I be more 'French'? – when things took a sudden detour.

"Mon Dieu!" shrieked Claire. She jumped up and waved her arms at one of the black Labs that had been stealthily skirting our perimeter all evening. The dog was now near the pool – about fifteen feet from us – and not far from the dining table that we were about to shift ourselves to. And, it had dropped a package from its mouth onto the deck. While our hostess continued to spew invectives in French, Alain got up and meandered

over to the area to investigate – with my hubby in tow, of course.

From where I sat, I could see that some sort of dead animal – over a foot long – had now joined our party. Specifically, it was the upper half – HALF – of an iguana. Gag!!

Alain casually scooped up the unfortunate reptile remnant with a dust pan and broom, then flung it over the wall.

Keith quipped, "Don't put it in our yard!"

To which Claire (who was again cool as a cucumber) replied, "There is one at your villa – but it won't bother you. It just shows up to drink from your pool."

Great. There went my plans of relaxing by the pool while Keith worked the next day. What would Barrett and I do with ourselves now?

Shifting gears, our hosts ushered us to the dinner table. Alain had prepared a lovely roast; but it was lamb – *dreaded lamb!* Once again, I would have to graciously skirt the main course. Claire had created her special bouillabaisse: a seafood soup with a creamy broth, fish, shellfish, vegetables, and a variety of Provencal herbs and spices. Thick slices of French bread and a few more bottles of wine accompanied the meal. Generally, one glass of wine is my limit, but I'd acquiesced to a second, and was starting to feel pretty good. I'd even managed to eat a few bites of lamb – with the help of an obscenely expensive Red (totally wasted on me; I am no connoisseur and it may as well have been Kool-Aid at that point).

Claire presented dessert – a nice quince crisp.

I raised my glass and announced, "*J'ai la patate*!" My quick study of French before leaving for this trip would now serve me well.

All three dinner companions looked at me quizzically.

"You have a potato?" asked Alain.

"Yes!" was my enthusiastic, if slightly slurred, reply.

Keith was busy consulting the translator on his phone. He looked up at me, puzzled. "Cath. Literally, you just said, "I have the potato."

Claire enlightened us. "Ah! Figuratively, though, that's a French expression meaning 'I feel good in my head.' "

"Apparently she does," concurred my husband.

Addressing our hosts, he added, "I think it may be espresso time – *oui?*"

CHAPTER 19

" *KEEEEITH!!* "

My husband came running – Barrett hot on his heels – into the bathroom of our villa. I was standing in the now-off shower, with a fuchsia-colored bath towel hastily wrapped around my body, water still dripping into my eyes. He stopped dead as he stared at the large, bare window before us. Dangling between the glass and the rock wall – spotlighted by the morning sun peeking through jungle foliage – was a dancing head wearing a grotesque expression.

Barrett barked furiously.

Keith stammered, "What the hell…?"

In an instant, the head disappeared upward, only to reappear again. Upon further inspection, we could see that it was a freakish mask of some sort (Taino Indian, we'd later learn) – human in shape, with 'skin' of bright blue; a vertical red stripe bisecting the face and wrapping around the forehead. Hollowed-out eyes, tusks protruding from nostrils, and a headdress of long brown and tan feathers completed the bizarre image.

My hubby dashed outside and around to the back of the villa (a barking Barrett in tow). Peering into the narrow crevice between window and rock, he found nothing – but when he looked sharply up toward the rock wall's ledge, he glimpsed a boy of about ten, peeking over the edge. And the little monster was in the process of reeling up the mask, via a fishing pole.

Having quickly thrown on a robe and flip-flops, I had ventured outside in time to witness this little scenario from the back corner of the villa, and was also privy to a loud shriek from Claire next door.

"Bastien!" she commanded. "*Laissez-les tranquilles*!" In translation, she was admonishing her son (as he turned out to be) to leave their guests alone. I guessed she was familiar with his MO.

My spouse turned to me. "That little bast…uh… Bastien is a real charmer."

"Agreed," I said, vowing to create a makeshift window-covering for the rest of our stay. Criminently!

Keith had a business meeting for part of the day, but first we drove to Cupecoy – on the Dutch side – for breakfast together. Specifically, we were at Porto Cupecoy, which was a posh marina community situated on the border of the two sides of the island. Shops and cafes lined a waterfront plaza with a large fountain as its centerpiece; we had a nice table outside, with beautiful weather. Barrett was happily lazing under my chair, watching the world go by. We were discussing our late afternoon plans; it looked like today would be the best day for spending time on Maho, watching the incoming jets land.

I was just putting a forkful of decadent Nutella crepe in my mouth, when I recognized Alain's booming voice.

"*Bon jour*!" he said cheerfully, as he approached our table and pulled up a chair to join us. "I thought it was you!" Snapping his fingers at seemingly nothing, a server magically appeared with a bowl – not a mug, but a bowl – of café au lait for him. This was followed by a large croissant, which Alain proceeded to break into pieces to dunk in his coffee. Seeing our two normal-sized coffee cups, and the puzzled look on my husband's face, our host explained, "Pfft! Cups are too small. We French like to have some dipping room!"

Indeed.

"So!" Alain continued, swiping at his mouth with his hand, pastry flakes flying. "I just had a call from my wife, and I want to apologize for our son's infraction this morning. Bastien's been a little overzealous lately about his school studies of our island's Indian history."

My ears perked up. "No problem!" I somewhat lied. "But we'd love to hear about the history. I understand that it's Carib, and Arawak – specifically the Taino?"

Alain nodded, and quickly pulled up a website on his phone, showing us the source: a blog from SXMdeals. com (SXM being the call letters for the island). Verifying what he already knew, he went on. "That's correct. Our island's first settlers – likely Ciboney Indians, who were a subgroup of Arawaks – date back to 3500 years ago. Then another group of Arawaks – the Taino – migrated from South America's Orinoco basin around 800 AD. Because the island was dense with salt-pans, the Indians called it 'Sualouiga', meaning 'land of salt'. Alternately, it was called 'Oualichi' – which meant 'land of brave and beautiful women'.

At that last sentence, Alain and my husband shared a knowing glance. I rolled my eyes.

Alain went on to explain that the Arawaks were mainly a farming and fishing society, and lived in villages of straw-roofed buildings that were strong enough to resist hurricanes. They were a tranquil civilization, who valued artistic and spiritual endeavors. Unfortunately, their lives were upended when Carib Indians – who came from the same region as the Arawaks – appeared.

"Caribs were a warrior nation, and they quickly killed the Arawak men and enslaved the women. By the time Europeans began to explore the Caribbean, Carib society had pretty much displaced the Arawaks." Alain shrugged in resignation.

I pondered the fate of the peaceful natives.

My husband had a more pressing thought. "I wonder if that's where the song *Orinoco Flow* comes from…?"

Alain and I looked at him with pause, simultaneously answering, "Sort of." Good grief.

We were parting for the morning, when Alain offered to drive me back to the villa, so that Keith could continue on toward his business meeting in Simpson Bay – also on the Dutch side of the island. "I'll be happy to take the scenic route back!" he offered with verve.

Sure? Why not?

I climbed the high step into the front passenger seat of Alain's well-worn clunker of a truck (a feat, since I was wearing a cute cargo skirt). I'd seen a rare Ford Mustang Shelby GT500 in our host's garage; this jalopy clearly showcased another side of him.

Hubby whispered in my ear, "Stay buckled and hang on tight." I wondered if I detected an air of finality in his goodbye kiss….

Barrett and I looked at each other in alarm.

Holding our pup with my thumb looped securely through his blue and white gingham harness, we shot off like a rocket, all four tires of Alain's truck seemingly going in different directions as we briefly hit the open and bumpy road. It was like riding a gangly Irish Setter at full speed.

Before I knew it, we'd entered St Maarten's rainforest, and were twisting and catapulting from one narrow, rocky road to the next. I was sure that Alain's old truck was throwing bolts and body parts along the way. Barrett's wide eyes reflected my sentiment – even more aptly so when barely into the thickest of the flora – guaiac trees, poisonous mancenilla trees, and orchids all around – our windshield was abruptly smacked with a resounding *PLOP!*

Alain let loose a string of expletives, followed by a tamer, "What the hell?"

I was momentarily speechless. Not Barrett, though, who barked ferociously (he'd never done that before!) at what appeared to be a gray monkey splayed across our windshield. Its black triangular face, ringed with white fur, was inches from ours and reflected our surprise.

Alain slammed the brakes in reflex. "Damn these stupid vervets! They're everywhere!" Gesturing wildly at the primate to remove itself, he admonished, "*Ouste*!" Apparently the monkey understood French, and leaped off the windshield and onto the hanging roots of a nearby tree.

I regained my composure. "Does this happen often? How many monkeys does this island have?"

Alain explained that the vervet is an invasive species, and that the government had approved a controversial plan to cull the entire population of the animal, as it had become an increasing nuisance. "When a species establishes a population in a non-native area, there are generally no predators to keep the numbers in control. The vervet is native to southern and eastern Africa, but on some Caribbean islands – such as nearby St Kitts and St Nevis – the population has grown to tens of thousands."

"Wow." I shuddered at the thought of thousands of monkeys leaping about every time I stepped out my front door. "When and how did they get here?"

"Sometime around the 17th century. European settlers were believed to have brought them over as exotic pets. Farmers in particular complain that the vervets raid their crops and destroy their livelihood. Well, off with their heads, I say! Pesky little animals."

At that, Barrett gave a whimper.

"Don't worry little buddy." Alain patted Barrett on the head. "There's always room on the island for one more Shih Tzu."

Now back at our villa and happy to be in one piece, I got out my laptop, hoping to produce a few more sentences for my first chapter – while awaiting Keith's return for the afternoon. Just a few! I would be happy with anything, given how slow my progress had been. My meager goal was 50 words – 50! – per day. How pathetic was that? Anyway, I had just situated myself at the dining table under the covered area by the pool, iced tea by my side, Barrett napping under my feet, bougainvillea swaying in the breeze.

Large iguana lying atop the stucco wall, staring at me.

"What the…?!" I skidded back my chair, and jumped up. Barrett followed suit, equally startled.

Scooping up my laptop and my dog – knocking over my tea in the process – I made a hasty retreat through the glass door into our bedroom and slammed it shut. The iguana – likely spooked by my quick movement – made a partial exit down the outside of the wall, then appeared to stop. At least a foot of its Technicolor tail still dangled over our side. UGH.

"Well, that's just great," I said to Barrett. "Now what are we going to do?" There was no way to get to the main living area – and thus, the attached kitchen for another iced tea – without going outside again, where the beast still lurked. No way was I going back out there.

It was a defeated wife and dog that Keith returned to an hour later, sitting on the bed and staring out to sea, so to speak – my mood to write having quickly disappeared with the iguana.

An hour later, we were sitting at the Sunset Bar and Grill for lunch, on Maho Beach. Things were looking up, as were we! Just a few yards in front of us, huge jets were skimming the beach, as they came in for a landing at the airport right across the narrow road. Barrett wasn't fazed at all by the sight, nor the sound.

"This is SO cool!" I said to Keith, taking another bite of my burger. I covered my mouth with my hand. "After we're done eating, let's go out onto the sand, and stand right under the jets as they come over – like everyone else is."

Planes seemed to appear on the ocean's horizon at intervals anywhere from three minutes to one hour. A surfboard cleverly placed upright in the sand, near the bar, posted in chalk the various airlines and their arrival times for the day: Ameriflight from San Juan; Insel from Curacao; Delta from JFK; Copa from Panama; Air France from Paris; American from Miami; and so on.

"Sounds good," agreed my husband. "It looks like we should be just in time for the next Air France plane."

Finishing up and leaving our table, we headed out onto the narrow strip of sandy beach, Barrett in tow – Keith holding his leash. There was no plane on the horizon yet, but about twenty beach-goers eagerly awaited the next arrival, spread about the small area on their beach towels. Some were sitting or lying prone; some were standing, ready to feel the full force of the experience about to happen. We stood, eagerly scanning where the ocean met the sky, phone cameras ready to capture the moment.

A small, silver dot appeared on the horizon, rapidly increasing in size as it approached. "There it is!" I practically screamed, as Keith fixed his lens on the incoming jet. All around us, people quickly stood – arms in the air, anchoring hats with one hand. I had my camera trained on the sky, as well.

WHOOOSHHHHH! Sand flew everywhere. So did any loose objects, as the blast from the huge silvery jet roaring overhead sent everything not anchored whirling. People scrambled to pick up their stray items.

"That was SO COOL!" I said to my husband. "We could practically touch the wheels! It couldn't have been more than ten feet above our heads!"

"I agree: that was awesome. Technically, though, that jet was about 90 feet above us – but it sure felt closer. I'm amazed that Barrett was so quiet."

We both looked down.

"*Barrett!!*" we yelled in unison. Where was he??

Before I could admonish Keith for letting go of the leash, we heard a yell from an older woman, about twenty feet away. She started off in a wobbly sprint toward the water – and she was topless. Topless in her eighties! Definitely an American, spreading her wings of freedom, so to speak.

"Barrett!!" yelled my husband. He took off after our wayward pup, who was gleefully dashing toward the surf – with two hot pink double-D cups in his mouth. As the irate owner of the bikini top flapped after him, Keith managed to zip in between her and Barrett, and intercept the booty (somehow, that seems appropriate…) from our delinquent canine. As he turned away from the water and daintily handed the prize back to the bared octogenarian, I snapped a photo. Of course!

We shepherded a sandy, wet Barrett back to our car.

I turned to Keith. "There. You've had your encounter with a topless woman on the beach. That should do it."

CHAPTER 20

"WHY ARE THOSE people plastered to the fence like that?" I asked my husband.

We were about to leave the Maho Beach parking area – Barrett now reasonably clean and dry, thanks to several bottles of water and a towel hastily grabbed before leaving our villa. Across the two-lane road from us was Princess Juliana Airport's runway – which began immediately on the other side of a chain link fence. Three college-aged kids – two guys and a girl – were hanging on for dear life, as the powerful back end of a Boeing 737 faced them just yards away, rumbling as it readied for takeoff.

"They're 'fence surfing'," explained Keith. "Stupid, stupid, stupid! People have been killed doing that." He pointed to a sign that was posted on the fence, which read: *DANGER! Toi la! Je t'aime! Jet blast of departing and arriving aircraft can cause severe physical harm resulting in extreme bodily harm and/or death.*

"Geez! Why do they do that?"

Before I could utter another word, the plane's engines revved up their roar, and the Boeing barreled down the runway, leaving a jet wash in its wake – pelting the white-knuckled fence-hangers with a high-powered barrage of tiny rocks and sand. This went on for a full minute, lifting all three humans off of their feet. The woman was unable to hold on for the duration and was thrown backwards – her head narrowly missing a strip of concrete block that divided the roadway directly behind. Good grief!!

"I have no idea," yelled my husband, above the roar. "Barrett has better sense than they do!"

Barrett harrumphed indignantly, turning his head away from the foolish human spectacle before him.

Back at our villa, we freshened up and changed for dinner – I, in a cute blue and green print dress that someone had once commented was 'very Versace' (appearances are deceiving); Keith in khaki pants and a pale green shirt; and Barrett looking very dapper in a tropical print bow tie – in blues and greens, of course. His little tie doubled as a collar, and I opted to skip his harness, as I didn't want to spoil the look.

"So where are we going for dinner?" I asked my husband. We were in the car, and heading down the steep driveway.

"Grand Case. You'll like it!" he replied, pulling out onto the coastal road. "It's known as the Culinary Capitol of the Caribbean." While Keith wasn't the restaurant enthusiast that I was, he had dined along this tiny town's Restaurant Row before, located on the French side of the island and stretching along a narrow beach overlooking the island of Anguilla. "My main experience has been with various lolos, but I've had dinner in a couple of the better places, too."

"The what?" I asked. "What are 'lolos'?"

As it turned out, *lolos* were the numerous open-air barbecue stands (my former-Texan hubby loves barbecue) that lined the beach. Part of the colorful history of the old fishing village that was Grand Case, they were very popular with locals and tourists, and served traditional Creole barbecued meat and fish along with other Caribbean specialties.

Our scenic drive came to an end, and we entered the short main strip of the village. I consulted my guide book. "Well, I hope we're headed to one of the gourmet restaurants. It says here that most of them are rated highly by Gault & Millau!"

Now it was Keith's turn to be enlightened. "Gault and who?"

"Gault & Millau – the gourmet restaurant guide. They're like Michelin, only French."

"What's a tire company got to do with it?"

Men.

With that, we parked in a sketchy-looking gravel lot (this was the Caribbean, where crime and posh coexisted side by side), and headed down Restaurant Row. We'd confirmed with Alain that dogs were welcome in most dining establishments, and Keith was carrying Barrett, whose furry little head whipped to and fro as he took in the sights and smells of the experience before him.

"I see Il Nettuno up ahead," said my husband. "It's good! Wonderful ocean view. The menu offers both Italian and seafood. You can choose your own lobster from the tank by the entry door."

"No!" I said. "I do love lobster – true – but I will *not* eat something that I've looked into the sad eyes of."

Barrett gave me a side-eye – which I believe he made as sad as possible.

Setting our pup on the ground, we continued toward the restaurant. As we approached, we could see a commotion near its doorway, as several pedestrians pointed at the sidewalk in front.

Before we knew what was happening, Barrett had slipped his collar and leash, and rushed into the fray.

Dashing to the scene ourselves, we were startled to see that a lobster had escaped the tank located just inside Il Nettuno's door, and was making a slow yet frantic escape down the sidewalk – that was, until Barrett intervened. Barking furiously at anyone who came near, our furry superhero attempted to shield the fugitive lobster. He had nosed the cowering crustacean against the wall of the building, and would not let the restaurant's employees anywhere near it. Eventually the chef appeared, and he and Barrett had a frosty stare down.

"*Ouste! Ouste!*" implored the little man, to no avail. He threw up his hands in disgust and retreated into the restaurant.

"*Barrett*!" I hissed. "Come here!"

Barrett gave me the impudent look of a teenager, before acquiescing. Keith scooped him up – stating sternly that going forward, a harness would be worn in public at all times.

The street audience, however, was on Barrett's side. "He's a hero!" someone declared.

"*Vive le Barrett*!!" said a second bystander. "Lobsters have rights, too!"

Several people had captured the incident with their phone cameras.

A lady with a wicker hamper knelt down and picked up the little red shell-shocked victim and tucked him in her basket. Taking him inside to pay, she was heard to say, "It's okay Little Red, I have an entire saltwater swimming pool at home, which my ungrateful family never uses. It's all yours."

Keith looked at me and shrugged as he held open the door to Il Nettuno. "I assume you'll be ordering the lasagna tonight."

The following day, my husband had a meeting at a jobsite on the island of Anguilla – and Barrett and I were going along. Accompanying us – escorting us, really – were Alain (it was his company who'd contracted the site), and two of his employees: Lucas and Remy. We could have taken Alain's personal speedboat over (as he normally did), but since Anguilla was British Overseas Territory, and Alain would be a Frenchman transporting two Americans privately, he preferred not to be involved in an immigration bungle. Thus, everyone agreed to meet at the Blowing Point Ferry terminal at the Marigot Port.

After another Nutella crepe breakfast – this could become a habit – we arrived at the port on time. Alain was waiting impatiently for us at the passport window, Remy and Lucas in tow. Alain quickly commandeered our passports, then had a hands-flying exchange with the agent at the window, expertly managing to expedite things for us. We already had a permit for Barrett to travel from St Martin to Anguilla, so we were good to go.

We boarded the small ferry, which was old and very utilitarian. Alain, Keith, Barrett (wearing an orange doggy life jacket), and I opted to sit in the cabin, which was three steps below deck. Remy and Lucas chose to tee-ter outside on the rim of the aft deck, a shared cigarette passing between them. It was a rough ride – Dramamine was my best friend – but the two young French guys had done this a million times and it was just another day at work for them.

The 25-minute journey to the island was beautiful: sunny, bright blue skies over sparkling turquoise and navy waters. A rare color combination, for sure! Lucas had said to me earlier (in an appealing French accent; this was another thing that he and Remy shared. Older Alain, well, his French wasn't as charming), "You will love Anguilla! The world's most beautiful beaches are there!" I would soon see for myself, because the plan was for the men to drop Barrett and me off at a beach resort before they went to their jobsite (a different resort, under construction) – then retrieve us afterwards, and we'd all go to lunch elsewhere. I wondered why we wouldn't just eat at the resort that we'd be waiting at, but didn't give it too much thought.

Docking on Anguilla, Alain urged Keith and me to be among the first off of the boat and into the immigration line. (The three Frenchmen had passes, thus avoiding the queue.) Alain and Remy then dashed out to the rental car lot, leaving Lucas behind to guide us Americans through official business, then to the car. Immigration went smoothly.

The rental car 'lot' should have been a clue of things to come. It was quite primitive – even by island standards. It consisted of a few older cars tossed among sand and scrubby sea grass. A handful of motley goats meandered about the lot, following us to our car.

"Hey!" I exclaimed. One of the hairy beasts had grabbed the hem of my flowered beach dress as I attempted to scurry to our vehicle. I was carrying Barrett, and could hear a low rumble emit from his chest. "Let go!" The more I tugged, the more the goat hung onto the fabric with its yellow bucked teeth.

My husband burst out laughing, while Alain looked annoyed at our delay.

"*La chevre mange l'hibiscous!*" observed Remy, with a chuckle. The young Frenchman's hottie-ness moved down a notch at that point, in my estimation. 'The goat was eating the hibiscus.' Got it. Now do something!

"Do something!" I implored my husband.

At that, Keith did what he often did: made a bad situation worse. Grabbing the hem of my dress – it was a gauzy material – he gave a tug. This gave the winning point to the goat, because a 4-inch raggedy square of my outfit simply ripped away, having already been tattered by teeth. The beast swallowed the fabric swatch in triumph – proof that a goat really will eat anything.

"Stupid goat!" I said, as it scampered off with its friends. Turning to Keith, I added, "Now what, Sherlock? Thank God I have a swimsuit underneath this dress, but still!" Men.

Meanwhile, the three Frenchman stood at the car – Alain looking perturbed, and Remy and Lucas avoiding eye contact with me as they clearly suppressed grins.

⬚

We'd been on the winding island road for 15 minutes, with Alain driving at breakneck speed – hot air whipping through the rolled-down windows – when we came to a screeching halt at a ramshackle shack on the edge of Shoal Bay Beach. As it turned out, this was the 'resort' that they were dropping Barrett and me off at – a mere hut on the site of a *future* resort. Surprise! It wasn't even built yet. It was manned, however, by a sad-looking, one-toothed island native called Badrick, whom Alain briefed as to why I was there. Badrick was told to find me a drink and to 'take care' of me. Keith looked quietly horrified, but I assured him that Barrett and I would be fine. There were a couple chairs and umbrellas dotting this otherwise deserted beach, and I had my eReader, so I would survive. I also had water and treats for Barrett – plus I had brought along his little crab-printed sun visor, with red doggy sunglasses attached.

Since my cell phone wouldn't work on the island, Keith gave me his, with instructions to call Alain's phone if problems arose.

Once our party left, it was just Badrick, Barrett, and me. It was about 150 degrees in the shade – and Barrett and I shared two broken lounge chairs under a spindly umbrella. Again, the ocean was a brilliantly colored aqua, green, and navy; perhaps Lucas was correct that the world's most beautiful beaches were here. I'd seen a lot of beaches, but this was among the best.

I turned my attention to Badrick, who was standing patiently by our primitive oasis. Handing him a twenty-dollar bill (and figuring on about fifteen dollars in change; I'd tip him from that), I asked him politely if he had a Diet Coke – wondering how in the world he would produce one on this isolated beach. He nodded, and headed off. In the distance, I could see what looked like a Styrofoam cooler in the sand, with a straw mat lying next to it.

Turning my focus to Barrett, I fixed a little pop-up bowl of water for him, and by the time I looked up again, Badrick was out of sight.

A half-hour later, there was still no sign of Badrick, a Diet Coke, or my money. I was also wondering where I might find a restroom. (Answer: nowhere.) Another hour passed; by then I had given up all hope of ever seeing our host again. I was also quite thirsty; the water in Barrett's bowl was starting to look good. Barrett was asleep on a towel in his chair…would he notice…? No! I wasn't that desperate. Yet.

The sun was now directly overhead, I had read all I cared to read for the moment, and I was starting to wonder if the rest of my landing party would ever return. Contemplating life alone on this island, I was running my foot through the powdery, pure white sand when I struck what turned out to be a large, Y-shaped piece of coral. I picked it up. Interesting! While it was mostly encrusted in white calcification, there were brilliant flecks of orangey-coral color showing through. I put the slingshot-sized sea treasure in my bag; I wasn't sure if it was legal to take it, but no one had told me otherwise…. Plus, I knew that there was at least one sizable coral reef off of the coast – surely a small piece wouldn't be missed.

WOOF! Followed by a louder, *WOOF*!! *WOOF*!!

Startled, I looked at my barking pup, who was standing on his chair in full alert, glaring at something behind me – and whatever it was, it was panting very close to my ear. Whipping my head around while simultaneously leaping out of my chair, I was even more startled to see a mangy-looking dog with muddy brown fur and yellow teeth, staring Barrett down.

"Shoo! Shoo! Go on! Scat!"

The relief I felt at hearing my husband's voice was palpable. At the wave of Keith's hand, the interloper turned away and headed down the beach.

"Good timing," I said shakily. "I have no idea where that thing came from!"

"I should have warned you about the Coconut Retrievers. Sorry."

"The what?"

"Coconut Retrievers. They roam the islands in this part of the Caribbean," explained my husband. "They're mostly strays, and Alain says they're a mix between retrievers, dachshunds, and bulldogs. What a combination. And, they're allowed to wander in and out of beach restaurants, resort lobbies, and such." He shrugged. "I guess they're fairly tame, if left alone."

No worries – I'd be leaving alone any Coconut Retrievers who crossed my path.

Shifting gears, I asked, "Where are the rest of the guys? I'm hungry! And, dying for a restroom."

Barrett wagged his tail in concurrence – probably on both counts.

Having borrowed the rental car from Alain to retrieve Barrett and me, Keith drove back to the jobsite, where his three colleagues were finishing up. The guys all piled into the car, and Alain took over the wheel. As earlier, Lucas rode in the front passenger seat, and my husband, I, Barrett, and Remy shared the small backseat.

"Now, for a light lunch!" exclaimed Alain with *joie de vivre*. He turned his attention to Keith and me. "You two will love this place. It's at one of the few resorts on the island. As you've probably noticed, Anguilla is not highly built-up – nor is it heavily inhabited. And it's small: only 16 miles long and 3 and a half miles wide – at its widest point. Essentially, one half is developed, and one half is mostly untouched."

" 'Anguilla'," I pondered. "Isn't that French for 'eel'?"

"*Oui*! Technically, it's *anguille*," confirmed Alain. "If you look at a map, you'll notice that the island is shaped like one of the beautiful little creatures. It was named in 1556, when the French explorer Pierre Laudonnaire sailed past. Then, in 1630 or so, the Dutch built a fort on the island, but that site has never been located. About twenty years later, English settlers from St Kitts and St Nevis colonized the island, and Anguilla has remained a British colony ever since. Today, the island's 16,000 residents are mainly of African descent, but there are many of Irish descent, too. The Irish came over from St Kitts in the 1600s to farm, but the limestone land was unfit for agriculture, so attempts at enslavement never lasted long. Anguilla, therefore, does not share the ugly history of slavery that existed among other Caribbean islands. And that, speaking of history, concludes our lesson!" Alain laughed.

"Perfect!" I said, already thinking of ways to incorporate Anguilla into my book. Now to just get past the first chapter….

Our 'light lunch' was over – and it was anything *but*. Alain, Remy, and Lucas had plowed through three courses, complete with three glasses of wine each. Keith and I abstained; alcohol during the middle of the day guaranteed the end of any further productivity – or even alertness – for us. So while we finished up the seafood platter we were sharing (sans eel – ugh!), the three Frenchmen leaned back in their chairs and moved on to their final indulgence: cigarettes and espresso. The two younger men reminisced over wild nights spent at Nikki Beach, a well-known night club and beach resort on St Barts – home to the rich and famous.

"Say!" said Remy. "You two should take a day trip over. By ferry or plane – either way is quick, and you won't regret it."

"That's the plan!" I was enthused.

"Isn't it just 'St Bart'?" asked Keith.

"No. No!" I rolled my eyes, 'It's St Barts. *Barts*!" I emphasized the 's' for good measure. "And there's no apostrophe before the 's' – in case you were wondering, which I doubt you were." (I'm a stickler for words; I can't help it. In contrast, my husband is the anti-stickler. It's a Texas thing.)

By now, Alain, Remy, Lucas, and even Barrett were looking at us – okay, mostly me – like we were daft. Likely thinking, *"Americans!"*

Even Barrett seemed to flaunt his British citizenship in that moment, turning his nose upward in disdain.

"CHIKUNGUNYA!"

"Chicken-what?" said my husband.

"*Chikungunya!*" I pointed at two warning posters gracing the wall of the tiny Customs office on Anguilla, where we were waiting for our ferry back to St Martin. "Look! Apparently we're in a high-risk area." The point was driven home by the first poster, which featured a caricature of a very menacing mosquito suspect, posing for his mugshot in front of a yellow wall. His name was Aedes – a type of his species – and he was holding a placard with relevant prisoner information: *Serial Killer* – followed by *Zika, Dengue, Fiebre Amarilla, Chikungunya*; a laundry list of offenses. More sobering was the second poster, which stated that Chikungunya is a potentially life-altering infection that poses a threat to any traveler where the disease-carrying mosquitos are found. To date, it existed in over 110 countries worldwide – the greatest risk areas being Mexico, Africa, Southeast Asia, and parts of the Caribbean.

I noted the last locale. "Great." Then I looked down at my arm – and the odd red spot near my wrist. "Hey! Does this look like a rash to you? It says that joint pain and a rash are common symptoms of Chikungunya. Aaaackkk! What the heck?"

My husband leaned in for a closer inspection. "Cath," he said, "remember the crab cakes you had for lunch? That's a dab of hot sauce on your arm."

Oh. Right.

Soon, our turn with the customs agent came up. The man wearing what I term 'standard Caribbean police wear' asked, "Any contraband, ma'am?"

"No, sir," I replied. In that moment, my eye caught a third poster on the wall; this one stated very clearly that sea life of any kind was not to leave the island. My mind instantly went to the slingshot of coral tucked in my bag. Was it considered sea life? Coral in the water is a living thing – so, yes. However, this particular piece was buried in the sand; it certainly wasn't a living creature anymore. Right? I didn't know, I definitely couldn't ask the men traveling with me (including my husband), and I had to think fast. The agent was opening my beach tote as we spoke.

A solution was presented for me. There was a sudden ruckus in the corner of the room, where a large mosquito buzzed around the heads of two sunburned women (Ohioan, I guessed) as they shouted and flailed their arms everywhere. Shrieks of, "Chicken mambo! Chicken mambo!" could be heard.

The distracted agent quickly closed my bag and motioned for me to move on.

I was saved by the crazy ladies – and the new dance they'd invented.

Back at our villa that evening, Keith and I were discussing plans for the next day, as we readied for another dinner in Grand Case. I had just dressed Barrett in a jaunty little French sailor shirt, when my cell phone rang. It was Charlotte – Barrett's temporary host from Harrods, who'd filled in between his late owner and us – and she was calling from London to check on the little guy.

"Charlotte! Hello! It's great to hear from you!"

Ears perked, Keith mouthed, *"Ask her about the red-soled shoes thing."*

After a few pleasantries, and my filling Charlotte in on all of our pup's adventures thus far – assuring her that he was a happy camper and a complete joy – I broached the subject of the Louboutin lunacy that occurred every time Barrett spotted a pair of the pricey footwear.

"Oh, that!" Charlotte laughed, and proceeded to explain.

"Uh huh, uh huh, uh huh. I see. Well, it all makes sense now. Thank you!" I promised to keep in touch, and we hung up.

"Well?" asked my hubby.

Barrett also seemed to await an explanation; perhaps he wanted to see if it jibed with the truth.

"So!" I began. "Remember when we were at Harrods, and passed all those designer boutiques within the store?"

"Yes." (Translation: 'No.' Of course Keith had no memory of what I was talking about. Men.)

"Well, anyway, you might remember the Christian Louboutin shop – plush red carpet, glossy white walls, red and black displays of various footwear, crystal chandeliers…?"

His eyes glazed over. Even Barrett looked lost.

I forged on. "Okay, work with me here. Charlotte said that there was a tall mannequin on a pedestal in the shop – wearing a pair of Louboutins, of course – holding a small stack of shoeboxes, each containing a pair of the red-soled pumps. Apparently, Barrett dashed in, bumped into the pedestal – and the mannequin, plus the boxes of shoes, all toppled over on him. He was caught in a Red Sea, so to speak – and it wasn't parting for him. He was pinned down by the offending 'woman' in the signature shoes, until a clerk rushed over and freed him." I added, "Thank goodness he wasn't seriously hurt!"

Keith and Barrett looked at me – Barrett's expression a mix of satisfaction and perhaps therapeutic breakthrough.

"Well, that explains a lot," concluded my husband. "From now on, the solution is simple: no more high-end shopping anywhere, ever."

I rolled my eyes. Faulty logic, mister.

⊡

Strolling up the sidewalk of Grand Case's Restaurant Row on this second night, we stopped at a French restaurant recommended by Alain and Claire. Carrying Barrett over the threshold, we did a double-take – while a few diners plus the maître d' grinned – as we made our entrance. It was soon obvious why: every server in the place was wearing a navy-and-white-striped French sailor's t-shirt – exactly like Barrett's.

"*Bienvenue!*" welcomed the maître d'. "Table for two-and-a-half?"

"*Oui, merci,*" I replied, feeling very French.

We were shown to a small bistro table, and Barrett settled happily under Keith's chair – a little bowl of water in front of him, courtesy of the server who took our drink orders. We perused the menu.

"Say," I began, "I've never actually tried escargot. Have you?"

Keith shook his head. "Let's try it. While we're not exactly in France, we're in French territory, so it has to be better here than at home. What have we got to lose?"

We placed an order for it, while deciding on our main courses.

"You know," I said, as we waited for our appetizer, "snails have been eaten since prehistoric times. I once read that the most commonly eaten snail is the *helix pomatia* – which is also known as the Roman snail. Roman! I like all things Roman – so it has to be good."

My husband was dubious.

A couple sips into our wine, our escargot arrived, artfully presented in their individual shells. We peered at the mushroomy, worm-like creatures, and dared each other to take the first bite.

I caved, and took the plunge.

While I generally like seafood with odd textures — squid, conch, oysters (not, not, not raw), and Ipswich clams — I was still taken aback by this spongy delicacy, once it was in-mouth. I gagged it down — with half a glass of wine. "Aaack! I feel like I just consumed Lowly!"

"Who?"

"Lowly! You know: Lowly Worm. Richard Scarry's cute cartoon character? You read his books to our kids when they were little. Remember?"

Blank stare.

"Never mind." I redirected, "Anyway, your turn."

By now, Keith was using his little snail tongs to pull the earthy beings out of their shells, then putting them on a bread plate — for Barrett. I followed suit, and we placed the offering on the floor, next to the water bowl. Barrett took one sniff, looked up at us as if we were insane, and turned his head away in disgust. In the end, we had the Lowly Worms packed up in a little to-go box, in order not to offend the establishment (although that may have already happened, once they saw their appetizer under the table), and dumped the contents in the sea, once we were outside.

My husband sighed. "17 euros for fish food. Perfect."

After dinner, we'd wandered up Restaurant Row in search of coffee and a treat. Now sitting outdoors at a little *boulangerie*, drinking espresso and sharing a *tarte tatin*, we continued our earlier discussion of tomorrow's plans: we were going to St Barts for the day, and needed to decide on the means by which we would get there.

"Well," I said, consulting my guidebook, "there are two ways to get to St Barts: by sea, or by air. Each is tricky, and one is particularly risky. But, I really want to go!"

"Go on…."

I took a sip of espresso. "The safest way is probably by ferry. But that means spending about 45 minutes on very bumpy seas – regardless of how good the weather is."

"You should be fine with that; you had no problem on the Anguilla ferry," reasoned my husband.

"True. But the passage to St Barts is considerably rougher, so we might want to consider the second option: taking a plane over. It's a very short flight: about ten minutes. However—"

"Sounds good to me," interrupted Keith. "Short is better. Especially with Barrett in tow."

"But wait," I continued. "Just like Princess Juliana Airport here in St Maarten, the Gustaf III Airport [aka St Jean Airport] on St Barts is on the *Top Ten Most Dangerous Airports to Land At in the World* list – with Princess Juliana being number one, and Gustaf III being number three." At this point, I wondered why we even contemplated flying in and out of *two* of the world's most dangerous airports – in the same trip, no less. St Maarten's was kind of unavoidable in this case (as in, either accept it, or don't go to St Maarten), but St Barts' was not.

My husband decided on the transportation mode for us. "Well, then, the ferry it is. I know you: if we fly this hop, your nails will be clamped into my arm the whole time. And Barrett will pick up on your stress; the pilot doesn't need a howling Shih Tzu over his shoulder for the entire flight."

I looked at Barrett in relief. He looked back – one tan eyebrow raised in slight offense.

The next morning, we drove to Oyster Pond, which has a large marina that harbors sizable yachts from all over the world. We were early enough to enjoy a stroll down the docks, reading the names and origins of some of the magnificent boats.

"This is interesting," said my husband. "While a lot of these yachts are from nearby St Kitts, St Barts, St Nevis, and Anguilla, I also see several from Spain and Portugal. I once read that the southern passage route from Europe to the Caribbean often begins in these two countries, for a smoother and more predictable sailing trip. And it takes about 15 days to sail from Lisbon to St Martin. Can you imagine?" He looked wistful.

I felt nauseous at the prospect. "Wouldn't work for me." I pointed at the name on the side of the large Benetti in front of us. It read *Ship Happens*. "Why tempt fate?"

Before boarding our ferry, I'd popped a Dramamine, and we were now underway and beginning to hit some big waves. Keith had a firm grasp on Barrett; our pup's orange life jacket coordinating nicely with his little goldfish-print sun visor and bright orange shades.

My main focus was on the horizon at all times. Uppp and down, uppp and down, the vessel went. On and on. I kept my white baseball cap pulled down to my dark sunglasses, and my disposable airsick bag open in my jute tote, just in case. I was wearing a new watermelon-pink t-shirt with white palm trees on the front, a cute white ripskirt, and pink jelly sandals – and I wanted to be sure my outfit made it through the day. There was no room for 'tacky' on St Barts, after all!

After sailing past the beautiful mountain scenery of the island of Saba, with its dormant volcano, the equally mountainous northern islands of St Barts finally came into view. Soon we could see gleaming white stucco villas with iconic red-tiled roofs, dotting the island's sun-drenched landscape. It was all in striking contrast to the bright blue sky and the deep blue sea.

"I love this!" I said to my husband, as our ferry docked in Gustavia Harbor, and my stomach unclenched. "Did you know that the whole island of St Barts is only eight square miles? And nearly all villas and buildings are limited to a single story of height? Anything that appears to be two stories is actually constructed into a sloping hillside, so it only looks that way."

"Good to know." Keith was preoccupied, as we disembarked the ferry and then walked through the terminal seeking the rental car stand. It was about 100 degrees in the shade, as we waited for what turned out to be a model-like French girl from the rental agency, to pick us up.

Following directions, we, Barrett, and another couple all piled into Colette's small vehicle. She then whisked us at warp speed through the town of Gustavia and out to the rental car lot, where we again waited in the blazing sun for our turn at a car. (The last of our small bottles of water was now in Barrett's little collapsible bowl; it was downed in no time.)

Finally installed in our own little Fiat Punto, we drove back into Gustavia for some lunch.

Several restaurants and shops were closed in the mid-afternoon heat, for siesta, of sorts. One exception was *Le Shipchandler du Port Franc*, and its open door beckoned us inside. Taking seats at a teak table near the entrance, we saw and heard (rather than felt) an anemic air conditioning unit chugging away.

A friendly server appeared and took our drink orders. She then asked, *"Voulez-vous de l'eau pour votre chien?"* We gratefully accepted her offer of water for our dog.

"Why is it that so many European restaurants leave their doors wide open in the summer, even with the air conditioning running?" I mused. Sweat was already forming under the brim of my hat, and the condensation from our drink glasses was dripping through the slats in our table.

"I have no idea," replied Keith, checking on our panting pup below, "but Barrett has learned to work the system."

I followed my husband's gaze downward.

Barrett had positioned himself in the perfect spot to receive a steady stream of cool drops: drip, drip, drip, landing right on his little tongue.

Back on the sidewalk after lunch, I decided it would be a good time to do some souvenir hunting, before setting out to see the island. I also had another hunt in mind. "I wonder if we'll see any celebrities."

"Why would we?" asked Keith.

Duh. "Because! You know: 'lifestyles of the rich and famous', and so on? St Barts is known for that. Everyone who is anyone comes here. Especially during the high season: December through April. They come for anonymity, and to see and be seen."

"Cath…isn't that a contradiction—"

"Yes!" I snapped. "But keep your eyes peeled anyway." Geez.

After first ducking into *Pati de St Barth* for a little shopping, we stopped at another souvenir shop a few doors down. I immediately headed to the back of the store, where I saw a rack full of doggy t-shirts with the words 'St Barts' on them. I began sifting through sizes and colors. Pulling out an extra-small in turquoise, I did a double-take.

"Look!" I handed the shirt to Keith. "What does this say?"

" 'St Barts'. What did you expect it to say?"

"Look again," I said.

He did. "Well, what do you know?" He held the shirt down low, for Barrett to see. Our pup wagged his tail enthusiastically. There, in bold print across the front, were the words, 'St Barretts'. Sold!

Taking our money at the register, the clerk also did a double-take. "Oh, I'm sorry!" she said. "No one here caught this misprint. Let me get you another one from the back."

Keith and I replied in unison, "No need; it's perfect!"

Barrett wagged in agreement.

Driving out of Gustavia, we began our exploration of the island.

"So what have you got, History Lady"? asked Hubby.

I consulted my copy of Fodor's. "Well, it says here that Christopher Columbus discovered St Barts in 1493. It was inhabited by the Caribs at the time, and called Quanalao, but the explorer renamed it for his brother Bartolome. The first group of colonists arrived in the mid-1600s, drawn by its spot on the West Indies Trade Route – but they were wiped out by the hostile Caribs. Then, in the late 1600s, another group of settlers arrived from Normandy and Brittany; this group prospered, with the help of French buccaneers, who took advantage of the island's protective harbor. Later, in 1784, the French traded the island to King Gustav III of Sweden, in exchange for port rights in Goteborg."

"Goatburg? Is it in Anguilla?"

"No! Geez. It's in Sweden! Today it's known as Gothenburg. Anyway…thus the name 'Gustavia' – as in, King Gustav III."

"Right," said Keith. "So it's French now; what happened? And how did it become 'the playground of the famous'?"

"I'm getting to that. Until the 19th century, the island thrived as a shipping and commercial center – but then earthquakes, fires, and hurricanes brought financial disaster. At that time, Oscar II of Sweden handed it back over to France. France briefly sold St Barts to America, then acquired it back again in 1877. Today, the island is a free port, and in 2007 it became a Collectivity – a French-administered overseas territory outside of continental France. Historically, it's been too dry, hilly, and rocky to produce sugar, thus it never developed much of a slave base. And, some of today's 3000 current residents are descendants of the sturdy Norman and Breton settlers of three centuries ago."

"Okay, but why the popularity with the hoity-toity?"

I did a quick Google search. "This source – uniquevillastbarth.com – sums it up: 'The combination of natural beauty, luxury accommodations, exclusive lifestyle, and high profile events makes St Barts a magnet for billionaires.' There you have it!" I shrugged. It made sense, to a point. But that was about it, as I am pretty sure there are multiple places in the world that could fit the same bill. Nonetheless, it's a stunning island, and we headed off in the little Fiat to explore it.

"Let's just beach hop," I suggested. The route was gorgeous. The sandy shorelines varied from rocky, to arid, to heavily-foliaged. Sea grapes, cacti, and acacia trees were everywhere, as were numerous flowers. The sea sparkled, and the sky shone brilliant.

Again, I consulted the guide book. "Listen to the rundown on these beaches. They all begin with the name 'Anse', which equates to 'cove' or 'bay'. In French, *anse* refers to a handle – like that of a cup or a basket. Anyway, Anse de Grande Saline is a favorite, though it's known for being quite windy." I hesitated. "We'd better have a good grip on Barrett if we stop at that one!"

Barrett burrowed further into my lap where he was riding, just in case.

I continued on. "Anse de Lorient is where the surfers are, with its big, rolling waves. It says here to beware of the level of the tide, which can come in very quickly. And Anse du Gouverneur is supposed to have pirates' treasure buried in the area. That would be a cool find!" I declared, then thought better of it, as I imagined going through Customs in St Martin with hidden doubloons in my bag. Or maybe I could hide them on Keith without him knowing it, I mused. No. Probably not.....

"What about Baie St-Jean?" asked my husband. "I heard something about that from Alain."

"Oh, yeah! That particular beach is considered to be like a mini Cote d' Azur."

"A what?"

"Cote d' Azur! You know: the French Riviera? Along the Mediterranean coast of France?" I thought for a moment. "We need to go there sometime."

"Let's focus on one trip at a time," came the practical reply. "For now, how about a stop on one of these beaches for a few pictures, then we'll head to the airport to watch the planes land, before we catch the ferry back. I want to see what all the fuss is about."

I did, too!

⊡

"Here comes one!"

A small plane appeared over a very high hill at the beginning of the runway.

We were standing in a strong breeze, watching from the parking lot of the Gustaf III Airport, and could understand its wide regard as one of the most dangerous airports on the planet. The extremely short runway (2100 feet) is sandwiched between a 150-foot hill one on one end, and mountains just across a small bay on the other end. French aviation authorities require special training, plus an endorsement for any pilot to land there. (One St Barts visitors' guide described the process clearly, advising, 'Don't do it on a windy day with a hangover.')

Hanging onto my hat and focusing intently on not missing subsequent planes as they came in to land, I was startled by a voice behind me.

"The gusts coming over the mountainous terrain out there made a bumpy ride across, that's for sure!" said a young man, somewhat shakily. He extended his hand, adding, "I'm Beau."

"Oh!" replied Keith, introducing us. "Were you a passenger just now?"

"No," said Beau, in his French accent. "I was the pilot. My first time on this run! We had no real room to add extra speed for gusts, and on top of that, we got the stall warning horn, too."

"Yikes!" I said. "I'm sure you've trained for that – but still."

"Yes," confirmed the new pilot, "but one of the challenges of this landing is that you're basically at very low power, descending rapidly in order to just barely clear the cars driving on the top of the hill. You then have to make a shallow turn to line up with the runway; 'flare', meaning gently raise the nose of the plane to slow the descent rate; then touchdown. If you float more than a couple hundred feet, you have to add power and go around, since there won't be enough room left to stop. Once you clear the road, the hill is slightly steeper than your glide angle— well, you get the idea. Sorry, folks, I didn't mean to go on and on."

"No, no – this is fascinating!" I said. "I'll bet you can't wait to do it again!"

"Negative," was Beau's reply. "I think I'll stick to flying cargo. St Martin is a big exporter of liquor; it's easier to fly the Morocco route, than to St Barts."

The next morning, we were back in our villa in St Martin, packing to fly home. It had been a great trip, and I was writing a little card to Claire and Alain, thanking them for their hospitality. I made a mental note to send them a gift once we were back in the States. I was just sealing the card, when Claire appeared at our glass door, phone in hand.

"*Bon jour!* Keith, I have a call for you. Apparently the caller was not able to connect with your number." She handed over her phone.

I heard my husband's end of the conversation, and gathered it was his boss calling from home. "Yes. Sure. Uhm hmm, uhm hmm, got it. No problem, will do. Go ahead and put me on the schedule, then. Cath will love this one! Thanks, Ray. See you in a couple of days."

After saying our goodbyes to Claire (we would see Alain at his office briefly, on our way to the airport), we loaded our bags into the car, buckled Barrett into his little seatbelt, and headed off.

I looked at Keith expectantly. "Well?"

" 'Well', what? Oh, yes. Ray said for you to remember to buy his favorite rum cakes at the airport." My husband stalled playfully. "And you'll probably want your coconut tea bags and some white chocolate truffles, too. And Barrett might want— "

"Never mind that!" I said impatiently. "Ray has another business trip lined up for you! Where to? And you *know* that Barrett and I are going along...."

"I'll give you a hint. Think about your master's thesis."

"ROME!" I said. "Yay, yay, YAY!" I began plotting a chapter of my book. "The Colosseum, the Pantheon, Hadrian's Mausoleum, the Roman Forum…."

"The pizza…." said my husband. He and Barrett had the same faraway gleam in their eyes.

CHAPTER 22

W E'D RETURNED HOME from St Martin on Friday, and had only the weekend to spruce up the yard and the house a bit, before heading off again the following Wednesday. For Rome! Normally, we had anywhere from a couple weeks' to a couple months' break between trips, but in this case, Keith's water-guy expertise was needed at one of the Eternal City's most famous fountains – ASAP.

While in the Caribbean the previous week, we'd lost one of the hibiscus that bordered our pool cage at home. There'd been a tropical storm, and minor landscape damage had resulted. Hubby was currently outside the screened enclosure, planting a new bush. Barrett was on the inside, supervising from the lanai. I was in the kitchen, occasionally glancing up from the salad I was prepping, to gaze out beyond the lanai at the large, rectangular pond that began just a few yards from the corner of the pool cage. It was a nice view; the center of the pond featured a lighted fountain, and the edge of the pond that started at our yard and extended past several more backyards was lined with lilies and other tall grasses that contributed to the water's health. This foliage also provided the perfect hiding spot for wildlife.

Barrett saw it first.

Simultaneous with our pup's ferocious barking, I abandoned the tomato I'd been slicing and dashed to the sliding glass door, throwing it open while shrieking, "KEITHHHHHH!"

My husband looked up, and in the process, glimpsed the cause of the commotion. He froze for a split second, before sprinting for the nearest safety: a lowish limb extending from one of the several huge, old, live oaks that border our property. (Our property line runs about 15 feet from our pool cage. It's a tiny backyard.) I've never seen him move so fast – and I haven't seen him climb a tree since our two grown kids were little. But he had no problem climbing now; the real problem was that the limb was only about ten feet off the ground. And lurking menacingly below the tree was a gator. A big gator. This one was at least eight feet long.

"Stay put!" I yelled to Keith.

"Where the hell would I be going?" he yelled back.

The behemoth reptile had stationed itself at the bottom of the tree, and was slashing its powerful tail back and forth. Jaws wide open, it proceeded to put its mud-colored forelegs on the trunk, and attempted to climb. This was scary, because alligators really can climb things, such as chain link fences – and tree trunks. Albeit, they can only rise as high as their tail will support – but this does allow them to scale fences, if they can get a foothold. (They can also show up on front porches – and ring doorbells. It's true.) At any rate, I had to rescue my tree'd husband. But how?

First things first. "BARRETT!" I shouted. "GET IN HERE!" I held the glass door open to the house, and he didn't have to be told twice. Good boy.

Then I went into panicked thinking mode. Grabbing an empty laundry basket – our laundry room is right off of the kitchen – I next opened the freezer door and began scooping every bit of packaged meat we had into the basket. Steaks, hamburgers, and chicken. Salmon, shrimp, and pork chops. For added insurance I grabbed tater tots – and a half gallon of ice cream.

Struggling with the full load, I ran out to the lanai.

Reluctant to open the screen door – yet really having no choice – I stepped out warily and began heaving frozen foods. The steaks, hamburgers, and chicken all missed their mark by a mile. Ditto for the salmon and the shrimp. Keith took a package of pork chops to the forehead.

"Hey!" he shouted.

"Sorry!"

So far, the gator was unfazed. He was more intent upon growling at his quarry. (Gators do growl – although it's usually a mating thing. Maybe this one thought my husband was cute.)

Down to my last ammunition, I lobbed the tater tots, then the ice cream, at the giant reptile. The second item got his attention, having clonked him on the head.

He paused his angry vigil, snatched the carton with his mouth, and stalked off toward the pond with it.

Who knew gators liked Rocky Road.

We'd loaded the last of the luggage in our car, Barrett was sitting in a cushy doggy seat affixed to the console between our seats, and we were ready to back out of the driveway. We were off to Italy!

"Hold on…." I said, nodding toward the house next-door.

Osman Kose approached my window, motioning for me to roll it down.

"Hi, guys!" He reached into his pocket. "I know you're off to Rome, and wonder if you'd—"

My husband cut him off. "Sorry, Osman, we've really got to go. Running late…."

Osman's face fell. "Oh. Okay. But geez, guys, I was hoping you would deliver this for me." He extended his hand, and stupidly I allowed him to drop its contents into mine.

I looked in my open palm. Keith and Barrett craned their necks to see the offering, as well. Barrett gave a low rumble.

I resisted the urge to fling the object out of my hand. "What is this?!"

Encased in a clear acrylic block, about the size of an ice cube, was a long, ugly, pointed tooth – in ghastly condition.

"It's a vampire tooth!" Osman was exasperated. "Geez, don't you guys know anything?"

"I know *this*— " began my impatient husband.

I signaled Keith to sit tight. "But why? What do you expect me to do with it?"

"I'd like you to place it at the base of Trajan's Column. In his Forum. In Rome. It's to let Trajan – the emperor – know that this particular Romanian [he tapped his chest for emphasis] forgives him for his conquest over us during the Dacian Wars." He then added, "We cherish our vampire symbols, you know."

"But, Osman," I said. "The Dacian Wars [Dacia later became Romania] took place in 101 AD and 105 AD. I hardly think forgiveness is necessary at this point."

Osman gave me his soulful eggplant look.

"Oh, alright. Fine." I tucked the incisor inside my purse.

Once on the road, I lamented to Keith, "Why did I agree to bring this gnarly canine?"

Barrett gave an offended *WOOF!*

"Not you," I replied. "The tooth."

Our flight to Rome had just departed Tampa. Barrett was riding cozy in his little gingham carrier, beneath the seat in front of Keith. Keith was tapping away on the seat-back screen in front of him, selecting his first movie for the 12-hour overnight trip ahead. I was reading an archaeology magazine – specifically, an article about a little-known gem off the Piazza Campo de' Fiori, in Rome.

I poked my plugged-in husband with my elbow.

"What?" he said, removing one earbud.

I pointed to the article. "We have to eat at Da Pancrazio while in Rome."

"You're choosing restaurants already?"

"This isn't just any restaurant." I then prompted, "Think: Julius Caesar."

"Caesar ate there?"

"No!" Men. "Of course not. But you could say that he was murdered in its basement. Sort of. The short story is that Pompey the Great – the Roman general and statesman – wanted to give Rome a new theater entirely built of marble, after having seen a similar one in Mytilene, Greece. In front of the theater, Pompey built a large 'Curia' – a meeting place – for senators who wanted to discuss politics during performances, for convenience. It was in that same Curia that Julius Caesar was murdered by Brutus and Cassius on the Ides of March, 44 BC. Anyway," I concluded, "if you eat there, you're then allowed to go downstairs and examine the ruins."

Keith missed the magnitude of the historical significance. "Well, I hope the spaghetti's good."

At that moment, the meal service trolley reached our row, and a flight attendant asked which entrée we'd like for our dinner: chicken, or ravioli.

"Chicken, please," we said in unison. Why taint our palates before the superior pasta that lay ahead?

We were half way through our flight, over the middle of the ocean, in the middle of the night. Keith and I were dozing off and on, as most of the passengers seemed to be – aided by the near total darkness inside the cabin.

Following one brief nap, I awoke to a soft chattering coming from Barrett's carrier. Bending down to check, I could see that our pup had his nose up against the mesh side. He appeared to be carrying on a quiet conversation. Sitting back up, I dug around in my tote for a mini flashlight – which I located, then bent back down to shine under the seat.

I gasped, and straightened back up quickly – pulling my feet up with me.

"Keith! Wake up!" I elbowed my husband twice for good measure.

He opened his eyes halfway. "Whaaa?"

"There's a rodent talking to Barrett!"

"You're ridiculous."

"I'm not! See for yourself!" I handed the flashlight to my husband.

He ducked down, and back up again. "Yep. You're right."

"That's it? I'm right? Do something!"

Before Keith could respond with another unhelpful comment, the situation escalated. A woman heading down the aisle toward the restroom screamed as the smallish rat darted across her foot. This woke sleeping passengers nearby, and a short chaos erupted as people tried to discern for themselves what the emergency was.

Four rows up, a small Italian boy came to the rescue. "Here, Giuseppe," he said in English, as he crouched in the aisle, holding a rat kibble – or whatever they eat. "Good boy," he then said, scooping up the wayward vermin and depositing it into its rat carrier.

"There," said my husband. "No harm done. It's obviously on its way back to Rome. I read recently that the city is home to approximately seven million rats. The area around the Colosseum is sort of their hotspot."

"Well, great," I replied. "I'll be looking forward to that. Maybe Guiseppe has relatives there. They can give us a tour."

After an exciting (to me) flight path over parts of France, Spain, and Portugal, our plane landed at Rome's Fiumicino Airport in the early morning.

I felt alive. "We're here! I can't believe it!"

My husband didn't share the same burst of energy, and I knew that mine would be short-lived. Even Barrett seemed a little blasé when we let him out of his doggy carrier in the airport to 'freshen up'. But still, nothing could dampen my enthusiasm for being in my favorite ancient spot in the world.

Keith drove our rental car – a Fiat 500X – onto the Autostrada A91, which is the main highway connecting the airport to Rome.

"You're on the wrong side of the road!" I shouted.

Barrett gave a yip of alarm from the backseat.

My husband swerved, then swerved back. A car coming up behind us honked in protest.

"Cath! Don't do that to me! What the heck are you talking about? I'm driving on the right side of the road."

"I know! The wrong right side! You're supposed to be driving on the left."

My jet-lagged husband sighed. He was tired, and in desperate need of a nap. "Cath. We're not in Britain. The rest of Europe drives on the right!"

Oh – right. Well, I was tired, too.

The drive to our hotel – albeit all highway – was beautiful nonetheless. "Look at those incredible umbrella pines! They're all over the countryside," I said.

"Yeah," said Keith. "I wonder how the Italians keep them trimmed."

I did a mental eye-roll. "They don't! The trees grow that way."

The umbrella pine – also known as Italian stone pine (Pinus pinea) – is a needled evergreen native to the Mediterranean region. It's known for its large mushroom-shaped canopy and reddish brown trunk, and while it starts out as a rounded shrub, it grows into a towering tree with a single trunk and umbrella-like branches. Fully mature, it can reach over 90 feet tall.

"Well, that's good," said my husband. "What man wants to waste his weekend on a 90-foot ladder, in the land of *amore* ?" He waggled his eyebrows at me. Men.

⊞

We'd checked into our hotel in the countryside, (it was lovely and we vowed to explore it later), had showers and a long nap, and were once again in our car – headed into Rome's ancient city center for dinner. We'd been advised to park near the Piazza Navona if possible, where we would also find plenty of cafes. Keith navigated the Roman traffic well (deceptively well, as we would later learn), found a parking spot several narrow, cobblestoned streets away from the piazza, and we were off.

The Piazza Navona was gorgeous. People – locals and tourists – were out for their evening meals, drinks, and strolls. Numerous *ristorantes* lined the piazza, as well as various shops, plus a beautiful, Baroque church – *Sant'Agnese in Agone* (St Agnes in Agony). Several street artists performed around the square.

We had our first glimpse of Rome's fabulous fountains, and I spotted Bernini's famed *Four Rivers* immediately. "We *must* choose one of the cafes in front of it!" I said to Keith.

"Yes, we must!" answered a man in my ear, with an oddly familiar accent.

Keith and I turned around. "Ewan! Sophie!" we said in unison. "What are you two doing here?"

Sophie laughed, and gave Barrett – who was wagging his tail furiously – a pat on the head. "We were going to surprise you with a call tomorrow – but here you are! Ewan was called to Maremma – just north of Rome – at the last minute for business, so we'll be spending a couple days here with you."

The four of us – five, counting Barrett – chose a table at Tre Scalini, overlooking the fountain.

"Chianti for all!" ordered my husband, when our waiter appeared. He then added, "And a bowl of *acqua* for the gentleman under the table, please."

CHAPTER 23

I HANDED BARRETT TO my husband as we stepped out of our hotel room and into the hallway.

Keith did a double take. "Why is Barrett wearing four blue Crocs?"

"They're wellies, of sorts. How else do you expect him to walk on hot cobblestones?" Sheesh.

He shook his head and said nothing, choosing to pick his battles.

Sophie and Ewan were meeting us for breakfast downstairs. They had moved to our resort – it was more of a resort than a hotel – for our remaining nights together, and had checked in bright and early.

"This place is really gorgeous!" I said, by way of greeting. I gazed at the expansive space around us. The opulent, glass-domed atrium began with the lobby, extended past a sleek, boat-shaped mahogany bar in the center of the long quadrangle, then continued on to a lovely restaurant at the end. La Brasserie opened fully to a panoramic terrace, overlooking Rome in the distance.

Most identifiable on the horizon was St Peter's Basilica, at the Vatican.

Sophie looked up at the 40-foot ceiling, where an arched mural descended, followed by a series of vaulted beams, which gave the effect of an inverted sailing ship from long ago. Many of Rome's historical highlights were captured in one massive painting.

"I agree," she said. "And our room is fantastic, too! Plush, sapphire blue carpet – with gold images of the constellations woven throughout. And, the bathroom is a surround of stunning red marble."

"Our room is spectacular, too – plus, it has two bathrooms." I nodded toward the males at our table. "That *is* a plus."

"Oh, yeahhh," concurred my sister.

Squeezed into our car, the four of us – plus pup – were back in the heart of Rome. We'd hoped to park near the same spot we'd snagged the night before, since anywhere close to the Piazza Navona was a good central starting point for wherever we'd want to walk to (and how far could it all be?). Fortunately, there was one tiny space left among several Vespas, and Keith managed to wedge us in.

The actual drive into town had been a little harrowing. Lots of traffic, lots of scooters, lots of *polizie*, and lots of rules – which no driver seemed to follow. And yet, we'd been warned by those in the know that it was very easy to inadvertently break a traffic rule in Italy – and then pay a stiff penalty for it.

We exited the car, said a silent prayer to the traffic gods, and started walking toward our first destination.

"Why did the drive in last night seem so much easier?" I asked, as I stepped my way carefully over the black, diamond-shaped cobblestones that originally paved all of ancient Rome – and much of its empire. These would take some proper shoes, for sure – and the sandals I was wearing didn't qualify. How did the gladiators do it? (I also made a mental note: one of these stones might make a nice paper weight for my home office….)

My husband replied to my traffic question with logic. "Because it was dark out. What we couldn't see, couldn't hurt us."

⊡

"Shhh…listen," I said. "I hear water. It has to be just ahead!"

We were walking along the Via delle Muratte – past scores of tempting little shops and cafes – on the last leg of our trek, which began about 15 minutes prior at the Piazza Navona. Everyone stopped and listened. No one else picked up on the faint gushing sound, except for Barrett. He gave an excited little bark and a tail wag.

Our pup looked very Italian in his little Gucci bandana (albeit not authentic — it said 'Pucci' instead of Gucci), with matching leash. The fabric mimicked the brand's signature tan, with brown monogramming

– though stamped PP, not GG. An iconic red and green 'Pucci stripe' was the finishing touch.

Keith bent down and picked up Barrett. "I don't trust you near this much water. Especially since it's technically my jobsite."

It was true. My husband had been hired as a consultant on an issue with the Trevi Fountain!

"There it is!" said Sophie and I together, as we rounded the corner onto the Piazza di Trevi. Straight in front of us was one of the most famous water features in the world.

"Wow!" said Ewan, admiring the gleaming, white marble sculpture of the Greek sea god Oceanus driving his shell-shaped chariot, which rose defiantly above the aqua blue waters of the fountain. The god was flanked by sea horses (not seahorses) and mermen (not mermaids).

"Right!" said Keith-the-water guy – likely dreaming of the ancient engineering that lay behind the scenes.

"I remember studying this fountain in one of my Art History classes," said Sophie. "Bernini sketched out the first designs, but it was architect Nicola Salvi who continued the project, in 1740. Unfortunately, he died before getting a chance to see his work come to fruition. It was finally completed more than twenty years later, under the oversight of sculptor Pietro Bracci."

"That's cool," said my husband. "Also cool is the fountain's other history. It actually sits on the site of an ancient Roman water source, and is made of the same travertine stone as the Colosseum. It lies at the convergence of three roads [*tre vie*, in Italian] and is the endpoint of an ancient aqueduct – Aqua Virgo – which was constructed in 19 BC. The aqueduct provided a critical source of water for the center of Rome, and its many public baths."

We made our way through the throng of tourists, to the edge of the fountain. I held out my palm to Keith. "Hand me a coin. I want to ensure another trip to Rome in the future!" I was referring to the movie *Three Coins in a Fountain*, which established the tradition of tossing a coin with the right hand over the left shoulder and into the water, in order to make this return journey come true. All around us, people were doing just that.

Hubby set Barrett on the low wall surrounding the fountain, while he fished around in his pocket for a eurocent, then handed it to me.

I turned my back to the water, and tossed the coin over my shoulder.

SPLASH! This was much louder than a coin hitting the water should produce. I was afraid to look.

"Stop!" A nearby *polizia* was at our side instantly. Luckily, he spoke English. And, he was cute.

Officer Fabio addressed us sternly. "Dogs are not allowed in the fountain! Please remove *il cane* at once. "

Barrett must have seen me toss the coin into the water, and mistaken it for a treat. Of course he felt compelled to fetch it.

"Barrett! Come here!" An embarrassed Keith gently tugged on our pup's leash, forcing him to swim (Hey! He can swim!) the short distance back to the wall.

"Don't let his wellies come off," I advised my husband.

He gave me a look.

"Never mind," I amended.

We now had a wet dog to contend with. I took off his fake-designer bandana, while he shook out his fur – all over the officer, who had by now softened and bent down to pet him.

He sat back on his heels. "Hey! I know you. You're Bennett…Beckett…Barrett!"

The four of us exchanged surprised glances. Barrett raised a tan eyebrow.

Fabio continued. "My wife and I were in London a month or so ago. We saw your story in *The Daily Mail*. Nice job, little guy!" He patted Barrett on the head.

Sophie mouthed to me, "*He's married.*"

"*So are we,*" I mouthed back.

After the officer left us, we glanced at our husbands, who were discreetly engaged in a contest to see who could toss a coin into one of the sea horse's open mouths.

Sophie rolled her eyes. "Our *Fabios*. Not."

⚓

After Trevi Fountain, we walked toward our next destination: lunch at Da Pancrazio. Barrett had dried quickly in the hot Roman sun; the husbands were debating who'd come closest to their coin-tossing mark; and Sophie had a question about the fountain.

"What happens to all of the coins that are tossed in the water?"

I knew. "There's a Roman Catholic charity called Caritas. Since 2006, they've collected around 3000 euros

– that's about $3400 – a day. The funds are used to provide food and social programs worldwide. A pretty good cause!"

All agreed.

We were silent for the next several minutes, as we were really beginning to feel the heat. Barrett was the lucky one: he was kept cool by frequent streams of water dispensed head to toe. Rome is home to more than 2500 outdoor drinking fountains, called *nasoni* or *fontanelle*, which provide free, fresh water for all. Most of them are cylindrical, cast iron columns with a protruding spout. And there's usually a little basin at the bottom, designed specifically for dogs. All Barrett had to do after getting a drink was take a little dash through the flow. He figured it out quickly.

I wiped a bead of sweat from my forehead. "I wish I could do that." I turned to Keith. "What do you know about these fountains?"

"Well, they're called *nasoni* because the curved spout resembles a nose. The water in these fountains comes from the same ancient aqueducts that have been supplying Rome for over 2000 years." He paused wistfully. "Imagine! And more importantly, the city tests for water purity approximately 250,000 times a year. Impressive."

Ewan chimed in. "Also, if you block the water flow with your hand, the water will come out through a small hole at the top of the spout, making it easier to take a drink directly."

"I think I'll stick to filling my water bottle from the spout," said Sophie.

Me, too.

Turning down a side street off Campo de' Fiori (where we'd later visit), we entered the cobblestoned Piazza del Biscione. Locating Ristorante da Pancrazio, we stepped inside – and back in time, over 2000 years. Soon seated at a table along a back wall of the main floor, we had a fantastic view of our surroundings. We were dining among ancient ruins!

"This is awesome!" I said. All around us were original travertine walls, weathered stone arches, marble busts of senators and emperors tucked in various niches, and bas reliefs. There were no windows, but the lighting cast a perfectly eerie glow.

We studied the menu. Starters included bruschetta; tripe; beef tartare; and lamb offal (heart, liver, kidneys, and tongue. There's a reason it's pronounced, 'awful'). Pastas included rigatoni with 'unweaned calf'; spaghetti with clams; ravioli; and paccheri with octopus. There were several salad choices, including a Caesar – of course! Seconds featured lamb; veal; octopus; and cockerel. And last but not least, desserts: tiramisu; ricotta cheese and sour cherry pie; caramel cheesecake; and chocolate cake. There were several other items on the menu, and we all settled easily on some really great food. Even Barrett made out like a bandit; seated cozily under Keith's chair, he had a fresh bowl of water – and a cup of doggy gelato.

We asked our waiter for the check. Once settled, he asked if we'd like to see the basement – the area directly under the restaurant that included a portion of the ruins of the Teatro di Pompeo; Pompey's Theatre.

Of course we would!

After descending a circular, stone staircase on our own – passing a large bust of Julius Caesar illuminated in the corner, backed by a curved brick wall – we emerged among the ruins. Entire columns stood intact, as did complete rooms with wall murals and barrel ceilings. It was magnificent.

Keith was carrying Barrett, not wanting to take any chances.

"Why don't you put him down?" asked Sophie.

I answered for him. "I did our research before coming to Italy. Good thing! While most of the rules make perfect sense – it's obligatory to keep your dog on a leash at all times, for instance – some of the rules are pretty strict. For example, dog owners must always carry a muzzle when out with their pup." Uh-oh; we definitely didn't have a muzzle in our bag of tricks.

Barrett looked indignant.

I continued. "And, get this: in 2005, Turin, Italy passed a law mandating that dog owners must walk their dogs three times a day. Three! Failure to comply can result in a fine of 500 euros! Turin is considered to have perhaps the strictest dog laws in all of Europe. Residents cannot dye their pets' fur, nor dock a dog's tail. (I have to agree with those two.) According to a local Turin paper, *La Stampa*, the reasoning for these last two regulations is to make it 'illegal to turn one's dog into a ridiculous fluffy toy'.

Barrett had a look of victory on his face.

"What's the law regarding how long a dog in Rome must be walked?" asked my husband.

"One walk per day," I replied.

Leaving Da Pancrazio, and now out on the piazza again, we set Barrett back down on the cobblestones. He'd certainly be meeting his quota.

"Where to next?" I asked the other three.

Sophie was quick to chime in. "The remaining ruins of the Theatre of Pompey! The outdoor portion."

I thought I detected a hint of mischief in her eye.

CHAPTER 24

THE SUN HAD gone behind a cloud, and more clouds were rolling in. "Finally, a break!" I gasped. "This heat is getting to me – even coming from Florida. Egads."

"I don't think it's that bad," said my sister. "True – it's hot. But it's kind of a nice break, coming from always-cold Scotland."

"Scotland's not cold," said Ewan. "You just think it is, because you moved there from Florida."

"Yeah, but—"

"Wait!" interrupted Keith. "Isn't this conversation going in circles?"

It was – as ours often do.

My husband glanced at his city map. "Anyway, it looks like we've reached the Theatre of Pompey."

Sophie, Ewan, and I looked at our surroundings, which were very much metro Rome. "Where?" we asked in unison.

"There." Keith pointed at a large open space before us – the Largo di Torre Argentina – situated among Rome's classic jumble of modern buildings and ancient ruins. (This juxtaposition was fascinating to me, in and of itself.) The area was sunken by about one street level, and was bordered by a low fence on all sides. It featured the remains of four Roman Republican temples, and the ruins of Pompey's Theatre. Located in the ancient Campus Martius, it was also one of the places that the *Argentario* – silver/money-men or bankers – used for their business.

"Look!" I said. "There are people walking around down there. Let's go."

We located a set of stone steps, and were soon roaming among the dusty ruins. Shortly, we came to our main destination: a solitary umbrella pine tree that marks the site where Julius Caesar was assassinated – the area since known as the Sacred Area of Largo di Torre Argentina. The setting on March 15, 44 BC was that of the Curia Pompeia – which was being used as a temporary meeting place for the Senate while the regular Curia in the Forum was under reconstruction.

"Beware, Cath." My sister suppressed a grin.

"I know. 'Beware the Ides of March'. Gee, I wonder how many times *that's* been said on this spot." I rolled my eyes. *Don't upstage the historian in me.*

Sophie looked past my shoulder, and gestured. "No. *Beware.*"

Our husbands – and Barrett – followed her gaze.

Barrett gave a startled *WOOF!*

I turned around, and jumped back. "What the heck?"

My disloyal companions burst out laughing. A few yards away, a sea of cats – CATS – roamed freely among this section of the ruins.

"We're in the Torre Argentina Cat Sanctuary," said Sophie, with glee. "I've been looking forward to this all day!"

I narrowed my eyes. *She would. Cat people.*

Located in what's known as Temple D, the shelter was founded in 1993 and offers sterilization and adoption programs for the estimated 350 cats who live there. Considering that Rome has a feral cat population of over 120,000, I was happy that only 350 were in my vicinity.

People were allowed to descend a set of travertine steps, into the cats' subterranean digs for a visit (and ideally, adoption) – so of course Keith, Sophie, and Ewan did so. Barrett and I stayed behind, neither of us feeling the feline appeal.

Taking a seat on an ancient step under the shade of a pine tree, I set Barrett down beside me, put out a couple salmon-flavored treats, and poured some water into his little travel bowl. Gazing out over the ruins and daydreaming of the days of Caesar, my reverie was suddenly broken when something heavy womped me on the shoulder.

"Aaack! Get off of me!"

A big, orange and white cat had pounced on me, and was eyeing Barrett's treat. Its claws were hooked into my shirt, and it was hissing at Barrett – who was naturally barking back.

Providentially, my party of deserters returned. Sophie, especially, was doubled over laughing.

"Keith! Get this creature off of me!"

My husband made a quick grab for the wily feline, but that just made it dig in all the deeper. Barrett got in the mix, and the cat unclawed me long enough to take a swipe at him. It succeeded in knocking off one of Barrett's little blue shoes, which went flying – landing in a nearby pile of ancient debris. The fur demon took that opportunity to grab one of Barrett's treats, and ran off.

"Good riddance!" I snapped, brushing off the remnants of 'cat' from my clothing. Then I noticed the large hole in the shoulder of my shirt. "Well, isn't that nice," I said in disgust.

Meanwhile, Sophie walked over to the pile where Barrett's little wellie had landed, and reached in to retrieve it.

"OUCH!" She quickly yanked her hand back – now sporting an angry, red scratch. "Damn cat," she muttered.

"Let's get that wound cleaned," I advised my sister. I thoughtfully added, "Oh – and next time, *beware.*"

We headed toward the next site on our list: the Pantheon. I was really looking forward to this! Hadrian was my guy, and this was one of his most famous contributions to the ancient world.

The Pantheon anchors an area considered to be the heart of Rome – extending as far west as the Tiber

River, running east through Campo de' Fiori and Piazza Navona, past the Pantheon, and ending at the Trevi Fountain. It was a 'neighborhood' that we were becoming familiar with.

Sophie made an observation as we walked. "Everywhere I look – in the roads, on the buildings, and in between – I see the letters 'SPQR' stamped about. They're etched not only into ancient ruins, but also on manhole covers and other modern plaques. What's the deal?"

"I covered that in a paper I once wrote," I said. "During the Roman Republic, Standards were imprinted with the letters SPQR, which was an abbreviation for *Senatus Populusque Romanus* – meaning 'Senate and People of Rome'. The Standard represented not only the legion which carried it in battle, but also the citizens of Rome. The Romans had a long-standing belief that people were 'free', and created a democracy where authority came from the people, rather than a single ruling power."

Ewan added, "There's another meaning, used today by London market traders. 'SPQR: Small Profits, Quick Returns'."

Ahh…the Brits.

Turning down a narrow *via*, we reached our spot between the Piazza Navona and the Trevi Fountain: the Piazza della Rotunda. This piazza was anchored by a beautiful fountain – Fontana del Pantheon – which is centered by an ancient Egyptian obelisk, dating back to the reign of Ramesses II (r. 1279-1213 BC).

"This fountain is fed by the same aqueduct that provides water to the Trevi Fountain," said Keith.

We all looked at Barrett.

"Don't even think about it," I warned.

We then turned our attention to the left of the fountain and the imposing structure before us. The Pantheon.

"Amazing!" said Ewan.

"Incredible!" I agreed.

Sophie recalled her university studies. "Wow. This is considered to be perhaps the most influential building in art history. Its dome was the model for the Duomo in Florence – Brunelleschi's Dome – and for Michelangelo's dome of St Peter's Basilica. Even Washington, DC's capitol building was inspired by it."

We gazed upward at the sixteen 40-foot high columns forming the massive portico's entrance. Each was made from a single piece of red-gray granite, taken from an Egyptian temple. Beyond stood a massive bronze door.

My husband turned to me. "Before we go inside, what's the history scoop here?"

"I thought you'd never ask! Well," I began, "if you look up at the huge triangular pediment above the portico, it says in Latin: 'M AGRIPPA L F COS TERTIVM FECIT' – which translates to, 'Marcus Agrippa, son of Lucio, three times consul made this'."

"I thought this was Hadrian's creation," said Ewan.

"I'm getting to that. Agrippa was the son-in-law and counselor of Emperor Augustus, between 27 and 25 AD. He originally had the temple erected in honor of all the Olympian gods, and it became known as the Pantheon, which is a Greek name meaning 'of all the Gods'. ('Pan', meaning 'all'; 'theo', meaning 'god' or 'divine'.) The temple in front of us isn't the original temple – that one was destroyed by fire in 80 AD. Later, between 118 and 125 AD, Emperor Hadrian, amateur architect among his many talents, undertook a complete reconstruction of the Pantheon – the one you see here." I paused. "Let's go inside, and I'll tell you more."

We walked through the great bronze door and into magnificence. Taking a moment to absorb it all, even Barrett seemed awed. We all looked up at the incredible domed ceiling.

"This dome was the largest ever made, prior to the Renaissance," I said. I consulted my guidebook for a moment. "It's as high as it is wide, at 142 feet – from floor to rooftop, and from side to side. The dome itself is made from a Roman invention: concrete. It gets lighter and thinner as it reaches the top; the base is 23 feet thick and made from a heavy mix of concrete and travertine – but near the top, it's less than five feet thick and made from a mix of concrete and lighter volcanic rock, or pumice. The coffered ceiling reduces the weight of the dome without compromising its strength. Genius!" I proclaimed.

Keith glanced back toward the open door, then up toward the center of the dome, where a 30-foot in diameter oculus – the Pantheon's only light source, and designed to protect against hinst earthquakes – opened wide to the sky. "Not to interrupt, but the forecast calls for brief rain today. What happens then?" At the moment, a sunbeam shone brilliantly through the 'eye-in-the-sky', creating a spectacular spotlight directly on one of the many tombs inside – including those of the artist Raphael, and of the first two kings of Italy.

"Not much," I said. "There's a strange physical phenomenon – the so-called chimney effect – whereby the hole creates an updraft, which helps to vaporize any drops of light rain. However, if the rain gets heavier, there are some grids in the 1800-year-old floor below the oculus, to help with drainage."

We walked to the center to look at the floor. Keith set Barrett on the ground – leashed, of course – and he quickly found a tiny puddle of water to lap up with his tongue. Apparently it had rained earlier for a moment, and we'd entirely missed it.

After circling the inside and studying all the Pantheon in its glory – religious and otherwise – I added a final history note. "While originally built to honor multiple gods, in the early Middle Ages, the Pantheon became a Christian church. It's functioned as such for 1400 years, making it the only ancient building in Rome continuously used since its construction. The interior survives in its original form – perfectly preserved – and is considered to be the oldest structure in the world to do so."

"Now for some modernity," said my husband. "Who's up for gelato?"

In this heat, we all were!

⬚

Our next destination was Trajan's Forum – not to be confused with the Imperial Forum. On our way there, we stopped at one of many shops that offered gelato and other small treats, as well as wine, plus some iconic culinary gift items, such as mini bottles of limoncello, small bags of multicolored pasta, cutting boards and other serving items made of olive wood, and more. Before going inside, Keith picked up Barrett and carried him over his shoulder.

A lot of baked goods were stored out in the open. In the front window of the shop, at eye level, there was a large sculpture of the Colosseum on display – totally made of bread. It was a real work of art – a masterpiece! – and not for sale.

The gelato line was long, but we got into it. Sophie and Ewan, then Keith and Barrett, then I. As we inched along, we scanned the various souvenirs for sale, and Sophie chose a couple of cute items for Ewan's niece and nephew. As we approached the glorious Colosseum of Bread, I prepared to take a picture of it.

CHOMP!

"BARRETT! NO!" I shrieked.

It was too late; the damage was done. Our puckish pup had taken a bite out of the top tier, bringing down half the Colosseum with it.

As my husband paid heftily at the register for the damages, he turned to me. "Well, Rome wasn't built in a day, but Barrett managed to bring down a huge portion of it in just two seconds."

CHAPTER 25

THE SUN WAS in full blaze again, as we walked down the Via del Corso, from the Pantheon to Trajan's Forum. The distance was just over a mile, but it felt longer in the heat. Keith was carrying Barrett, who was wearing a doggy sun visor – in a white and blue 'gladiators print', to match his little wellies. (Whenever he was being carried any distance, we took the wellies off to give his paws some air.) Barrett wasn't panting, but the rest of us were.

I pointed ahead. "Trajan's Column is coming up. Yay! See…? It's surrounded by Trajan's Forum – and there's Trajan's Market in the background."

We soon reached the emperor's forum, which was across the street from the better known Imperial (aka Roman) Forum. Trajan's Column, at a towering 140 feet, was the magnificent centerpiece of this ancient site.

After entering, we explored the grounds of Trajan's ruins – a brilliant combination of marble, travertine, concrete, and red brick.

"Why two different forums?" asked Sophie.

"Actually," I said, "there were several forums, each sort of an extension of the previous. The original Roman Forum was constructed to create more space than existed in Rome's political and administrative center at the time. This was near the end of the Republican period, during the first century BC. It was begun under Julius Caesar, and became known as the Forum of Caesar. Fifty years later, the emperor Augustus (previously known as Octavian) – Caesar's adopted son – added another forum just to the east: the Forum of Augustus. Then, 97 AD produced the Forum of [Emperor] Nerva. The last of the Imperial Forum additions was the Forum of Trajan, built in 112 AD – with his famous column created in 113 AD." I steered our group toward the colossal pillar. "Which reminds me...."

Standing in front of the monument, I made a sweeping arm motion. "This whole area is Trajan's commemoration of his triumph over the Dacian barbarians – the people who inhabited what is now Romania."

We studied the massive column.

"The elaborate carving is amazing!" said Sophie.

"Yep," I agreed. "The whole design is actually a spiral relief flowing upward, showing Trajan's exploits during conquest. If laid out flat, it would be more than 600 feet long – and there are over 2500 figures carved in it." I pointed skyward. "That's a figure of St Peter standing on top – but originally, a bronze statue of Trajan stood in its place."

Keith put Barrett's wellies back on, and set him on the ground, leash in hand. "This is definitely awesome," he concluded. "Where to next?"

My group turned toward the site's exit.

"Wait!" I fished around for an object in my crossbody bag. "I'm not done here...."

A look of recognition dawned on my husband's face. I heard him mutter "run" to Sophie and Ewan. Even Barrett was poised for flight.

Sophie glimpsed Osman Kose's vampire tooth in my hand, the acrylic cube encasement having yellowed with age – which made it look even more disgusting. "What is that horrid thing?"

"I'll explain later." I glanced around furtively. Good. The closest tourists were many yards away, focused on reading stone inscriptions. I inched forward – about to lean over the short railing and tuck the wacky Romanian offering into some weeds at the base of the column.

"Ma'am!" shouted a security guard, out of nowhere. "*Stai facendo?*"

"He asked, 'What are you doing?'," translated Sophie.

I glared at my sister. "I know that." I turned and took a step toward the guard, intending to explain – but my sandal caught on the edge of a small rock and I tripped. The brittle acrylic cube flew out of my hand, shattering on the stone below. The vampire tooth flew out.

"Barrett! No!" yelled Keith, attempting to restrain our pup by his leash.

It was too late. The pooch was on the booty.

By now, a small crowd had formed around our little fracas. Barrett looked up at his new friends – tail wagging. He gave them his best smile.

A small girl screamed. "It's a big, furry bat!"

She had a point. Barrett's little lopsided grin flashed a perfectly placed vampire tooth.

Explaining, I smiled sheepishly at the guard. "A canine among canines – so to speak."

❖

"I'm famished," said my husband.

We'd made our way to the colorful Campo de' Fiore. In ancient times, it was the 'Field of Flowers' – an open meadow that Christians passed through on their way to the Vatican, thus becoming a prime spot for a bustling market. Today, the piazza is known for its large fruit, vegetable, and flower market in the morning, and its cafes and bars in the evening. And right now, our aim was to choose a café for dinner.

"How about the one with the red-and-white-checkered tablecloths?" said Sophie.

"Which one?" asked Ewan. "They all have that tablecloth."

Almost.

I pointed. "Well, how about that one at the far end, by the statue?"

We agreed, strolled down the piazza, and were soon seated at two small, wobbly tables pushed together. A waiter brought our drinks: Moretti beer for the guys, and

Barolo wine for the girls. "And an *acqua* for the furry gentleman," he said, placing a bowl on the ground in front of Barrett, before walking away.

Ewan raised his glass. "*Saluti!*" He took a sip, then nodded toward the enormous bronze statue that towered – and glowered – nearby. "So, who is that?"

"That's Bruno – Giordano Bruno," answered Sophie. "He was a 16th-century Dominican friar, who was also a philosopher, mathematician, poet, and cosmologist. In the eyes of the Catholic Church, he was a heretic. In the late 1500s, he was imprisoned on several charges of heresy – including denial of the doctrine of transubstantiation. His crimes included the notion that the earth revolved around the sun, and speculating about life on other planets. He was put on trial by the Roman Inquisition, found guilty, and condemned to death. After being locked up for six years, he was burned at the stake – on this very spot – in the year 1600."

We were quiet for a moment. Then Sophie said, "Three hundred years later, the Roman sculptor Ettore Ferrari unveiled this statue. It was meant to face the sun, but at the last minute the decision was made to erect it facing the direction of the Vatican, which lies to the north. Thus, the friar's face is perpetually shaded." She added, "The monument is also a memorial to eight other figures who were persecuted by the Catholic Church for their beliefs during that dark time."

Again we paused to contemplate all of this. Soon, the solemn mood was lifted by the arrival of strolling violinists – and large plates of pasta.

"*Buon appetito*!" said our waiter, refilling our drinks.

"*Grazie*!" we all replied.

Two hours, some tiramisu, and an espresso-each later, we were still at our table, chatting away and enjoying the people-watching.

Sophie turned to me. "Cath, how's your book coming along?"

I groaned. "Don't ask. I've barely made a dent. I haven't even completed the first chapter. So many interruptions, every time I begin."

She considered my dilemma. "I know you're wedded to the idea of a non-fiction historical work – but have you ever thought of writing something less daunting? Maybe a book of short historical essays? You already have several from your Master's work."

Our husbands ended their chat, and joined our conversation.

"Here's another idea," offered Keith. "What about writing short pieces for museums and such? You can still write history – so to speak – but on a more manageable scale. It's easier to accomplish several 10-page pieces, than one 300-page book – right? And, you could use your past papers as a springboard."

My mind was whirling. I had an idea! "You know, I think I'll email Annabelle Pargetter when I get home from this trip."

My tablemates were blank.

"Think: from the British Museum?"

A resounding *WOOF!* came from under the table.

"Well, Barrett certainly remembers her," I said. "She rewarded his historical contribution with a pretty nice meal ticket!"

⚏

The next morning, the four – make that five – of us were having breakfast at the hotel, outside on the terrace. We'd been to the lavish buffet, and were enjoying cappuccinos, cheeses, pastries, fruits, eggs, bacon…the whole gamut. At least once, I saw Keith slip a piece of bacon to Barrett.

"This food is so scrummy," said Sophie.

"What's wrong with it?" asked my husband.

Sophie looked puzzled. "Nothing. I said it was scrummy. You know: 'scrumptious meets yummy'. Scrummy. It's a British thing."

Keith and I looked to Ewan for confirmation, who simply shrugged. "I'd say it's blasta."

"Blasta?" said Keith. "That sounds pretty bad. So Sophie likes it, but you don't?"

"Wrong," said our brother-in-law. "Blasta is a common Scottish word for 'good'."

I picked up the chocolate croissant I'd been working on. A piece fell off, and landed in my cappuccino. "Well, this pastry is too crumby for me," I commented, setting it back on my bread plate.

My husband was further confused. "Crummy? I think the food here is great."

"Not crummy. Crumby. *Crumby*!"

It didn't register.

"Never mind." I pushed back my chair, and stood up. "Time's a-wasting. Let's *vamos*." (It was Spanish, not Italian – but close enough.)

"Ah!" said Keith. "Vamoose. Finally a word I understand."

My husband was getting pretty good at driving in Rome. A tad overly confident, in fact. Our first stop of the day would be the Roman (Imperial) Forum, and we'd been told that the best area to park in was near the Capitoline Museum, which sounded perfect, because that was to be our second destination of the day – plus, we'd planned on lunch there, too, at the museum's rooftop café.

Following a line of cars, we began to turn down a side street – as directed by our GPS.

I could barely get the words out fast enough. "ZTL! ZTL! Stop!" I shrieked.

Keith hit the brakes in panicked realization, glancing in his rearview mirror to see if there was enough backup room to change course. Thankfully, there was just enough space behind us to throw our car into reverse, and abort the situation. Cars honked, but we didn't care.

A bead of sweat trickled down Hubby's forehead. "God. That was close."

ZTL (*Zona a Traffico Limitato*) zones in Italy are a driving tourist's nightmare. An expensive one. Essentially,

they're restricted traffic areas in a city's historic center –
and in some other areas. Private cars are generally not
allowed in ZTL zones – but the rub is that residents,
taxis, vehicles with handicapped placards, and those
with special permits are allowed in these zones. So simply
moving along with traffic and following 'normal-looking'
vehicles can lure you right into disaster. While there
are ZTL traffic signs posted, they are sometimes (read:
almost always) hard to see, until it's too late. Fines are
typically assessed based upon ticket-cameras, and greet
the unsuspecting traveler once he returns home – and
receives a foreign citation forwarded by the rental car
company, which has tacked on additional fees, of course.
The amount of the fine varies greatly: anywhere from
80 to 300 euros – about $90 to $350. And, in order to
incur a fine, the entire vehicle doesn't even need to have
crossed fully over the invisible line; just the nose of the
car poking into the ZTL zone is enough to qualify for
this unlucky prize.

An hour later, we'd crawled the five miles' distance
from our ZTL debacle to the area of the Capitoline
Museums. Most of that time was spent slowly circling
the nearby Colosseum. Repeatedly. Because the large
roundabout skirting the historic arena was fraught with
too many cars, too many lanes, and too many Romans
who didn't see a need to acknowledge separate lanes in
the first place. Plus, there was no clear way to exit the
merry-go-round – at least, to a distressed American
driver. (Note: a couple years later, all traffic would be
banned on this road, to protect the ancient monument

from vehicular pollution and damage.) Finally, finally, we found a way off, and had the Capitoline Museums in sight – high on the Capitoline Hill.

"My God," said my husband, consulting the GPS. "It's completely surrounded by ZTL zones!"

It was true – and thus we found ourselves instead in the Colonna parking lot on Via Santa Maria – a 15-minute walk from the Museums. As well, it was a 16-minute walk to the Forum, which was our first destination.

"Sixteen minutes. Right. That will be thirty for us," grumbled Keith. The sun was inching high in the sky, and it would soon be sweltering on the ground. "So glad the Forum is outdoors. Not!"

We put Barrett's little wellies and sun visor on him, gave him some water, and off we went.

It was going to be a long, hot, dusty morning among the ruins.

CHAPTER 26

TOOK IN THE vast, haunted landscape of ruins from millennia before me. I was almost speechless – though not enough to prevent a history tutorial.

"Imagine!" I said to my family. "Rome was born right here, on this very spot. According to legend, it was founded by Romulus and Remus – twin brothers born to the first Vestal Virgin, Rhea Silvia, and the god Mars. The infants were abandoned, nursed by a she-wolf (*lupa*), then raised by a shepherd – Faustulus – on the Palatine Hill. Once grown, they built their own city; eventually, intense feuding between the two led to Remus's death at his brother's hands. The result? Romulus became the first king of Rome, in 753 BC."

"That's some sibling rivalry, alright," observed Keith.

Sophie and I glanced at each other. We'd had our moments.

We walked among the ruins – which covered the size of a football field. While the dense, green, pine forest of the Palatine Hill was adjacent to the Forum, the site itself was stark: ancient stone ruins, and a lot of dirt – with some scraggly scrub spotted here and there. In no time, Barrett went from being a black dog with a few tan spots, to being a tan dog with a few black spots.

I nodded toward our pup. "Remember *Harry the Dirty Dog* – the book we read to our kids?" I asked Keith.

He searched his memory. "Oh, yeah! He was red – and huge. Right?"

"Wrong! That was *Clifford*." Sheesh.

Back to the topic at hand.

For almost a thousand years, the Imperial Forum was the heartbeat of Rome. What remains today are mostly broken arches and columns – and many are enormous. It's very easy to sense the magnitude of what once stood here.

Ewan read an informational plaque. "Here's a basic overview: From 500 BC to 500 AD, Rome grew from a small tribe of barbarians into a vast empire, before slowly diminishing to city-size again. For the first 500 years, Rome was a republic, governed by elected senators. During the second 500 years – a time of world conquest, followed by eventual decline – it was an empire ruled by military-backed emperors." He paused. "And that's 'The Rise and Fall of the Roman Empire' in a nutshell."

"Sort of," I said. I then elaborated a bit. "Julius Caesar bridged the gap between republic and empire. When his [adopted] son Augustus succeeded him, 'Caesar' became a title, in addition to a family name. Thus, the first emperor – Emperor Augustus – was also called Caesar Augustus." I paused. "A side note here: as emperor,

Augustus ushered in the Pax Romana (Roman peace), which was an era when Rome reached its peak and controlled a realm reaching from England to Egypt; from Turkey to Morocco. Between One AD and 200 AD, unprecedented peace and prosperity existed throughout the Empire."

We continued exploring, as the morning grew hotter. Crossing what was once the main square, I said, "Imagine – under this bright sun – blinding white marble buildings, 50-foot columns, and shining bronze roofs. Plus, rows of marble statues painted in realistic colors. And, processional chariots clattering down the Via Sacra – right where we're standing." I pointed at the ancient, large basalt stones under our feet. "Julius Caesar walked on these!"

We rushed through several landmarks that morning – not taking as much time as we'd have liked, due to the heat, and time constraints. The Temple of Julius Caesar (his body was burned here after his assassination); the Temple of Antoninus Pius and Faustina (later converted to a 7th-century Catholic Church); Caligula's Palace (aka the Palace of Tiberius); and The Curia (Senate House) – to name a few. We also saw the Rostrum – the infamous 'Speaker's Corner' where Mark Antony rose to offer Julius Caesar the laurel leaf crown of kingship (which Caesar publicly refused – while privately turning dictator). The Arch of Septimius Severus (commemorating the African-born Roman emperor's battles in Mesopotamia), and the Temple of Saturn (the Forum's oldest temple), almost rounded out our morning.

There was one last piece of antiquity that I did not want to miss.

"The Temple of Vesta, and the House of the Vestal Virgins," I said. "We have to see them! Their history is fascinating."

Halfway up the Forum's west side, bordering the Palatine Hill and not far from Caligula's Palace, lay the ruins of the Vestals' lives. Figuratively and literally.

We entered what is considered to be Rome's most ancient sacred spot.

"Wow." Viewing the grounds before me, I contemplated the lives of the girls and women who had lived, served, benefitted, and suffered there. There was a ghostly silence about the place, as the sun shone directly overhead on the crumbled past. A faint whispering could be heard from the pines on the Palatine, and it wasn't hard to imagine the eerie sound being the voices of the long forgotten.

" 'Wow' is right," said Sophie. She turned to me. "Enlighten us, Cath. This is right up your alley."

It was, as I'd written a paper on the subject in college.

We found a small spot of shade under a bit of foliage, overhanging a crumbling brick wall. Sitting on a broken column section that doubled as a lumpy bench of sorts, we appreciated the break, and each went for our water bottles. Barrett, too, imbibed from his little collapsible bowl.

"The beginning of the Vestal Virgins, during the 7th century BC, was attributed to one of Rome's first kings – King Numa Pompilius," I said. "During that time, the Temple of Vesta was built and dedicated to Vesta, the goddess of the fire and the hearth, who was the protectress of the family and also of the State. Within the temple, Vestal Virgins were charged with guarding a sacred and eternal flame, which symbolized the eternal life of the city. As long as the flame burned, Rome would not fall. Not surprisingly, the temple was frequently rebuilt over the centuries, due to destruction by fire. The last reconstruction came at the end of the 2nd century AD, by Julia Domna, the wife of the emperor Septimius Severus."

"What about the lives of the Vestals?" asked Sophie. "How were they chosen, how did they live, and so forth?"

"They lived in the House of the Vestal Virgins – we're sitting in its courtyard right now – which was a long, two-story building surrounding this central quadrangle, with these two pools as part of the design." I pointed at the shallow pools, with their murky water and film of leaves. "Naturally, it's next to the Temple. The resident priestesses – as Vestals were also called – not only guarded the sacred flame, but they performed the rites connected with the cult of the hearth, such as preparing the *mola salsa* – a toasted grain flour with salt, used for the sacrificing of animals. There were always six Vestal Virgins in number, and they entered as novices between the ages of six and ten."

Sophie and I shuddered at the thought.

I continued. "These little girls were chosen by the supreme religious community of the State – the *Pontifex Maximus* – and at first, only Patrician females were eligible. Later, the honor was open to girls of Plebeian families, too. The Vestal Virgins took strict vows of chastity, and they served a term of thirty years. Ten years of apprenticeship, ten years of service, and ten years of teaching."

"Thirty years!" said Sophie.

"It gets worse," I went on. "On the one hand, the Vestals received a large dowry from the State, and were allotted every honor, including having their own box opposite the emperor in the Colosseum. They were revered by the citizens, too. However, they also lived under constant fear of horrible punishment. The two worst infractions were: allowing the sacred flame to go out, and violating their vow of chastity. Should either of these things happen, the guilty Vestal Virgin was to be buried alive – with a loaf of bread and a lamp – in a small underground chamber, in the 'field of the wicked' (*Campus Sceleratus*).

"Good God!" said Keith. "Why the extreme cruelty?"

"That's the most bizarre part," I explained. "By law, no one was allowed to spill the blood of a Vestal Virgin, so to solve that problem, it was decided on live burial instead. This led to another problem, because no burials were allowed within the city of Rome. The solution was to give the condemned woman enough food to keep her alive for a few days – so that her grave could simply be called a 'room'. Thus, she was not buried alive; she was simply sent to a room with some provisions, where she would die a natural death." I concluded, "The last Vestal

Virgin to serve was Coelia Concordia. In 391 AD, by decree of Emperor Theodosius I – and with Christianity on the rise – the practice was ended. Oh – and regarding the number of Vestals buried alive, historians estimate that there were only four. A relatively small number – unless you were one of them."

We were all silent for a moment. Even Barrett had a hang-dog look.

Ewan finally spoke. "Geez. Well on that cheery note, I think we're done here. Who's ready for some lunch?"

Barrett's tail-wag spoke for us all.

It was a short walk to the Capitoline Museums. On our way there, we stopped at one of Rome's *nasoni* – drinking fountains – and quickly 'showered' Barrett. He was now dust-free. He was a new man, with a spring in his step.

"I wish I could have a shower," said my husband. He pulled his (cooling?) fishing shirt away from his sweaty self, hoping for a breezy moment. Soon, he was distracted. Several yards ahead on our path lay an open manhole cover – and there was a ladder protruding partway from it.

Hubby wasted no time, trotting ahead to investigate. He said over his shoulder, "There's got to be a water guy down there. I'd love to see the systems below a Roman street!" In a matter of moments, we saw him descend the ladder. He gave us a quick wave before disappearing from sight.

"Oh, brother," I said. "Those poor Italian workers. He's going to blab them to death – and they won't even understand the language."

Sophie weighed in. "That could work in their favor."

Ewan and I nodded in assent.

Ten minutes passed. "I wish he'd hurry up," I said. We were standing under the shade of a large umbrella – which was attached to a street vendor's cart. In exchange for the convenience, we'd bought four new bottles of water – and a fried rice ball. In another minute, we'd have to up the investment.

"These aren't bad," said Ewan, his mouthful of rice, mozzarella, and tomato sauce.

Watching for our absent group member, Sophie announced, "Here he comes. Finally."

Water Guy approached.

We all did a double take.

"What happened?!" I asked.

Keith stood in front of us – soaking wet from head to toe. "It was a stormwater pump station. The guys were working on a valve – and it burst." He added, "I was leaning in for a closer look when it ruptured."

The three of us couldn't suppress our laughter any longer.

I knew my husband. "Well, of course you were!" I said. "At least you got that shower you were longing for. Now let's go."

During the remaining trek to the Capitoline Museums, Keith dried out – mostly.

Our first destination beyond entry was the Terrazza Caffarelli. This covered, outdoor cafe was located on an observation deck, and the view overlooking the Roman Forum immediately below was spectacular!

I stood up from our table for a minute, leaning my elbows on the travertine-capped wall, to get a better look. This was a sight that would remain one of my very favorites, from all of our travels. (As I would later learn, my husband captured a candid picture of this moment – my face partly obscured in the lower right corner of the shot, as I contemplated the epic scene before me. This is a memorable photo for two reasons. One, it reminds me of the way I felt on this profound spot. Two, the image obstructing the side of my face appears to be a menacing, black UFO of frightening stature. In reality, it was a gangly bug on the lens of Keith's cell phone camera – magnified to ridiculous proportions. Still, he was proud of his 'sighting'. Men.)

The conversation at our table brought me back into the moment.

"What's with the potato chips?" asked Sophie, reaching into a small black bowl at the center of our table.

"You mean, crisps," corrected Ewan.

"Potato chips to an American; crisps to a Brit; *patatine croccanti* to an Italian. Same thing." Sophie shrugged. "Anyway, why are we seeing them all over Rome, served with aperitifs – and often gratis?"

Good question. They seemed inordinately popular.

"I don't know, but nobody can eat just one," declared Keith, as he reached for his fifteenth.

WOOF!

"Sorry!" said my husband. Two chips promptly made their way to *il cane* under the table.

"Where to first?" asked Sophie, as we approached the exhibit areas of the Capitoline Museums – which are collectively one museum, and are recognized as the oldest public museums in the world, dating back to 1471. Composed of two palaces, Palazzo dei Conservatori and Palazzo Nuovo, they flank one of the most famous statues in the world, which we would soon see.

"Follow us, ladies," said our husbands, as they led us to the original equestrian statue of Emperor Marcus Aurelius – an enormous sculpture, done in gilded bronze, and standing about 14 feet high. It was stunning. The 1800-year-old piece, displayed in a huge atrium, is mounted on a raised platform which is about shoulder-height to an adult – increasing its looming effect even further. It's amazingly well-preserved, and the reason for its survival during a time when most bronze statues were being melted down was that it was originally mistaken for Constantine. Both emperor and horse give off an aura of calm, combined with powerful command.

After Ewan, Keith, and Barrett posed for a picture as close to the underside of the statue as possible, Keith set Barrett on the ground for a moment, near the back end of the horse. We consulted our museum map for our next direction, then turned and walked away. About ten steps later, we heard a child's voice, in British English – near the rear end of the statue.

"Papa, look! That horse isn't potty-trained!"

Slowly, the four of us turned and looked at the marble floor under the horse's tail. Sure enough, Barrett had left a deposit.

Mortified, I pulled a blue plastic bag out of the little holder on Barrett's leash, and handed it to Keith. Along with a disposable wipe – or three. "Here," I said. "It's a dad thing."

My husband skittered over and took care of doody-duty. He turned to rejoin his gang, finding we'd already fled the scene – leaving him holding the bag, so to speak.

Hidden from view, the three of us received a group text. "Cowards," it read.

The rest of our time at the museum was spent hitting the highlights, since we were – once again – limited on time. Sophie led us to the famous *Dying Gaul* – a fascinating marble sculpture of a wounded warrior from Gaul (later, France), showing every muscle and every bit of pain in the man's expression. A Roman copy of the lost Greek original, it's extremely realistic.

"I'd like to see the she-wolf," said Ewan, referring to Rome's most famous symbol, the *Capitoline Wolf.* While there are many copies throughout the world of this renowned *lupa* nursing the twins Romulus and Remus, this bronze statue is the original. The consensus is that while the wolf herself is likely of Etruscan origins – thus having little to do with the legendary founding of Rome – the infant twins were probably added to the sculpture sometime during the 15th century.

Barrett wasn't keen about the massive wolf before him, and burrowed deeper under Keith's arm.

Sophie wanted to see *Bernini's Medusa*, and as we stood before the polished stone sculpture, my sister filled us in. "This work is believed to date between 1638 and 1648, and is rooted in classical mythology, as cited in Ovid's *Metamorphoses*. Here, the beautiful Medusa, one of the Gorgon sisters, was caught in the process of transforming into a monster. Her hair was turned into writhing snakes, as punishment from Minerva for having had an affair with Neptune, god of the sea. The punishment also dictated that anyone who looked at her would turn to stone."

"Well, snake hair. It doesn't get much worse than that," I mused.

Keith led us to the Hall of Emperors, where rows of marble heads faced us down from the centuries. 67 imperial portraits (busts) lined the shining hall. "Look at the sneer in Nero's eyes!" said my husband. "I can definitely see him fiddling while Rome burned."

"It wasn't exactly like that…. Never mind. That's for another day." I said, before switching gears. "You can easily recognize Hadrian, though! He was the first emperor to wear a beard. See?" Sure enough, there it was.

We finished the Hall.

"Okay, Cath," said my husband. "We have time for one more exhibit. What shall it be?"

"That's easy," I said. "*The Head, Hands, and Feet of Constantine*. I first saw it when I was here as a teen, and it left such an impact on me. It's so awesome. Let's go!"

Near the entrance to the museums – we'd originally bypassed it somehow – was an outdoor courtyard that featured the enormous, ruined body parts of *The Colossus of Constantine* – Rome's first Christian emperor. 1700 years ago, this statue stood in the Forum's huge Basilica of Maxentius. It rendered the emperor Constantine more than 40 feet high – and he was seated! Today, the museum has a lineup of Constantine's head, right hand – index finger extended; foot, elbow joint, and various other parts. The head sits atop a tall pedestal of stone; Keith stood in front of it for a photo, yet his own height fell several feet short of the top of the pedestal, where Constantine's neck and head began.

"How did this statue fall?" wondered Ewan.

I knew. "At some point, the statue was believed to have been deliberately broken and pillaged for bronze, before its rediscovery in the 15th century, following an excavation at the Basilica Maxentius." I thought for a moment. "Man, I wish I had remembered to look around the bases of the ruins in the Forum. There could have been a tiny marble fragment for me to take." I was soon cheered by another thought. "However, tonight is our underground tour of the Colosseum, after dark. Certainly, I can pick up something there!"

"Sure," said Keith. "If you want to get thrown to the lions."

Barrett had been walking between Keith and me. He halted suddenly, and made a huge leap into my arms. He didn't like the sound of lions, one bit.

CHAPTER 27

"**I**T'S GOING TO be amazing," I said. "I can't wait!"

The four of us were drinking Chianti, having just ordered dinner at a café near the Colosseum. Discussing the evening ahead, we wondered what touring the huge amphitheater would be like – underground and after dark, no less!

"Ditto," said Sophie. "But first, I want to savor the pizza. It's truly different from pizza at home – be it Scotland or America."

She was right. True Italian pizza is made with a thin, crispy crust – rolled flat to within an inch of its life. Topped to the rim, then baked in a wood-fired oven. It's generally eaten one of two ways: either cut with a knife and fork, or folded and held by hand. There's no way to simply pick up an open slice and take a bite – it's way too floppy for that. It's delish!

Between the four of us, we'd ordered Italy's top three pizzas – Margherita being number one. Ham with mushrooms ranked second, and Gorgonzola with salami came in third.

Our pies arrived.

"Hmm," I said. "I'm not so sure about the ham, now that I think about it. The menu said prosciutto *crudo* – which is different from prosciutto *cotto*. 'Crudo' is raw. Ugh. 'Cotto' is cooked. Even though the raw ham is 'cured', I just don't know…."

We looked at the glistening pink and white flesh on Pizza #2, and felt green.

Keith and Ewan solved the problem by rearranging the toppings. The ham came off, and some salami from Pizza #3 took its place.

"What should we do with this ham?" asked my husband, loaded forkful dangling mid-air.

Beneath my chair, a tail thumped against my ankle.

"Barrett will eat it. He's a pig about…well, pig."

Problem solved.

⚏

With an hour to spare before the Colosseum tour, we lingered over our drinks. At one point, Keith stood to visit the restroom – knocking our rickety table, and toppling my drink glass in the process. (Sophie and Ewan were unaffected; as usual in Rome, we had two tables pushed together.) Red wine splashed all over my yellow top and skirt.

I looked at the damage. "Well, this is just great. I'm wearing Gorbachev's forehead!"

My husband apologized and dipped his napkin into his glass of water, offering a 'clean cloth' as remedy.

"Never mind," I sighed. "The 'wrath of grapes' and all…."

"Cath," corrected my sister. "That's *The Grapes of*—"

I shot her a look, squelching the literature lesson.

It was dark outside as we approached the Colosseum, and the sight was spectacular. The ancient arena was dramatically lit – an eerie yellow glow emanating from arches surrounding the amphitheater on all sides and levels. This was emphasized by the black sky behind it.

We all said "Wow…." in one form or another.

Waiting near the spot where we were to meet our tour guide, we were accosted by a gladiator.

"20 euros for a photo!" was the gruff demand in Italian-accented English.

I'd read about these guys, in their cheesy but realistic costumes.

Barrett growled – then lunged.

Keith held fast to the leash. "Barrett! No!!"

It was too late; our furry little protector now had a big scrap of red cape in his mouth.

Suddenly it was ancient Rome all over again. The gladiator snarled and made a grab for Barrett. "I ought to throw you to the— " Fortunately, he missed. This guy was really unhinged.

A *polizie* appeared, and shooed the guy off. He apologized to us, stating that legislation was underway to ban these con artists from Rome. (It later passed.) 'Gladiators' of this sort hung out at popular sites, preying on tourists after posing for photos with them – then aggressively demanding payment. Incidents of wallets being stolen – and female tourists being groped – had occurred.

Mildly shaken – on behalf of Barrett – we pulled ourselves together, just as our tour guide arrived.

Graciela was an archaeologist, and she welcomed our small group of fifteen with a brief history lesson before we would enter the arena. "Originally called the Flavian Amphitheater, construction was begun in 72 AD by Emperor Vespasian – and completed in 86 AD by Emperor Domitian. The resources necessary for this enormous project – money and slaves – came from the spoils that the Romans secured with the destruction of Jerusalem and the Temple of Jews, in 70 AD. What you see today is about one-third of the actual arena. Over the centuries, earthquakes destroyed some of it, and during the Middle Ages and the Renaissance, many of the pre-cut stones were carted off to make other buildings that still stand in Rome today. The exterior was built of 3.5 million cubic feet of travertine stone. It took 200 ox-drawn wagons shuttling between here and Tivoli —18 miles northeast of Rome – every day for four years, just to bring the stone here. Imagine!"

Our guide continued. "With eighty entrances reserved for public access, the arena could accommodate

50,000 spectators: 45,000 seated, and 5000 in the top area – mostly standing. There was an elaborate removable awning to protect from sun and rain, called the 'Velarium'. Statues embellished each arch starting from the second level, and there were five levels. Seating was segregated; at ringside, the emperor, senators, Vestal Virgins, and VIPs occupied marble seats – some with their names carved on them. The next level up was for those of noble birth; above that were the Plebeians (ordinary free Roman citizens). Up at the very top, there were wooden benches, and standing room, for the poorest people: foreigners, slaves, and women." She paused. "And now, if you'll follow me, we'll head inside and go subterranean. Please watch your step, as the dirt floors are very uneven, and rocks, stones and wooden planks may protrude. As well, the lighting is very dim." She switched on her flashlight.

We stepped inside the imposing arena – and seemingly back in time. Oval in shape, we learned that it was 280 feet long, by 165 feet wide. An enthusiastic math teacher in our group pointed out, "That's the Golden Ratio! 'Five to three'. Since the days of the Greek mathematician Pythagoras, artists have considered that proportion to be ideal, with almost mystical properties." Which seemed somehow fitting.

Looking at the arena's floor, we saw numerous underground passages beneath the performance area, partially exposed. Following our guide down a series of wooden stairs and dusty ramps, we eventually landed in the dimly lit labyrinth of dirt rooms and cells which had held gladiators, prisoners, and wild animals almost 2000 years before.

Sophie and I looked at each other and shuddered. Keith and Ewan were agog. Barrett had his head halfway tucked under Keith's arm – one eye peeking out.

Graciela began this portion of the tour. "The underground rooms here contained facilities, and stored stage equipment for some of the shows. Scenery was elaborate, especially for the animal hunts: stage managers created hills, woods, and even small lakes. For transporting prisoners and animals up to the arena floor, 'elevators' were made, using weights and counterweights. Ramps were then used, from the open elevators to the arena. Gladiators had barracks next to the Colosseum; they accessed the arena via an underground passage."

We moved along the dim corridors, as Graciela talked. "Obviously, the Colosseum is known for its violent history. It was inaugurated with a 100-day festival in which 2000 men and 9000 animals were killed. Generally, shows took place during the summer for 18 hours a day, and during the winter for 15 hours a day – two or three times a year, in cycles of a week or more. Admission required a ticket which was a small clay tablet – often a pottery shard — marked with entrance, section, row, and seat number.

Fighting involved man against man; man against beast; and beast against beast. (The arena floor was covered in sand, to absorb the blood.) Gladiators were usually slaves, criminals, or poor people who got their chance at freedom and status in the arena. They learned to fight in training schools, and the best were rewarded with great wealth and fame."

"What about the poor animals? Where did they come from?" asked a woman in our group.

"The animals came from all over the world," said our guide. "Lions, bears, tigers, crocodiles, hippos, panthers, bulls, mastiff dogs, wild boars, and elephants. Mornings were reserved for fights among the wild beasts; afternoons were for the gladiator battles."

A man asked, "The Christians. Were they really thrown to the lions?"

"Sadly, yes. They were not only thrown to the lions, but also made to fight gladiators. However, there's no evidence that this actually occurred in the Colosseum. But it did happen in other venues."

We continued our walk through this strange underground world, before reaching the end and ascending back to ground level. When we emerged, the night sky was full of stars, shining down on the open arena – the jagged ruins of the Colosseum walls forming a haunting silhouette.

"There's one more thing of interest here," said Graciela. "Between 80 AD and 86 AD, Roman authorities often staged naval battles in the Colosseum. There were gladiatorial combats on actual boats. The arena would be flooded for the occasion using a complex hydraulic system, bringing in channels of water from Lake Nero."

Keith the Water Guy was impressed by this. "I wonder if there's anything left of the system that I can get a private tour of...?" he said to no one in particular.

"No! That's a recipe for trouble," I said – as I surreptitiously bent down and picked up a piece of ancient stone. The irony was not lost on me.

Before leaving the area for the night, we walked to two nearby sites: the Circus Maximus, and the Arch of Constantine. The Arch came first, situated between the Colosseum and the Palatine Hill – and spanning the Via Triumphalis, which was the route taken by triumphant military leaders when they returned to ancient Rome in a victory procession.

"This thing is huge," said Ewan. He glanced at his guidebook. "It says here that, dedicated in 315 AD, it's the largest of the triumphal arches – at 69 feet high, 85 feet wide, and 24 feet deep. The construction is of brick-faced concrete, covered in marble." He turned to me. "What's the history, Cath?"

"Glad you asked!" I said. "So, beginning in the late 3rd century, the Roman Empire was ruled by four co-emperors: two seniors, and two juniors. This was done in effort to bring political stability, after the turmoil of that century. However, in 312 AD, Constantine took control over the Western Empire by defeating his co-emperor Maxentius at the Battle of Milvian Bridge – thus becoming sole emperor. The night before the battle, Constantine had seen a vision of a cross in the sky. His mother (later to become St Helena) and sister were

Christians, and at this moment he decided to legalize Christianity."

We discussed the impact of Constantine, as we reached our next stop.

After dark was not the best time to view what remains of the Circus Maximus. "Where is it, exactly?" asked Sophie.

We peered at an enormous, rectangular green, with a vague sand track running around it. Along one side, the ruins of a long, red brick entertainment complex were eerily backlit by the night sky.

"Right in front of us," I said. "While barren today, it stood for almost a thousand years as a famed spot for chariot racing. At 2100 feet long – chariot drivers had to complete seven circuits before reaching the finishing line – it accommodated 300,000 spectators. The complex itself went through several major reconstructions; the last one was undertaken by Emperor Trajan – although it was later enlarged by Emperor Caracalla, and restored by Emperor Constantine. Some of the seating – presumably higher up – was wooden, and frequent collapses occurred. One such incident, during the reign of Antoninus Pius, killed 1112 people. Another, under Diocletian, killed over 13,000."

Suddenly, out of the total darkness of the Palatine Hill, came a mournful howl.

Barrett gave a small whimper in response.

"*Lupa*," said Sophie in a low voice.

"You know," I said, scanning the desolation around us, "it's a long walk back to where we parked this morning…."

Making a hasty retreat back to the bustling traffic around the Colosseum, we hailed a taxi to take us to our car. We were done for the night.

Finishing our cappuccinos at breakfast the next morning, we discussed the day's plans. My husband, who was tired of battling Rome's crazy traffic, suggested that we take the hotel shuttle – a tour-sized bus of sorts – into the city center. There was a standard drop-off point for these shuttles, and it happened to be very near our first destination for the day: Castel Sant' Angelo – which was originally built as Hadrian's Mausoleum. We would be spending the morning with Hadrian! At least, in my mind.

"That might be a good idea," said Sophie. "On the one hand, the shuttle runs every hour on the hour, until 10:00 PM. We could stay in town as long as we like—"

"On the other hand," I finished the thought for her, "it will mean a lot of walking. A LOT. We won't have our car to bridge any gaps."

Keith noted that the day before, we'd parked in one spot and never saw our car again until we were ready to leave the city. He had a point. "And, while it's a half-hour ride in, the bus is well air-conditioned, so we'll be comfortable."

We gathered our things for the day – mostly Barrett's. Leash; harness; sunglasses; and visor. (He'd shunned the gladiator-print one after his harrowing incident, so I brought his red-and-white checkered one, with the 'pupperoni' pizzas on it, instead.) Treats; food; collapsible bowls; and blue wellies. We were ready to go.

Twenty minutes later, we were crammed on the shuttle bus with thirty other tourists. Large windows and a huge glass roof afforded views all around.

Ten minutes after that, we reached the end of the winding driveway – ready to pull out onto the Italian cypress-lined highway.

Five minutes on the road, the bus's air-conditioning conked out, never to be felt again.

"Good God," said my husband. "We're trapped in a rotisserie on wheels."

CHAPTER 28

WHAT SHOULD HAVE been a cool thirty-minute journey to the city turned into a scorching one-hour trip, the glass bubble we were riding in having become a hothouse worthy of growing exotic flowers. Traffic was congested on the Via Aurelia, just before it became the Viale Vaticano, which skirted the Vatican City walls. Pretty much everyone on board had downed their individual *acqua* supply – us included. I was careful to reserve enough water for Barrett, but had just poured the last of his bottle into his little bowl. He, too, was in thirst-overdrive.

I glanced at my husband, alarmed. "Are you okay? You look pale and flushed at the same time."

He croaked, "I need water…."

I turned to Sophie and Ewan, sitting behind us. "Do you guys have any water left? Keith isn't looking well."

They shook their heads, then searched around for assistance – in that way that you do when you already know there's no solution nearby, but you make a hopeful attempt anyway.

I did the same. "Here!" I finally said, offering my husband the only remedy available. "Drink this."

He looked at me like I was crazy – for about one second. Then he took Barrett's silicone water bowl from my hand and greedily lapped up what was left – a mixture of relief and disbelief on his face.

I received the empty bowl. "You have a dog hair on your nose. Then, "Oh – wait!"

I snapped a picture before he could object.

🧳

Castel Sant' Angelo stood before us, on the right bank of the Tiber River. A glorious rotunda, it was once the tallest building in ancient Rome, at 210 feet high and 292 feet wide.

"Hadrian!" I called out. "I'm home...."

Ewan and Sophie shot looks of sympathy toward my husband, who simply shrugged.

Designed and built by the emperor as his own tomb, between 134 AD and 139 AD, Hadrian's Mausoleum – as it was first called – was a massive cylindrical structure that was originally topped by a full, circular cypress grove. A huge statue of the emperor riding a golden quadriga (a chariot drawn by four horses) once crowned the impressive structure.

"What an undertaking – no pun intended," said Ewan. "And what an ego."

I knew there was more to it. As we walked toward the entrance, I explained. "Hadrian was actually inspired by the emperor Augustus, who built his own mausoleum in 28 BC. Its ruins are nearby, in the Campus Martius – the level area between several of Rome's hills and the river. Hadrian's intention was for this mausoleum to enshrine not only his immediate family, but also the remains of succeeding emperors. The last recorded deposition was of Emperor Caracalla, in 217 AD."

Inside, we would begin the hike of stone stairsteps and ramps lining the massive 'drum' – but first, we walked the square base of the building, following the route of Hadrian's funeral procession.

"Interestingly," I said, "this mausoleum was incomplete at the time of Hadrian's death. He died a year earlier, at his villa in Baiae, on the Gulf of Naples. (His wife, Vibia Sabina, preceded him in death by two years.) The emperor was first buried at nearby Puteoli, on an estate that had once belonged to Cicero. His remains were later transferred to Rome, where he was reburied close to the almost-finished mausoleum. Once the tomb was completed, Hadrian's body was cremated, and his ashes were placed together with those of his wife, and of his first adopted son, Lucius Aelius – who had died the same year as Sabina."

"You said, 'first adopted son'?" observed Sophie.

"Right. As an emperor, Hadrian needed a successor – but he was childless. (That's a whole other story.) Since his first adopted son had died, he sought a replacement heir. On his deathbed, he preferred Marcus Antoninus – who would later become Marcus Aurelius, but who was still too young to become an emperor. So instead, Hadrian adopted 51-year-old Antoninus Pius – on the condition that Antoninus Pius would adopt Marcus Antoninus at the same time. Later, Marcus Aurelius Antoninus further secured his claim to the throne, by marrying Antoninus Pius's daughter, Faustina the Younger."

"Well, that was complicated," said my husband.

"Yep," I concurred. "Nothing was simple with the Romans."

"Where in Hades are the damn urns?" I said.

We'd been circling and climbing inside the massive structure for over an hour. It was getting warm, and even I had begun to have my fill of the large quantity of statues and busts of my beloved Hadrian – and that's saying a lot. There are around 150 known surviving images – and it felt like they were all there. (They're not, of course. They're scattered throughout Europe, the Middle East, and America – mainly in museums.) That said, naturally I had to pose in front of a couple of them.

Keith consulted his site map again. "They're supposed to be in the Treasury Room. We're bound to come upon it soon; we've covered pretty much the entire area. And those two guides we asked along the way? No help there."

This was true. And about fifteen minutes later, we finally stumbled upon our quarry – only to learn that the urns were no longer there. How did I miss that key fact in my research?

Located deep within the building, the Treasury Room – as it would be called during the Middle Ages – was a small, dark, round chamber, surrounded in various ancient stone tile patterns. It could be viewed only from the cordoned-off doorway. In the center of the room, three large 14th-century treasure chests stood empty – but during the Renaissance, by which time the Vatican had converted the mausoleum to Castel Sant' Angelo (as a papal refuge during Charles V's Sack of Rome in 1527), the iron-studded chests would have held some of the papacy's most valuable jewels and relics. As well, walnut cupboards lined the walls; these were the pope's secret archives.

I was disappointed, but quickly did an online search. "It says here that the contents of the tomb and most of the Hadrian's Mausoleum embellishments were lost over the centuries. And when the Visigoths sacked Rome in 410 AD, the urns and ashes were scattered." I frowned. "Well, of course they were. Stupid Goths!"

"Cath," said my husband, handing me a yellow packet of gold, "have some Peanut M&M's. I think your blood sugar's dropping."

Barrett wagged his tail, a hopeful expression on his face.

Once outside, Keith gave him a doggy treat, water, and a pit stop. "Now, let's get some lunch among the horses. I'm starving."

Sophie and Ewan looked puzzled, and Barrett raised a furry eyebrow. But I knew where we were headed!

It would be a three-mile walk to our lunch destination.

The trek eastward took us first across the Tiber, then to a brief stop at the Ara Pacis. (Augustus's 'Altar of Peace'.) The small, gleaming Carrara marble temple had been excavated and relocated in 1938. It was moved again in 2006, then a sleek glass museum was constructed around it, protecting it from humidity and pollution.

Entering the museum, we climbed a short marble staircase into the temple, and up to the altar itself. After several minutes spent studying the elaborate relief carvings fronting inside and out, we contemplated the monument's purpose.

"It's ironic," said Ewan, "that an altar dedicated to peace was in fact used for the sacrifice of sacred animals."

"Well, that's ancient Rome for you," I said. "A contradiction at every turn."

Barrett wasn't mollified by my explanation. He jumped out of Keith's arms, tugging toward the exit. It was time to move on.

Not far from the Ara Pacis, we passed the Mausoleum of Augustus. It was under restoration, thus partially obscured by scaffolding and a chain link fence – which we peered through briefly. At this point, we were only halfway through our journey, and it was hotter than blazes. We hailed a taxi to take us the rest of the way.

Keith gave our destination to the driver.

"No way!" exclaimed the art history lover in Sophie.

"Yep!" I confirmed. "We're having lunch at Ristorante Atelier Canova Tadolini. It should be really cool!"

Just northwest of the Spanish Steps, we exited our taxi on the Via del Babuino, and walked through the doorway of the former *atelier* (workshop and studio) of the famous 19th-century Neoclassical sculptor, Antonio Canova. Our jaws dropped.

"This is stunning!" said Sophie.

She was right.

Once inside the intimate restaurant, we were surrounded on all sides and from all angles, by larger-than-life marble sculptures. Massive goddesses, ten-foot patricians, soldiers on horseback, and more. Plus busts, friezes, reliefs, plaster casts, and sculpted body parts of every kind. Accentuating the drama, the walls of every room and on every ancient floor were painted a deep crimson red. Among the sea of sculptures, small tables with white linen tablecloths floated between popes, kings, saints, and pagan divinities. Overall, there were about 400 works on display.

"*Saluti a tutti*," said the maître d'. He showed us to our table – setting a petite ceramic bowl of water on the floor for Barrett.

"*Buona sera*," we all responded. (By now we had learned that even if you know nothing else of the local language, it's key to at least greet an individual in their native tongue, before embarking upon further conversation.)

Studying the menu, we were startled by a bark from Barrett – followed by another, then another. He had popped out from under Keith's chair, and was staring high up the wall behind me.

We followed his gaze upward – I, craning my neck around to do so.

"Egads!" I said. "No wonder he's upset."

Looming over my shoulder – large and menacing – was a man of marble, leaning forward and ready to lunge. And, his eyes had an eerie glow, due to strategic gallery lighting.

"I hope he's well-adhered!" I said. I resolved Barrett's angst by picking him up and keeping him on my lap – under the drop of the tablecloth.

After we'd ordered, Keith turned to Sophie. "So tell us about Canova. And, where does the name 'Tadolini' come in?"

"Sure!" Sophie made a sweeping gesture. "As you can see, Antonio Canova was an incredible sculptor. By the early 1800s, he was at the height of his European fame; one of his most famous and scandalous works was the nude sculpture of Pauline Bonaparte Borghese – Napoleon's sister. The work was commissioned by her husband, Camillo Borghese, 6th Prince of Sulmona [in Italy's Abruzzo region]. Canova portrayed her in the guise of the victorious Venus, in *The Judgement of Paris* – but it still caused a stir among contemporaries. Anyway, in 1818 the artist secured the property we are now in, solely as his *atelier*. His most gifted protégé was Adamo Tadolini; he considered the student to be his spiritual heir, and together they formed a strong collaborative relationship. Under Canova's strict supervision, Tadolini was handed commissions to reproduce some of his tutor's most famous works."

At this point, our meals arrived. Keith and I shared *spaghetti alla carbonara*, while Sophie ordered the 'Tadolini salad' – featuring lettuce, chicken, bacon, *emmental* cheese, and corn. Ewan had the sea bass baked in a sea salt crust. Everything was delicious.

My brother-in-law pointed his fork at Sophie's salad. "What's mental cheese?"

My sister rolled her eyes. "EH-muhn-taal. *Emmental!*" she pronounced. "It's French."

We all learned something.

⊞

Before leaving the restaurant/*atelier*, we wandered through the rest of the interconnected rooms, Barrett on foot. There was a chamber in the back where tools were displayed that the famous sculptors once used. It was fascinating and creepy at the same time.

"Wow," I said. "This could double as an ancient medical museum of torture."

We turned and left the room – just in time to see Barrett make a dash up the set of old stairs in front of us – leash trailing behind. We knew that the stairway led to another dining area, also sculpture-lined.

"Barrett! Stop!" I shouted. The four of us were in hot pursuit – single file up the creaky, narrow steps.

We reached the top, and searched the labyrinth of small dining rooms. There were a few diners – but no dog to be found.

Keith was beginning to sweat. "Where is he?" he whispered frantically to me.

Room by room, nothing. Just a forest of white marble against a red backdrop.

We came to an area with a loft of sorts, high above the diners' heads. It, too, was crammed with invaluable marble busts. It was at this moment that one of the diners caught our eye. The woman gave a subtle nod of her head, urging us to look skyward.

"Good God!" said my husband.

Sophie, Ewan, and I followed his gaze – horrified. Tucked among scores of fragile, priceless heads, was Barrett. He had wedged himself behind a scowling pope, and was barely visible. Were it not for the fact that popes generally don't have black mustaches made of furry, swishing tails, no one would have spotted him.

It took a very patient manager, and a piece of special cheese, to entice our problem child out of hiding.

"Now I know why it's called 'mental' cheese," grumbled Keith. "That dog is certifiable."

CHAPTER 29

"DON'T SIT ON the steps!"

Our little group had made its way from Canova Tadolini to the Piazza di Spagna, without incident. I was hoping to keep it that way.

Sophie and Ewan looked up from where they'd plopped themselves on the third step of the famous site.

"Why not?" asked Ewan.

"It's illegal. Sitting on the Spanish Steps was banned recently, after a major cleaning and restoration effort." I added, "Bulgari – that Italian jeweler with the classic *Serpenti* design – funded the 1.5 million-euro project, in celebration of their 130th anniversary." While I don't like serpents in general, I wouldn't turn down a bracelet as a gift – although with a $12,000 price tag, one is unlikely to come my way….

Built in the 1720s, the Spanish Steps – all 138 of them – later became a Roman icon, as well as the widest staircase in Europe. They were called 'Spanish' simply because the Spanish Embassy to the Vatican was located there.

Sophie stood. "Speaking of Bulgari, let's see the stores on the Via dei Condotti – just for fun. The guys can stay here and people-watch."

Keith had a different plan. "Better idea: let's grab some gelato first, then we three men will have a nice table in the shade while you two window shop."

"You mean: *shop*," I corrected.

"*Window* shop," countered my husband.

My silence signaled that negotiations had ended – in my favor, of course.

⚏

"This gelato is fantastic!" said Sophie. She took another bite of her favorite flavor, *mandarino* – aka tangerine. We were seated outdoors at Giolitti, on Via degli Uffici del Vicario, where the rest of us enjoyed *cocco*, *lampone*, and *fico caramellato* – coconut, raspberry, and caramelized fig. Barrett was happy with his little IceBau – a dog-friendly ice cream.

I took a demi-spoonful of *cocco*. "I have news," I said. "Sort of."

My tablemates looked up expectantly.

"Last night at the hotel, I emailed a couple of my historical essays – as writing samples – along with an inquiry, to Annabelle Pargetter."

"Who?" asked my husband.

"Annabelle Pargetter! The representative from the British Museum. The one who so kindly secured Barrett's artifact deal?"

"Oh, right!" said Keith. "Go on…."

"Well, I told her that I was interested in possibly writing pieces for museums – but that I'm open to any form of authorship, as long as it involves history. I figured it was a longshot, but that in her position, she might have some contacts for me. Who knows?"

"Good for you!" enthused my sister. "There are numerous avenues for writing about history. Maybe this one fits you better, timing-wise. You're pretty busy these days, with your travels and all."

"I know," I said wistfully. "But it's always been my dream to write a book."

⊞

Sophie's eyes bugged. "Cath…a Louis Vuitton dog collar? Seriously? At 350 euros, that's $400! Keith will have your head."

"Yeah…you're probably right. That would be a little ridiculous, I guess." We were in the designer's shop on the Via dei Condotti. While I already had a well-utilized LV bag at home, I just wanted 'a little something' from one of their most famous store locations in the world, too.

I sighed. "Well, shoot. With Scrooge McDuck waiting for me outside, my wings are pretty well clipped."

I scouted around, and soon made a selection. We got in line at the posh counter, behind a gaggle of teenaged girls from Singapore. One by one – arms loaded with merchandise – they made their purchases. We watched, our jaws mentally dropping.

"Egads!" I whispered to my sister, "Each one spent nearly six figures!"

My turn at the register came, and I paid for my paltry purchase.

We headed out the door.

"You do realize," said Sophie, "that your new credit card holder cost as much as the dog collar would have."

"Yep," I said. "And if Keith finds out, I won't have any cards left for it to hold."

We laughed – the Sister Code of Silence, a given.

At dinner time, we found ourselves on the Piazza Navona. Again, we were seated near Bernini's *Fountain of the Four Rivers*, admiring the Baroque masterpiece of travertine marble.

"Which four rivers are these?" asked my husband.

Sophie pointed at the sculpture. "The river gods – holding up the Egyptian obelisk – represented the four known continents in 1650. The Nile, the Ganges, the Danube, and the Rio de la Plata – located in Africa, Asia, Europe, and the Americas."

"And the symbolism?" I asked. "Presumably, the animals and plants throughout the sculpture reflect each country?"

"Correct," said my sister. "And if you look further, there's more. The Nile's head is draped with a loose cloth, meaning that no one at the time knew the exact source of the river. The Danube touches a papal coat of arms, since it's the largest river close to Rome. The Ganges carries a long oar, representing the river's navigability. And the Rio de la Plata (*plata* is Spanish for 'silver') sits on a pile of coins – a symbol of the potential riches that America might provide Europe."

"Well, speaking of riches," interjected Ewan, "here comes our food."

He was right. Yummy salads and pastas soon overflowed our two tiny tables.

While eating, we watched various street performers around the piazza. Musicians, portrait artists, clowns, and more. Keith and Ewan were impressed by all; Sophie and I rolled our eyes at some. Barrett was unfazed, well-fed and snoozing under my chair.

One act in particular fascinated our husbands. Two men wearing orange turbans and *kurtas* (long, loose-fitting tunics and matching pants) sat on the piazza before us – and it was the way that they were sitting that was interesting. The first man posed on the ground in a lotus position – holding a wooden pole about five feet high. Atop the pole sat the second man – also in the lotus position. The arrangement of his tunic created the illusion that he was almost floating. Very Zen, they stared peacefully ahead.

"Well, that's clever," I said, finishing my espresso. I turned to Sophie. "Let's visit the leather shops across the square. Barrett's still asleep, and the guys are eyeballing the dessert menu."

We scooted back our chairs and were off – leaving the guys to relax at the table.

A half hour later we returned to our spot, only to find no husbands. Instead, two strange men sat at our table, counting a pile of euros – and an American dollar. They were laughing and pointing, enjoying the performance before them. An old shopping bag sat on an empty chair – a bit of orange fabric spilling out.

We followed their gaze – and did double takes.

Two males had taken the place of the original men-in-orange. They were wearing white togas rather than *kurtas* and turbans. The one sitting atop the pole had a prop in his arms: a little ball of black fluff – wearing a Roman laurel leaf crown on its head. The prop was smiling a furry, lopsided grin.

"Criminently," I said to my sister. "Men. You can't take them anywhere."

⌂

During breakfast the next morning, we discussed plans for our last day in Rome.

"I have some minor bad news," I said. "Dogs are not allowed in the Vatican. That cancels out the Vatican Museums, and St Peter's Basilica, for us. However," I said to my sister and brother-in-law, "you guys should go ahead! Sophie, you especially shouldn't miss highlights such as the Sistine Chapel, and Michelangelo's *Pieta*. Nor Bernini's *Baldachin* – the huge bronze canopy over St Peter's tomb. They're right up your alley."

"Nonsense!" replied Sophie. "We can see those during our next trip here. We want to spend this last bit of time together – the five of us."

Barrett gave a little yip of assent.

"Well, if you're sure…." I said. "But, there is one thing I need to do at the Museums. If I could have fifteen minutes inside one of their shops, that would be great! I'd like to pick up a gift for our elderly neighbor, Frank. He's Catholic," I added.

Everyone agreed that we would make the short stop, before heading to the last destination of our trip. We finished our meal – tucking away a few bananas and little Nutella packets from the buffet for later (whenever the need for potassium and chocolate struck). Soon, we were in our car and driving toward Vatican City.

The Vatican Museums shop (one of several) was full of choices. I specifically wanted something that would please Frank, the cat-lover. I knew that felines were considered sacred by the ancient Romans; this was influenced by the followers of Isis, an Egyptian goddess who was widely worshipped in Rome at the time. Thus, many artifacts depicting cats existed, and there were several nice replicas for sale. I chose a copy of an 'Urn for the Mummy of a Cat' – the original being in bronze, and dating between 945-712 BC. It was about two feet tall, and fragile, so I opted to have it shipped to our home by the museum.

Standing at the register to pay, I witnessed the clerk enter the title of my purchase in her computer, along with my address. Just as I handed her my credit card, there was a power glitch, and all of the lights on the floor went out. After about two minutes in total darkness, the lights came back on, but the registers were still down. The clerk took my credit card information by hand, then gave me a written receipt and a friendly apology. She assured me that my purchase would arrive at my home within a week. That was service!

I exited the museum, and found my chariot.

"How'd it go?" asked my husband.

"Great!" I said. "Frank will really be surprised when he sees what I bought for him."

"To the Parco degli Acquedotti!"

"Wait," said the Water Guy. "I thought we were going to the Park of the Aqueducts."

I sighed. "We are." Water Guy will never be mistaken for Word Guy.

We drove nine miles southeast, from the Vatican to the Via Lemonia. Just outside of Rome, on the Appian Way, lay our destination.

"WOW." I said. "Wow, wow, *wow.*"

"It seems…suspended in time," said Sophie.

Keith was speechless.

We parked, then walked several yards. Standing before us was a huge, open space – quiet and desolate, under a bright blue sky dotted with slow-moving white clouds. The only sounds were the faint chirpings of birds, and a haunted whistling among the umbrella pines that lined a section of the Appian Way (to the right of where we stood). This scene was the backdrop for one of the most stunning sights we'd come to yet: a long, broken trail of ancient Rome's crumbling skeletons – the enormous Aqueducts – extending both left and right as far as the eye could see.

We climbed over a low wall – a two-sided, rickety metal staircase had been provided – then walked to the arch and pillars of one of the nearest aqueducts. Barrett was on his leash, and clearly enjoyed gamboling through the tall grasses, and the red and yellow wildflowers, that grew among large patches of dirt.

I turned to my husband. "Over to you," I said.

"So," began Keith, "here are some massive remains of several of the ancient aqueducts that were built during the Roman Empire. These marvels were so well constructed, that many have survived; they can be found all over Italy, as well as Spain, France, Germany, Turkey, and Israel. The technology was highly specialized, and remained unsurpassed for more than 1000 years after the Empire's decline. At its height, Rome had eleven of these superstructures – covering 300 miles. By the year 52 AD, there was enough potable water flowing into the city daily to provide for its nearly one million inhabitants." He paused. "Impressive!"

"Definitely," agreed Ewan. "How were they built? And how did they operate?"

My husband continued his water tutorial. "Well, one of the most prominent examples is right here: the Aqua Claudia. It took eleven years and 30,000 men – many were slaves – to build. Roman cement (*pozzolana*) was used – the same material comprising the dome of the Pantheon. Strong and able to harden even underwater, it was one of the greatest building innovations in antiquity. As for how the aqueducts worked, they operated without any pumps or generators, of course. Instead, the simple answer is that they functioned on the principle that water will always flow downhill. From their sources in the hills around Rome, they were built in such a way that there was always a small but consistent incline. "

We walked around for a while, contemplating the enormity of it all. At one point, a jet flew high overhead, then another, and another. The international airport was not far, and the aqueducts were in a flight path. I could have watched this all day, because the juxtaposition of two of my favorite things – huge planes and ancient ruins – felt very profound to me. It was something I would always remember. What would Hadrian think, I wondered, if he could see this?

Lost in thought, we turned to head back to our car. "Where's Barrett?!" I asked Keith in alarm.

Once again, our furry delinquent had slipped his bonds. We spotted him in the short distance; he was headed down the Appian Way – happily running alongside two joggers who had just passed by.

Hearing us call for our dog, one of the joggers stopped and scooped him up.

Keith trotted up to the woman, and retrieved our furry fugitive – who had managed to gain a yellow wildflower, stuck to one ear. My husband apologized and thanked her profusely.

"No problem at all," she said, in a British accent. She took a closer look at our pup, now in my husband's arms. "Say! Is this Barrett, by any chance? I read about him in the *Daily Mail*...."

Hearing this story from Keith, I shook my head in amazement. "You know, this little guy could be destined for big things."

CHAPTER 30

"**I**'M REALLY GOING to miss you two," I sniffed. We were at Fiumicino Airport in Rome, getting ready to head our separate ways. Keith, Barrett, and I were off to Tampa, and Sophie and Ewan were going home to Scotland.

Sophie hugged me. "Me, too! But don't worry; we already plan on meeting you guys at some point during your next trip – wherever that may be." She knelt down and gave Barrett a hug. "Be good, little guy!"

He wagged his tail in assurance.

Keith and Ewan patted each other on the shoulder – followed by a quick hug. Barrett plopped down between their feet, not wanting to be left out.

I watched as my sister and brother-in-law walked off, toward their gate at the opposite end of the terminal from ours.

Sophie turned and gave me a thumbs up. *"Keep writing,"* she mouthed.

Our Boeing 787 had just taken off on its transatlantic flight. Barrett was snoozing in his gingham doggy carrier, tucked below the seat in front of Keith – his furry little head resting on a new toy that Sophie had bought for him. Italian by design, it was a red, white, and green stuffed cat. (It was fitting for Rome, so I ignored my feline aversion.) I was staring out the window, embracing my last view of Italy.

Leaning back from the glass, I covered one eye with my hand, then looked out again. "You know," I said to Keith, "this could be an augury window."

My husband removed one earbud – already tuned in to his first movie for the long flight ahead. "A what?"

"An augury window! Augury was the ancient Greco-Roman practice of observing the behavior of birds and their flight patterns, in order to receive omens. Basically, it was divination. The augur – the person who read the signs – was considered a spiritual leader, capable of advising officials on important matters. Watching the sky, he would trace an imaginary window with a *lituus* – a crooked wand – to mark out a ritual space, called a *templum*. The passage of birds through this 'window' indicated divine favor (or disfavor) for a specific plan or undertaking." I gestured to my right. "So any portal to the skies would do the trick!"

"Ahh."

Had I 'the gift', I might have divined a mental eye-roll with that reply.

Turning back to my window, I looked out in time to see us fly over the Park of the Aqueducts. It was a breathtaking sight. I wondered what an ancient augur would have thought, had he spotted our huge silver bird in his templum.

⟁

Midway over the Atlantic, the skies became as choppy as the waves below. I called to mind the 'Jello Analogy' that I had come to rely on in times of heavy turbulence. It didn't help. My next strategy was to pull up a short video of *The Snowman* on my phone; specifically, my favorite scene where the boy and the snowman fly over the ocean hand-in-hand, as majestic whales breach the sea below. That helped a little – mainly because it was set to the beautiful but melancholy song, *Walking in the Air*, and I was now distracted by the tears trickling down my cheeks.

My alarmed husband took out both earbuds. "Good grief! What's wrong? What happened?"

I showed him my phone.

"Ahh," he said. He'd been this route before.

⟁

The skies smoothed out, and I settled in with an iced tea, and a copy of *Minerva*. Reading an article entitled, 'Harboring the Past', about the ancient port city of Ostia Antica (about fifteen miles southwest of Rome), I made a mental note to visit the site, the next time we were in the area.

The calm was interrupted by the PA system overhead. "Is there a physician on board? If so, please identify yourself to the nearest flight attendant."

Keith and I looked at each other. Uh-oh.

That announcement was followed shortly after, by a second notification from the cockpit. "Ladies and gentleman," said the captain, "we have a medical emergency on board. Just to be on the safe side, we will be diverting to Newfoundland, Canada. We're sorry for any inconvenience, and will make every effort to be on our way to Tampa from there, as soon as we are able to do so."

"Oh, no!" I said. "Whoever the passenger is, I pray they're going to be okay. How awful to be seriously ill, at 35,000 feet in the air. I hope they have family with them."

Thinking about making lemonade out of this temporary lemon, I said, "Newfoundland…. We've never been there. I wonder how long our layover will be. Depending upon the time, maybe we could—"

"Cath. Forget it. We are not leaving the airport for any reason. None. Zip. *Nada*."

Drat. Back to the drawing board. "Well, there has to be a way to have a Newfoundland experience."

Keith ignored me – but I felt a little paw from below, tap me on the ankle.

We landed at Gander International Airport. After the ailing patient had been taken off the plane on a stretcher (it turned out to be appendicitis), the rest of the passengers deplaned, also. We had a three- hour layover ahead.

"Just as well, I guess," said Keith. "Barrett can have a meal and a potty break, and we can all stretch our legs."

"Right," I said. "And we can have a decent dinner, too. Then we'll skip the 'mystery meat' on the next flight."

We chose a nice pub – with seating along one half, a long bar in the middle, and an open-view 'show kitchen' behind the bar. Keith ordered fish-and-chips (his happy meal), and I ordered French onion soup. Barrett was leashed, under my chair. I vaguely noticed that a few feet away, there was another bit of black fluff dining under its owner's table.

We'd just received our drinks, when we heard an almost imperceptible *Woof* from below. We glanced at each other, then down at Barrett, who appeared perfectly quiet.

Woof!

"There it is again," said my husband. "What is he doing?"

We checked our pup a second time. He returned an innocent look.

WOOF! This *woof* did not belong to us.

In a millisecond, there was an explosion of black fur under our neighbor's table – from what looked like a small bear. (Actually, not that small.) It barreled out of its cave, and made a beeline for the kitchen. Barrett, not being one to skip a party, slipped his harness (again!) and joined in the rollicking fun. Apparently, he and the enormous Newfoundland had cooked up some quick plans together, as soon as their eyes had met.

The next few moments passed in slow motion – at least, for us. Diners sat dumbfounded (and let's face it, laughing) as sounds of crashing and banging reverberated from the kitchen.

A chef was heard yelling, "*Sortez, vous les betes!*" (Our server translated for us: "Get out, you beasts!")

Before we could act, the hulking Newfoundland came slinking out of the kitchen, head hung low, covered in warm Hollandaise sauce. Barrett trotted out behind him – happy as a clam, wearing a small saucepan upside down on his head. Johnny Appleseed would have approved.

"Well," said my husband. "There. You've had your Newfoundland experience."

We'd been home for a few days, and were settling into our regular routine. The weekend had come, and we'd both slept in. Barrett was up early, of course, and watching his favorite cartoon: *Scooby Doo*. (We'd discovered that if we set it up for him the night before, and left a special remote for him with only one working button to push….)

Anyway, after showering and making our coffee, I opened my laptop.

There was an email from Annabelle Pargetter.

I read it.

"Keith!" I hollered down the hallway. "Come out here! I've received a reply from Annabelle Pargetter!"

I read the email again – and again. I could hardly believe it.

My husband trotted into the kitchen. "Well, what does it say?"

I turned my screen toward him.

Dear Cath Keith,

It was lovely to hear from you. Thank you so much for your writing samples, which were excellent. Given your talent, your knowledge of history, and your incorrigible but endearing dog, I have located a publisher who would like to offer you a contract. They are proposing that you write a series of children's books, starring Barrett as your lead character. He will romp his way through history, so to speak.

Please get back to me if you are interested,

Sincerely,

Annabelle Pargetter

Keith gave me a big hug. "Hon! This is fantastic! Congratulations!"

I sat in stunned silence for a moment, before speaking. "I don't know…." I said. "I mean, it's a fantastic opportunity, of course. But – what about my other plan? My dream?" I paused. "I really wanted to write history – with a twist of 'art imitating life'…."

"Cath," said my husband. "You're there. It's right here before you."

It took two days to come to terms with my new path to authorship. It would certainly involve more travel, more history, and more writing – three of my favorite things. And bringing fun to it all would be Barrett. I was in the middle of composing my answer to Annabelle Pargetter, when the doorbell rang. Keith was bathing our pup, so I answered the door.

It was Osman Kose. He struggled with a heavy box, about five feet tall. It had the word *FRAGILE* stamped all over it, and it was from Italy.

"Hey, there," said our neighbor. "The DHL driver left this package with me, by mistake."

"Oh, good! Thanks!" I took the box from him and set it on the floor in our foyer. "It's something I purchased for Frank." I was anxious to see the replica of the 'Urn for the Mummy of a Cat', and hoped that it had survived the overseas trip intact. Based on the oversized container, it was probably well-packed.

"Good old Frank," said Osman. "He's a nice guy." He hovered, waiting to see the contents.

"Yep," I said absentmindedly. I cut carefully into the box. The first thing I came to was a shipping receipt on the inside. It was addressed to The Louvre. I was confused. "The LOUVRE? The museum in Paris?" I muttered.

The sender line read, 'Enzo Bianchi, Collector'.

I suddenly remembered the power glitch at the Vatican, when I was paying for Frank's gift. Uh-oh.

I began cutting deeper – and more rapidly, though carefully. Soon I came to the goods. I sat back on my heels, speechless (this was becoming a thing).

Osman found his voice first. "Gee! You guys bought a human mummy for Frank?"

Our neighbor was out the door.

"Keeeeeith!" I called out. "Come quick!"

"Whaaaat?" He came dashing in, a towel-wrapped Barrett in his arms.

I pointed at the four-foot mummy.

"Call Air France, please. And book three seats."

THE END

About the Author

Rhonda Bellows Summerford is an author of humorous fiction, and a lover of antiquity (with a penchant for ancient Rome and Britain). She travels extensively for research; every trip is a history trip – and no trip is without folly! She holds a dual BA in Psychology and History, and an MA in History. She and her husband live on the Gulf Coast of Florida, with their beloved Shih Tzu, Zoey. Rhonda is a member of WFWA (Women's Fiction Writers Association) and is a steering committee member of a local history club. She's also a hospital volunteer, as well as a supporter of veterans' causes, children's charities, and various animal rescues. When Rhonda isn't writing, she can be found at the beach – with a book, of course.